Pride Publishing books by Jennifer Moffatt

Falling Hard
A Hard Sell

I0565630

Falling Hard

A HARD SELL

JENNIFER MOFFATT

A Hard Sell
ISBN # 978-1-80250-764-5
©Copyright Jennifer Moffatt 2024
Cover Art by Kelly Martin ©Copyright March 2024
Interior text design by Claire Siemaszkiewicz
Pride Publishing

A HARD SELL

Dedication

For my mom, Teresa (1952–2013), who always let me take as many books as I could carry out of the library, then carried a whole bunch more.

Acknowledgements

I would like to thank my parents for raising me to love books, and for always supporting and believing in me no matter what, and my husband and kids who cheered me on while accepting the fact that I spend almost all my free time at my laptop now.

Thank you to the people who said yes: my agent Jordy Albert and my editor Anna Olson, as well as the team at Totally Entwined who worked with me to make this book happen.

I started writing during the COVID shutdown, and the incomparable Hanna Kubicka has been with me since my very first word. She's read everything I've ever written, and my work is better because of her. I am so grateful for her love, support, and friendship, and I can't wait for the day when an ocean no longer separates us. Hanna, 'thank you' is not enough.

So, so many thanks to John who beta read for me, provided some much-needed cheerleading when times were tough, and who designed my beautiful website: jmoffattwrites.com.

Heartfelt thanks to Rebekah Rodriguez-Lynn, Lotte, Jo Ellsworth and K.C. Carmine, who beta read, pep-talked, and supported me in countless ways with countless messages (and memes).

I would also like to thank Tyrell Johnson, Alexander James, Debra, Patrick and Hana who offered help, suggestions, and kind words on my query letter and sample pages.

Thank you to my friends Amanda, Cheryl, Jo and Andrew who have never stopped rooting for me and replying to screechy messages with appropriate levels of excitement (or despair) at every step of this publishing journey.

I would like to send thanks to Sally Thorne for writing *The Hating Game*. That book is one of the main reasons I started writing. I wanted to give others the same warm, fuzzy, falling-in-love feeling that *The Hating Game* gave me.

Finally, I would especially like to thank everyone who read *A Hard Sell*. I hope it made you smile.

Chapter One

The Big Bad Wolf

Ding.

The elevator doors slid open and Luka Moreno bounced out, a ray of sunshine flooding the dim reception area. He paused when he caught a glimpse of himself in the mirrored 'Breakpoint Advertising' sign on the wall, straightening the collar of his checkered dress shirt. It peeked out from beneath his purple sweater and matched his navy trousers. His honey-toned skin was glowing. He grinned at his reflection. Sometimes, he just killed it.

A rhythm thrummed through his veins as he strutted down the hallway, drumming the beat on his thigh. His first stop was his best friend's office. He poked his head in. "Morning, gorgeous."

Tawney looked up from her desk where she was highlighting a report, markers in three different colors clutched in her hand. "Hey, cutie."

He blew her a kiss and continued down the hall, throwing a smile at the adorable rumpled sandy-haired hottie from IT. He didn't pause to say hi, though, because Luka was fairly certain that particular hottie was straight, and, even if he wasn't, Luka was not going to date anyone from work. Not again, anyway.

Luka waved at the colony of interns scurrying to and fro in the bullpen and exchanged pleasantries with the other designers as he passed their desks.

"Did you get my email, Luka? I'm dying to know what you think!"

"Moreno! I saw your new soft drink spot last night. You killed it!"

"Luka, I'm making an iced coffee run, you want?"

He grinned and winked and demurred his way through the pack until he reached his office and sank into his chair. The storyboards he was working on sat waiting for him in a neat pile. He'd have plenty of time to finish those up today, with hours to spare. Maybe he'd even get ahead on a few other projects, do some sketching or even inking if he was lucky. He could hardly believe he got paid to be creative all day, to turn his ideas into little packages of art for the world to see. It was a dream.

* * * *

Thud.

Luka looked over from his computer screen to the stack of files Tawney had just dumped on his desk.

"Sorry." She smiled apologetically. "For the new account."

Luka was unable to stifle a groan. "Ugh." He rubbed his eyes. "What time is it?"

"Almost eight. You should get out of here."

He pouted at her. "I'm not the only one still at work."

"I'm on my way. Wanna grab some food?"

The panels on his screen blurred as he blinked at them. His stomach was growling, but... "I said I'd have these storyboards finished today."

"You're still working on those? You were almost done this morning!"

"Well..." Luka gave Tawney a sheepish look.

"Oh, no. Don't tell me." Tawney folded her arms and glared at him.

Biting his lip, he nodded, unable to say the words.

"Luka! Why do you keep helping him?"

Luka moaned and flopped his head onto the desk. "Because I'm pathetic." His reply was muffled.

Tawney nodded in agreement, her tight brown curls bouncing emphatically. "Yes. Yes, you are. But so is Morgan. You need to stop."

"I know," Luka admitted. God, did he ever know.

"Because, once again, you spent the entire day doing his shit, and now —"

He interrupted her with a tortured moan. "It's okay, babe. I already hate myself." *Never* would he *ever again* date someone from work.

Tawney softened. "Okay, but don't stay too much longer. You need some rest. Tomorrow is a big day."

Luka looked at her, mind scrabbling for purchase. "Remind me..."

"You poor thing, it may be too late for you. The Big Bad Wolf, Luk! He's here tomorrow!"

Luka smacked his forehead. "I knew that. Shit, this week has been insane. I *should* get out of here." He would just come in a little earlier than normal to finish polishing the storyboards. Because it actually *was* a big day. Thomas Badgley, a.k.a. 'The Big Bad Wolf,' was a company legend. A VP known for swooping in and working his magic for the major clients. And their office had just landed the Sartini account. It was *major*.

"Yes, you should. I hear he's intense. You don't want to be half-asleep when you meet him."

"I guess you don't get a nickname like 'Big Bad Wolf' by being a giant ball of fluff."

"Guess not. See you tomorrow, Luk." Tawney gave him a wave and eased out through the door. The office was dark, the empty desks and chairs now just humped, silent shadows. Last one out, again. Then his stomach growled, more insistent this time, and he decided that the smushed granola bar at the bottom of his bag was not going to cut it. Time to go home.

He struggled to keep his eyes open on the train, then grabbed an order of red curry from the Thai place he hated, just because it was fast and on the way. Luka dropped his keys on the side table, dumped his laptop bag on the chair then went straight into the kitchen to find a fork. A minute later he was digging into his dinner in front of *Breaking Bad*. He let himself sink into the meth-dealing shenanigans, his exhaustion temporarily forgotten.

But by the time the episode was ending, Walt's current predicament seemingly beyond hope, Luka's eyelids were drooping. He turned the TV off as soon as the credits began to roll, before the next episode could suck him in. He meant to go to bed, but somehow he found himself picking up his guitar from its stand by the couch. He plucked a few notes, a melody that had been winding through his head all day, the metal of the strings cool under his thumb. He strummed again, closing his eyes, letting the vibrations wash over him.

His mom had started teaching him piano before he could even reach the pedals, and the violin and guitar had followed soon after. Music was woven into the fabric of his soul, but it was a part he didn't share with many people. Not since the *Say Hi* Horror, anyway. Besides his family, the only people who knew about his musical talents were Tawney and Finn. Though now, against his better judgment, Morgan had been added to that group.

He put his guitar back on its stand and went to bed. It took him just a minute to fall fast asleep.

Unfortunately, Luka had the annoying habit of waking up well before his six a.m. alarm. There would be a moment, usually around five, sometimes even earlier, when he became aware that he was awake. A switch would flip, and his brain would begin whirring away. Mostly things to do at work — *Shit, I never got back to accounting about the hours for the Boyer file. Is the meeting with the casting director at nine or nine-thirty? I have to remember to check with Finn about the font for the catalogue...* But there were other random things, too. *Did I have five cups of coffee yesterday? Is that too many? Do I need to buy more coffee? Ooh, it's my sister's birthday next week. Should I get her a gift certificate for a massage? Wait, is that what I got her that last year?*

Sometimes, just for fun, his brain would start flipping through the stack of index cards that meticulously recorded all the embarrassing or stupid things he had done in his life. Secretly fucking Morgan for months was at the top of that stack right now, and the *Say Hi* Horror always made an appearance.

On rare occasions, when he was really worn out, he would manage to shut all that noise down and drift back to sleep. Of course, then he began his day being jarred awake by the alarm at six. He wasn't sure which was worse. This Friday morning, however, he must have been extra exhausted, because for the first time in years, he turned his alarm off and fell back asleep without even realizing it.

When he woke up a while later, feeling refreshed, he picked up his phone to look at the time, then threw himself out of bed with a shriek. "Fuck! Fuck fuck fuuuuuuuck, fucking fuck!" It was 8:07. He was supposed to be at his desk by eight-thirty. That was not happening. Of all the fucking days to be late for work for the first time.

He dashed into the shower to scrub clean, then yanked on the first clothes he got his hands on. A bagel thawed in the microwave while he brewed his coffee, since there was no functioning without it. Then he was out of the door, travel mug in hand, swearing again when the coffee sloshed onto his shirt.

Collapsing into a seat on the subway, he texted his boss.

Hi Ilona – I'm so sorry, it seems I slept through my alarm, I'll be a little late…

He held his breath after he had hit 'send' then sighed with relief when it went through. His boss was beautiful, polished and more than a little intimidating. Some days he still couldn't believe Ilona had hired him, a fresh face with not much more than a charming smile and a padded resume. And that was when he wasn't running late for the most important meeting of the year.

Then the lights flickered and the train began to slow down, before grinding to a halt in the dark tunnel. Luka joined the other passengers in groaning loudly. How could this be happening? The speaker crackled to life and a disinterested voice explained there was a technical problem causing a short delay and thanking them for their patience. Luka added another text for Ilona, leg jittering as he tapped on his phone.

And my train just stopped.

This one didn't go through. *Fuck. No signal.* He sighed and pressed his head to the cool glass, willing the metal tube back to life. *Oh, God.* He pictured everyone sitting around the conference table, staring at his empty seat, Morgan as smug as ever.

It was an excruciating fifteen minutes before they were moving again. Luka had been starting to wonder if he could pry open the doors and climb up to a manhole cover, but that was rendered unnecessary when they lurched back to life. As the beleaguered train was finally pulling into the station, two messages popped up. One was a reply from Ilona.

Come to the conference room when you arrive.

The other was from Tawney.

Where are you???

He dashed up the stairs and sprinted the three blocks to his office, dodging cars and what seemed like exceptionally slow-moving foot traffic. Eyeing a crowd waiting at the elevator, he bounded up four flights of stairs, his heartbeat echoing louder than his footsteps. White spots were floating in front of his eyes by the time he arrived in the foyer, sweaty and heaving like a racehorse. He dabbed a sleeve at his forehead and made his way down the hall, attempting to get his breathing under control lest someone call nine-one-one on account of his imminent heart attack.

Pausing outside the conference room, he caught a glimpse of the packed space, all eyes focused on a person at the front he couldn't see. *Fucking. Hell.* There was nothing to do but go in. He took another ragged breath, smoothed his jacket then pushed the door open, oh so quietly.

Every head in the room whipped over to stare at him. Luka froze, an awkward smile on his face, determined to avoid making eye contact with a single person. Another bead of sweat trickled down his forehead.

"So sorry," he stage-whispered, embarrassment flooding his face. The room was jammed with just about the entire office, extra chairs crammed in another ring around the table and wherever else they would fit. There was an open seat right next to Tawney. However, it was on the other side of the table, through the dense sea of people. "Excuse me," he whispered to the first person he had to squeeze past. And again, "Excuse me," to the next. Every pair of eyes watched him in silence. *Fucking kill me now,* he thought to himself, mouthing "Sorry," again.

Seventeen million years later, he fell into the chair. It screeched like a car wreck. He closed his eyes, not quite ready to risk a glance at the head of the table.

"Well, now that Luka is settled," Ilona said dryly, "please go ahead, Thomas."

Luka dared to raise his eyes. Then he saw Thomas Badgley for the first time. *Oh...my fucking God.* It was like in movies when the rest of the world faded away to an irrelevant gray blur, and all that was left was one perfect person bathed in heavenly light. Luka was sure he made an audible wheeze, the breath he had barely gained back gone again. Tawney shot him a concerned look, but he didn't care.

How *could* he? Because Thomas Badgley was the most insanely gorgeous man he had ever seen in his entire life. It was impossible to look away. And Thomas was staring back at Luka with a smooth face and phenomenal eyes, a warm, shining golden brown. But just for a split second, then Thomas' gaze returned to the rest of the room.

Luka continued to drink him in, his mouth gaping. Thomas had wavy hair, a rich chocolate-brown, long enough to be pulled back into a small bun. He was at least six-foot-two, with ivory skin, a strong, chiseled jaw, a heavy brow and a wide, muscular frame that tapered into a narrow waist. His thick shoulders and arms looked ready to burst through his expensive, charcoal-gray fitted suit jacket. *Big Bad Wolf, indeed.*

Thomas was speaking, although Luka had no idea what he was saying. He was lost in the way Thomas' lips formed around each sound he made, the flashes of a pink tongue and the deep baritone of his voice vibrating the hairs on Luka's skin.

Then he realized everyone was staring at him again, right as Tawney kicked him under the table.

"Sorry?" Luka choked out.

Ilona cleared her throat and arched her eyebrow. "I was just saying, Luka has finished up those storyboards, haven't you?"

Fuuuuck. "Yes. I mean, no. Almost. The subway..." His cheeks flared up again.

"Hmm," Thomas grunted. He didn't look impressed.

"Well," Ilona said, shooting him a disapproving frown, "the design team can meet again later today. But I think the rest of us are clear on next steps. Thanks, everyone."

This time he caught the sympathetic glance Tawney threw at him.

Fuck me.

Chapter Two

Demonstrating Competence

Tawney followed Luka into his office, grimacing.

"Did I just...?" he started. How was it possible he had screwed up so badly? His brain pulled out another index card to add to the pile of shame. It might even take two cards.

"Mmhmm." She bit her lip.

But before she could close the door, a mane of curly red hair poked through. "Moreno!"

Luka sighed. "Finn."

His other best friend, graphic designer extraordinaire and chaotic bisexual, wiggled through the opening. Finn managed to blow out a breath, shaking his head while still grinning. "Jesus."

"So..." Luka nodded. It wasn't promising if Finn was this amused. "It was as bad as I think."

"Worse!" Finn chortled. "First of all..." He put a hand on Luka's shoulder and studied him at arm's length, rubbing his beard. "What the fuck are you wearing?"

Luka had no idea. He looked down at his clothes. A forest-green blazer, burgundy trousers and a buttery yellow button-down dotted with blue flowers, done up crookedly, topped off with a large coffee stain.

"Second—"

"You know what, you can stop. I was there." Luka yanked his blazer off while Finn cackled.

"It wasn't so bad," Tawney piped up.

The two men stared at her.

"I mean…" she stammered. "We all know that was not usual behavior for you."

Luka fell into his chair with a groan. "Thomas Badgley does not know that. Thomas Badgley thinks I'm a screw-up who dresses like a sloppy clown, shows up late and doesn't meet deadlines. Could it be any worse?"

"You, um"—Tawney cringed—"actually have some toothpaste." She pointed at the corner of her mouth. "Just here."

"I *what*?"

Then, the cherry on top, Ilona appeared in his doorway, as immaculate as ever, thick raven hair cascading onto her shoulders.

"You don't even need to say it," Luka told her, wanting to weep. He wiped at the toothpaste.

She pursed her perfect plum lips. "Design team meeting after lunch." She turned to go, then paused to look at him again. "That means one o'clock sharp. And can you change?"

* * * *

Luka marched into the conference room at 12:49, storyboards tucked under his arm. On time—Check.

Thankfully, he kept a pale blue dress shirt hanging in his closet at work for occasions such as these. Well, maybe not *just* such as these. The blue made his eyes pop and went with the burgundy trousers. He had touched up his soft chestnut waves over the lunch break, sweeping his bangs just so over one eye. The sloppy clown was no more. He knew he looked good. Next up—Demonstrating competence.

Luka faltered a step, almost tripping over an errant chair, when he saw Thomas was already in the conference room. His suit jacket was gone and he was bent over the table, sleeves rolled up, arranging some papers. Luka was surprised he was there already, not to mention distracted by the way Thomas' shirt pulled tight over his shoulders. He fought hard not to let it all show on his face.

"Oh, hello, Thomas," he said, enjoying the way the two syllables fell off his tongue, hard and soft at the same time.

Thomas looked up with a flash of recognition and took in Luka's improved appearance. "Luka, I believe?"

"Nice to meet you, officially." He offered his hand.

Thomas took it, his grip firm, but not excessive. Luka's hand tingled. Thomas' cologne, something citrusy, but with a rich, spicy underlayer, sent a dizzying swirl down to his gut. The man was a walking sex pheromone. Every cell in Luka's body was responding to Thomas at a biological level.

"You too," Thomas rumbled.

Luka made himself let go of Thomas' hand and placed the storyboards on the table. He opened his mouth to apologize for his performance that morning, when the door swung open behind them. They both turned and Luka groaned inwardly when Morgan sashayed in.

"Oh, Luka," Morgan drawled. "You made it on time. And thank God you changed."

"Morgan," Luka replied through gritted teeth as the fine-boned blond breezed past him in a cloud of overconfidence and the aftershave that Luka hated.

"Morgan Di Meo," he announced, thrusting his hand at Thomas. "I have to tell you, Mr. Badgley, I am such a huge fan. The work you did on the U State campaign? I practically enrolled myself." His laugh was much too loud. He ran the fingers of his free hand over his short hair as they shook.

Thomas nodded politely. "Nice to meet you, Morgan. Please, call me Thomas."

Luka seethed.

"Anyway," Morgan continued, "we're just thrilled to have you here. I know I was in the conference room *at least* twenty minutes early this morning because I was so excited."

That motherf— Luka began thinking, when he was interrupted by Finn barging in, telling Tawney the punchline of an inappropriate joke with his usual volume. Ilona and the rest of the design team filed in behind them. They found their places around the table, Luka fiddling with the corners of his storyboards while trying not to stare at Thomas.

"Thanks for gathering again, everyone," Ilona started, joining Thomas at the head of the table. "Luka?" She wasn't one for preambles.

Luka took a breath as he spread out his designs. Sartini was a prestigious wine label that had recently expanded into the fine-dining business. They had chosen Breakpoint as their new advertising firm, and the team had been working around the clock getting ready for their first presentation. He had mapped out their ideas for three different commercials, and was feeling pretty good about his work. He liked to keep ads simple—primal even. Strong images and sounds that would connect with something deep inside.

Thomas watched with a blank face, offering a small nod when Luka was finished. Then it was Morgan's turn. Luka simmered as Morgan played the rough cut of the music for the commercial that Luka had actually—secretly—written most of. He felt Tawney's gaze on him as he tried not to squirm.

The tale of Luka's relationship with Morgan was a sorry one. Morgan had arrived at Breakpoint a few months ago, handsome and charming, with striking cheekbones and wandering hands. Luka had been flattered when it started with some innocent flirting by the photocopier.

"Luka, is it?" The melodious voice came from behind him. He whirled. Damn. "Sure is. I haven't had the pleasure?"

"Well, I have," the new face purred, gray eyes cool and confident. "Morgan Di Meo." They shook hands, then he reached out and ran a finger down Luka's sleeve. "I love your shirt."

Luka flushed. It was an ordinary dress shirt, but that didn't matter. He was already sold. "Thanks."

Morgan eased closer, dropping his voice. "It matches your eyes...and my bedroom floor."

Okay, maybe the flirting wasn't that innocent. But he was still taken by surprise when Morgan ended up giving him a hand job in the supply closet a week later. He went in for some staples and Morgan followed, pressing him up against the shelves and kissing him quite convincingly. Luka kissed him back, knowing it was a bad idea, but it all felt rather sexy and dangerous. Then Morgan unzipped Luka's pants, and, well, that was how it began. Morgan came back to his place that night. And came at his place that night.

The whole affair was very Secret Agent — they left the office at different times and even took separate trains. Because the thing was, Breakpoint Advertising was not a big fan of interoffice dating — or, he would have to assume, supply closet hand jobs.

Tawney warned him early on. "Not a great idea, Luk. You have to tell HR — there's a stack of forms and a sexual harassment module, for starters."

"It's fine." Luka waved her off. "It's super casual." So casual, Luka thought, that maybe they didn't need to disclose anything. They mostly just fooled around at Luka's place, then ordered delivery and streamed a show. But as time went on, the guilt of keeping it a secret started to weigh on him. Plus, it might be nice to be seen in public with the guy he was sleeping with on a very regular basis.

Except whenever he tried to float the idea of an appointment with HR, Morgan brushed it off and changed the topic.

"Did you see that new place that opened up by the Main Street station? With all the disco balls in the window?" Luka asked one night after he finished his lettuce wraps. "That might be fun to check out sometime."

"Mmhmm," Morgan replied, not even taking his eyes off of the TV.

"Once we have a meeting with HR..." Luka tried. He stopped when he saw the tension in Morgan's shoulders.

"Ugh, these new places all try way too hard to be irreverent." Morgan rolled his eyes and picked up his wine. "Like, disco balls? Am I a teenage girl decorating my bedroom in the late nineties?"

Eventually Luka gave up asking. So it went, for several months. Sex, food, TV, awkwardly playing it cool at work, repeat. At least the sex was fantastic, he consoled himself, because there wasn't much else to it.

Then one day, when they were unpacking their dinner order, Luka's entire meal was missing. Morgan had offered a half-hearted "Aw, sucks, babe," before digging into his pad Thai without another thought.

Luka watched Morgan, inhaling his noodles and flipping to the next episode of their show, and it hit him. He was in a secret shallow relationship with a man who didn't care about him all that much and was definitely not worth getting fired over.

The breakup didn't go well. At first, Morgan just scoffed, thinking Luka was trying to make a point. "Oh, God, is this because I said I didn't want Indian tonight?"

"No, Morgan. It's because this isn't even a real relationship. It's just sex. You and I both know there's no real feelings here. I'm just... I'm done."

Then when Morgan realized Luka was serious, he got pissy. "Fine. Your dick is nothing special, anyway. Good luck finding someone else who wants to bother with it." He stormed out, taking the rest of his dinner with him.

Luka sighed. Honestly, the supply closest? What was I thinking?

He was looking forward to putting the whole situation in the rear-view mirror. No harm, no foul, no angry boss frowning at him next to an HR rep. It would not do to have this loose end flapping in the breeze.

Except the loose end refused to make things easy. Morgan sulked around, glaring at Luka across the conference table and doing shit like letting the elevator door close just as Luka was running for it. When his favorite coffee mug went missing, on a hunch, he found it in one of Morgan's desk drawers, along with some of his best watercolor pens. Total nightmare.

Luka was so desperate to fix the situation that when Morgan asked for a bit of help with a jingle, he said sure, hoping it would smooth things over. But then a few days later, there he was, leaning on Luka's door frame. "Hey, do you mind taking a quick look at this score?" Eyes wide, blond hair rippling just so.

Then a week later… "You don't mind giving me your thoughts, do you? You're the best." More and more now, Luka found himself pushing his own projects aside to help Morgan with his. It was all fucked up, and it was all his fault.

Thomas spoke this time when Morgan finished playing the music. "Good start. I like your use of the lone violin. It's very…engaging."

I know, right? Luka held his breath, wondering if Morgan would at least throw a little bit of credit his way.

"Thank you so much, sir." Morgan preened, avoiding looking in Luka's direction.

Apparently not. Luka slumped in his chair, imagining all the ways Morgan should suffer a slow death. *Bury him in an anthill coated in honey? Throw him into the lion enclosure during feeding time at the zoo? Drop a hundred hornet nests on him? …Wait, why do these all involve animals?* He did his best to ditch the grisly nature channel fantasies as the rest of the group shared their progress and bantered about some ideas for the direction they wanted to take the campaign. Thomas didn't say much else beyond a few non-committal grunts. Luka had no idea what he was thinking about any of it.

After everyone had presented, a lull in the conversation hit, and heads turned to Thomas and Ilona at the front.

"Did you need anything else, Thomas?" Ilona asked.

"I'd like to take another look at everything, if you don't mind. I'll find you if I have any questions."

They stared at him. He stared back. "Does anyone have any questions for me?"

Are you single? was the first thing that popped into Luka's head. He didn't see any rings. Then he admonished himself. *Christ, Luka, have you learned nothing? Calm the fuck down.*

When no one said anything, Thomas nodded once. "I appreciate your hard work. We'll meet again soon."

"Thanks, everyone." Ilona dismissed them.

It took Morgan about two seconds to stand and saunter over to Thomas. Luka recognized that head toss, the predatory appraisal in his eyes. His insides rolled. He couldn't stomach watching Morgan put the moves on Thomas. He scrambled out of the conference room as fast as he could.

Finn followed, providing distraction by yammering on about the latest numbers from analytics. Their new head of that department was Rory—tattooed, pierced, nonbinary and brilliant. And Finn had started talking about them a *lot*. His current update was all "Rory thinks" this, and "Rory says" that. Luka listened, amused.

When Luka had arrived at Breakpoint four years ago, Finn had stood out as the only other openly queer man in the office, with shining red hair, a big voice and broad shoulders. They had gravitated toward each other instantly, and Luka asked him to go for a drink after work almost right away. It could have been considered a date, but of course, at the time, he didn't realize how serious Breakpoint was about their dating policy—not that he was able to use that excuse three and a half years later.

Luka sat across from Finn at the bar, worrying that the butterflies weren't there. Finn's hair gleamed in the low lighting but it made Luka wonder what conditioner he used, not what it would look like spread out on a mattress.

"So, where did you go to school?" Luka asked before taking a sip of his cocktail.

"U State, you?"

"Bryerson."

"Nice. I dated a couple from Bryerson once."

"Like...at the same time?"

"Not exactly. I went out with her first a few times, and then him, but when he brought me home, she showed up."

Luka grimaced. "Awkward."

"It was at first, but then we had a threesome."

Luka tried not to inhale his drink. "How did that go?"

Finn looked mighty pleased with himself. "It became a bit of a competition between the two of them to see who could get me off first, so...really, really good." He grinned while Luka laughed.

In fact, Luka's cheeks hurt from laughing at the end of the night. So it turned out to be okay that there was no romantic spark, no burning passion, because the warm glow of friendship was perfect. He got Finn's complete hair care regime out of him, too. He ordered the whole product line when he got home.

Now Luka relied on Finn for his blunt takes on life and reminders not to take anything too seriously. And his hair had never been shinier. But this, the softness that emerged when he talked about Rory, who had joined the firm a few weeks earlier...this was new.

The first time they had met Rory, Finn hadn't done much beyond mumble hello and shake Rory's hand. Luka remembered looking sideways at Finn, shocked that he hadn't cracked some joke about number-crunching nerds or commented on Rory's tattoo sleeve.

Then when Rory had spilled coffee in the staffroom, Luka's jaw had dropped when Finn had done nothing but scramble to help clean it up. The last time Luka had spilled something, Finn had asked if he was drunk and called him "Spilly Talker" for weeks. He had been at Finn's house, and he had been drunk, but that was beside the point. And he had definitely noticed Finn staring at Rory during team meetings. Finn was not subtle.

"Anyway, Rory said they weren't too worried about it, so I figure it will be fine," Finn summed up as they arrived in Luka's office.

"Mmhmm. Are we going to talk about it?" Luka asked, leaning back in his chair with a teasing smile. It felt like the time to offer Finn a blunt take of his own.

Finn ran a hand through his curls as he leaned against the doorframe a little too casually. "Talk about what?"

Luka's grin widened. "You want me to say it?"

"Don't know what the fuck you're talking about."

This man, for all his loud-mouthed bluster, was just fucking adorable. "Your undying love for Rory."

Finn's face turned as red as his hair. "I don't... I— what..." he stammered.

"I'm sorry, what now?" Luka cupped a hand around his ear. "You don't...?"

"Fuck off," Finn mumbled, fighting off a bashful smile. He pushed himself off the frame and marched out, eyes on the ground.

Luka chuckled to himself. Pining was good and all, but Finn would have to face his feelings eventually.

Chapter Three

Shut Up, Morgan

Luka spent the weekend thinking about work way too much. Well, their new client specifically. Okay, it was Thomas. He was thinking about Thomas.

Does he get those suits custom-made? Luka wondered while he loaded the dishwasher. *Each one must cost more than my mortgage payment.*

God, his hair is so sexy. I don't think I've seen an exec with long hair before... as he perused the grocery aisles.

Lying in bed and trying to fall asleep on Sunday night, he thought, *I should ask him what he does to be in such good shape. Is there a non-creepy way to ask that? Fuck, imagine him shirtless...*

Luka's imagination was happy to oblige. He dreamed of Thomas, wearing nothing but a tie, stretched out and gleaming on the conference room table. He woke up sweaty and aroused, the image burned onto his brain.

But Luka made sure he was at his desk bright and early Monday morning, unruffled, and sweat-free. He dove into his tasks for a productive morning until he was startled out of his zone with a rap on his doorframe a little before lunch.

"Luka," Thomas greeted him, his deep voice reverberating through Luka's chest. "May I come in?"

Luka's mouth dried out as naked Thomas flashed before his eyes. "Sure," he managed to stammer, mortified to feel his cheeks heating up. *Okay, this is starting to be a problem. Sure, he's blisteringly hot, but he's probably a jerk, all bulging muscles and raging ego.*

Thomas had the storyboards with him and set them on Luka's desk before taking a seat. For such a heavy, thickset man, his every move was smooth and graceful. Luka imagined him in hand-to-hand combat, whirling in a roundhouse kick, hurling someone over his shoulder in one fluid motion, before throwing two torrid punches into a hapless opponent, all without breaking a sweat.

"I was able to speak with Aleandro Sartini this morning, and it looks like we'll need to make some changes," Thomas said.

"Oh?" Luka blinked back to reality, focusing on the man in front of him sitting in an office chair.

"We're taking a slightly different direction. Let's meet with the team after lunch to brainstorm."

"Okay." His cheeks burned even hotter. *I fucked up again. He must think I'm a total joke.*

Thomas nodded and got to his feet. "I'll see you then." He opened the door to leave and nearly collided with Finn, who was barreling in.

"Excuse me," Thomas muttered.

"No problem." Finn shut the door in Thomas' face.

"Finn!"

"What?" He dropped into the chair Thomas had just vacated and stared at Luka.

"That was rude."

"Nah." Finn leaned back, running his hands through his hair. "He's a busy, important man, places to be. He's already forgotten it."

Luka rubbed his forehead. "I just don't know if closing the door in the new VP's face is the best move."

He readied himself for a retort, but Finn didn't even appear to have been listening. Finn was, in fact, squirming, scratching at his beard, and, for once, struggling to find words.

"Can I help you?" Luka asked after the silence began to stretch into awkwardness.

"Look," Finn growled, scrubbing his face. "About…Rory." He reddened.

Luka did his best to suppress a smile. "Yes?"

"I'm not—It's…" He took a deep breath and fiddled with the seam in his pants, then looked up at Luka pleadingly. "You won't say anything, will you?"

Luka softened. "No. But if you really feel that way, you should."

Finn scoffed. "What would Rory ever want with me? They're so…gentle and quiet and sweet, and I…" He trailed off, staring at the wall, then realized Luka was watching him and scowled again. "Anyway, like you're one to talk."

"What does that mean?"

"Why's your face so red, eh?" Finn grinned. "I've seen the way you look at the Wolf."

Finn didn't know a thing about the Morgan situation, and the agony of the lesson Luka had learned. He had kept telling himself he was going to say something to Finn as he and Morgan got more involved, but the secret kept getting bigger, until it was impossible to share.

And now the last thing he needed was for Finn to get a hold of this bone. His interest in Thomas was just the average intense sexual attraction and he would get over it. Hopefully very soon. "I don't know what you're talking about. Thomas is my boss. And it's red because I shat the bed and the storyboards are garbage. We have to redo them all."

"What?" Finn furrowed his brow. "Thomas said they were garbage?"

"Well, no."

"What did he say?"

"He said he talked to Aleandro and we need to go in another direction."

"So?" Finn shrugged. "You did the work based on the information we had at the time. Now we know more, so we adapt."

Luka blinked at him. Being an expert bullshitter himself, Finn could also cut straight through it. "I guess."

"Just means more time working with him." Finn waggled his eyebrows.

"Anyway," Luka said, ignoring the way Finn never failed to see right through him, "speaking of work..." He gestured to his paper-covered desk.

"Yeah, yeah," Finn grumbled, getting to his feet. "I know, 'Fuck off, Finn.'" He paused at the door and turned back with soft eyes. "Thanks, Luka."

"Any time, bud."

* * * *

Luka rounded the corner to the printer and cursed under this breath when Morgan was standing there waiting for his stack of papers.

Morgan saw him coming and smirked. "Just be a minute, babe."

"Don't call me that," Luka muttered.

"Aw, too many painful memories?" Morgan asked with mock concern.

Luka pressed his lips together and leaned against the counter, determined to wait in silence.

But the annoying little twat kept going. "So, the Big Bad Wolf, huh?" Morgan fanned himself. "I'd like him to huff and puff and blow my house down, if you know what I mean."

"Even the printer knows what you mean, Morgan." *Ugh*. He hated that this man knew things about him that only a handful of other people did. He hated that he had been so vulnerable in front of him.

"What's wrong?" Morgan asked, blinking his soulless gray eyes innocently. "Jealous? Regretting letting me go? No tears, Luka, darling. *You* broke up with *me*."

Luka started counting to ten before he said something he'd regret.

When he got to nine, Morgan grabbed his papers and flounced off, calling over his shoulder, "I know you like to watch me walk away."

Luka shuddered as he grabbed his lone sheet, then turned and collided with a massive, solid frame. *Thomas*.

"Oh, shit! I mean, shoot. Sorry," Luka stammered, straightening his blazer and smoothing back his hair. Jesus, that man was rock-hard.

"It's fine." Thomas tilted his head and examined Luka.

Then he realized what Thomas had just heard. *Fuck*. His mind raced. "Um..." he gulped. "Morgan's not... I assure you — We aren't..." Not wanting to lie, he trailed off, staring at Thomas helplessly.

He leaned past Luka to pick up his printing and grunted. "I didn't hear a thing."

Well, that's definitely not true. Thomas' dizzying scent washed over him. "Okay…but…"

"See you in there." And off he went.

Luka slumped against the counter and closed his eyes. *At this point I wouldn't blame him if he told Ilona to fire me.*

He took a moment, doing his best to rally, before slinking into the conference room. The single empty spot was next to Thomas. His insides jangled as he huffed and took the seat. He could feel Morgan's gaze on him from the other end of the table, and he studiously kept his eyes down.

"Thanks for coming," Thomas started. "I spoke with Aleandro Sartini and I wanted to update you all on the direction we're hoping to take."

Luka started to feel a little bit better as Thomas spoke. It turned out, after additional focus-group testing, Aleandro had decided to more strongly associate the new restaurants with their already well-established wine label, and wanted to shift the focus to include it in all their promotional material. Maybe he wasn't a total idiot after all. And despite himself, his mind began to whir with new ideas.

"I'll work with Luka on the new storyboards," Thomas continued, and Luka deflated.

The Big Bad Wolf split the room into teams and assigned tasks, all while Luka sat there, stewing over the fact that Thomas thought he needed a babysitter.

Once the room cleared, he forced himself to meet Thomas' honey-brown eyes. "Shall we work in my office?" he asked.

Thomas nodded once, face impassive. "Fine."

And he's clearly dreading it…

Luka led Thomas to his office, for some reason painfully aware of his gait. *Am I walking too fast? Now is it too slow? Am I wiggling my ass too much? Not enough? What do I do with my arms?* Thomas glided along beside him, part runway model, part ninja. Luka almost tripped over his own feet. He waved an arm at his desk. "Did you want to take this half?" It was a large L-shape and there was room for Thomas to pull up a chair on the other side.

"Mmm." Thomas set his bag down and began unpacking his laptop and a stack of files.

Luka cleared his throat. Might as well plunge in. "Did Aleandro give you that focus-group research? I'd love to have a look."

A glimmer of what might have been approval flashed across Thomas' face. "I already forwarded it to you."

Luka dropped into his chair to scroll through his email. "Terrific, thanks." He clicked the document open and grabbed his sketchbook, tucking one foot up on his chair. Thomas was watching him. "Oh…is it okay if I read it now?"

Thomas' lip quirked with the first hint of a smile. "Mmm. I'll go do a lap and check in with the other teams. Coffee?"

"Sure, thank you. Two creams, two sugars, please."

His fingers itching to sketch, he turned his attention back to the screen and lost himself in the report. He had already filled two pages with notes and drawings, but it felt like just a few minutes had passed when Thomas placed a mug next to him.

"Oh, you're back already. Thanks!" Luka took a grateful gulp. He sighed happily. The first taste was always the best. He wasn't proud of his caffeine dependence, but figured there were worse drugs.

"What was that song you were humming?" Thomas asked as he sat again.

"Was that out loud?" Luka flushed. "Sorry. Bad habit."

"No, it sounded nice. Sort of...familiar."

Luka paused, hearing it in his head again. This was a new one today, something a little sweet and sad. He had scribbled the chords down in a notebook this morning, but it wouldn't leave him until it was fully formed. "Sometimes a melody or a riff just comes to me and I can't stop humming it. It won't go away until I turn it into a song. It's weird."

"It's not weird. You write music?"

"Uh..." Luka panicked. "Not really. I just mess around."

"Hmm."

He did, in fact, write music. He just didn't share it with anyone. The only people who had ever been privy to his original songs were his parents, and those had been clumsy childhood attempts. Even Tawney and Finn, who had seen him play covers and gushed about how good they were, had not heard his original material. And neither would Thomas.

Luka couldn't think of anything to say, so he bobbed his head and took another drink.

Thomas did the same. "The coffee here is really good."

"Isn't it?" Luka agreed, relieved for the easy topic change. "Not to brag, but that was my doing. It was undrinkable sludge when I started. Ilona put me in charge of improving the situation when she'd had enough of my complaining. So I did my research, taste-tested every coffee place in town... I mean, there were interviews and spreadsheets involved." He chuckled. "And, well, this is what I went with."

Thomas' eyebrows were raised, but his lips were almost-smiling again. "Excellent choice."

"Thanks." Luka grinned at him, then the thing that had been niggling at his brain since before the meeting came out of his mouth. "Look, I don't want you to think I'm hiding anything. Morgan and I were seeing each other, but it was *extremely* casual. Embarrassingly so, in fact. It was a while ago, and, trust me, I learned my lesson. I would never date anyone I work with again."

Thomas took another sip of his coffee, holding Luka's gaze over the brim. "I assure you, I have no idea what you're talking about. And if I did, I wouldn't hold it against you."

Luka rolled his eyes. "If you knew Morgan, you would."

This time Thomas' eyes crinkled as he nodded toward the sketchbook. "Can I hear your ideas?"

Chapter Four

5K

Luka and Thomas redesigned the commercial storyboards over the next couple days, but Luka still found the Big Bad Wolf hard to read. He was polite but stoic, and he ignored or sidestepped most of the questions designed to get to know him better.

"So, where did you grow up?" Luka posed as they were waiting for the elevator.

"Here and there. Blue Lake for a while." Thomas watched the numbers above the door.

"Oh, nice. Never been there, myself. I hear it's beautiful."

"Mmm," was all he replied.

* * * *

The next day as they were eating lunch, Luka asked, "Watching anything good lately? I need something new to binge after my *Breaking Bad* rewatch."

"I don't really keep up on the latest shows." Thomas shoveled in another forkful of salad and flipped to the next page of the report he was reading.

Luka got a chance to see a glimmer of the man behind the Wolf when their staff meeting drew to a close on Thursday.

"Don't forget, the '5K for Hope' is this Sunday," Finn announced from the head of the table. "If you have any donations that weren't online, you can bring the cash and pledge forms with you. The run itself starts at nine, so please try to be there by eight-thirty. I'll have your shirts for you tomorrow. And"—he turned to Luka—"I need to congratulate Moreno who, once again, has raised the most money in the office."

"Oh." Luka hunched his shoulders as the room applauded. "It's nothing."

"It's not nothing," Finn insisted. "That money will make a difference to people with cancer. You did a great job."

Later as they were eating lunch in the staffroom with Finn and Rory, Thomas showed some interest in something that wasn't the Sartini campaign. "How much money did you raise?" he asked Luka.

"Um, just over five thousand," Luka murmured.

Thomas' eyebrows shot up. "That's incredible."

"It's not anything I did. My sister's asshole ex actually chooses to *not* be an asshole on occasion. He makes a big donation every year."

"Yeah, but it's not just him!" Finn piped up. "Luka works hard collecting from a lot of people."

Luka shrugged. "I just send lots of emails and harass everyone on my socials. It's a good cause."

Thomas nodded. "Well, I'd love to join you. Is it too late to sign up?"

"Not at all!" Finn answered. "I'll send you the link. We should have an extra shirt…" He raised an eyebrow at Thomas' frame. "A double-XL, hopefully."

"Great. I'll be there."

* * * *

Sunday dawned bright and clear, although with a definite late September chill in the air. Luka put on his run shirt and a hoodie, and, after a brief internal debate, shorts. His summer tan was still valiantly hanging in, and he might as well show it off. The starting line was at a park not far from his place, so he decided to walk for a good warm-up. He bought a coffee along the way and found himself smiling at nothing in particular, energized and looking forward to the day.

He joined a growing stream of racers as they approached the park, then tracked down the Breakpoint group under a tent with their name on it. Finn was in peak form, making the rounds, cracking jokes and handing out stickers and balloons for the kids.

Morgan was also there, sweatbands on his forehead *and* wrists, running belt around his waist, carrying two water bottles and multiple packs of protein gel. He was alternating between jogging in place and swinging his arms around in gigantic circles. His running shoes were glowing white, clearly experiencing their first contact with the outside world.

Luka rolled his eyes and waved at Tawney when he saw her chatting with Ilona. He turned in a nonchalant circle. Thomas should be easy to spot over the crowd but he was nowhere to be found. Then, just when he was worried that Thomas wasn't going to make it, the bodies parted in front of him, and there he was, crouched down helping a little boy tie his balloon.

When he stood, Luka saw it in slow motion, his brain clinging to the long black lines of Thomas' running tights, thick legs unfolding and stretching on forever, muscles rippling under the shining fabric. Luka gulped, short on air. Finn had indeed found an XXL shirt for him, which was at its breaking point over his shoulders and chest, but loose around his waist. *How* was the word that came to mind. *How is he possible?*

"Hey," Luka said as they met, willing his eyes to stay on Thomas' face.

"Good morning, Luka."

The man was a fucking god, descended from a sacred mountaintop, swathed in fabric spun from midnight, skin burnished and glowing...absolute divine perfection. *Am I drooling?* Then he shook his head to clear it. *Shit, Luka. Get it together. You're here to fund cancer research, for God's sake. Now is not the time for your dick to be in charge.*

But before he could say anything else, Finn climbed up on a chair and called for their attention. "Welcome to Breakpoint's fifth annual 5K for Hope!" He paused for a round of enthusiastic applause while Luka imagined he could feel the heat from Thomas' body standing so close to his. "Thanks to your fundraising efforts and a last-minute anonymous donation, we have smashed our previous best for a total of just over twenty-six-thousand dollars!"

The cheering grew louder.

"You're all making a real impact! Don't forget to stay for the closing ceremony, drink lots of water and have fun out there!"

A pair of bubbly blonds bounded onto the main stage to lead the group in a warm-up. Luka's eyes were drawn back to Thomas' legs. The sharp lines of his calf muscles looked like they were carved from marble. Thomas was bouncing up and down on his toes, light as a feather, then lifting each foot back one at a time to stretch his quads. Luka tried not to stare when Thomas lunged into a calf stretch. Luka did his best to copy his movements instead.

"You a runner?" Thomas asked, lifting one eyebrow.

"Oh, you know… Sometimes." He had run from the subway just a few days ago, hadn't he? Luka normally walked the race with the families and dogs and strollers toward the back, but…the idea of keeping up with Thomas in those tights was appealing. It was only five kilometers, the shortest of all the charity run distances. How hard could it be?

They followed the herd to the start line, but ended up toward the back, losing their friends — and Morgan — in the crowd. One of the blonds counted down the start, then sent them off with a whoop.

He fell into stride with Thomas, enjoying the morning sun warming his shoulders and the explosion of brilliant red, yellow and orange leaves all around them, sharp against the searing blue sky. The first kilometer that looped around the park was okay…sort of. Thomas seemed to be setting a brisk pace and Luka's body grew heavy quickly. He pulled off his hoodie and tied it around his waist as his temperature spiked. The ache in his thighs was concerning as Thomas breezed right on by the first water station.

The ache extended well beyond his thighs by the second kilometer. Particularly into his lungs. He was also sweating, a lot. Thomas looked like he had just leaped from the pages of a high-end running catalogue. Not even a single drop of sweat marred his chiseled brow line as he cast a sideways glance at Luka. "You okay?"

"Fine," Luka gasped. He would have added more — a breezy 'Just a bit rusty!' or 'Hammies are a little tight, is all' — if he had any oxygen to spare.

By the third kilometer, Luka was suffering profoundly, ready to find a hole he could crawl into and die if he had the energy for doing anything beyond collapsing right there on the pavement.

Which he got a chance to do when a dog of indeterminate but trendy breed — a something-doodle, no doubt — changed directions ahead of him, its neon pink leash stretched out across Luka's path.

Had he not been near death's door, off-balance and hand pressed to the sharp pain in his side, it would have been a small matter of sidestepping it. But his legs didn't respond to his brain's sluggish command in time, and he went right over the leash, elbow-first onto the road. The owner lost her grip and the dog yipped and bolted, fleeing across the street.

"Luka!" Thomas said with alarm, hovering over him in an instant. The stream of joggers parted around them as he knelt next to Luka's sprawled figure. One hand came to rest on Luka's shoulder. "Are you okay?"

"Oh my God, I'm so sorry!" the dog owner cried at them as she chased after her dog and vanished.

Luka grimaced. His elbow and knee were hurting something fierce, the skin scraped open on the gravel, bright red blood welling up. But his ego was in much worse shape. *Can I do anything right?* Thomas was already signaling a race official.

"Oh, no, I'm fine," Luka protested, trying to scramble to his feet, mortified.

"Easy," Thomas said, locking eyes with Luka. "Let's make sure you're all right."

Luka swallowed hard, settling back into the pavement. "Okay." Thomas' eyes were molten gold, impossible to look away from. He forgot about the stinging wounds for a moment, and just felt...safe.

He tore his eyes away when a woman wearing a First Aid uniform approached and gave him a quick, calm assessment. Once she had determined that everything was as it should be, minus the scrapes, she began cleaning and bandaging them.

Still embarrassed, Luka looked up at Thomas standing and waiting as she worked. "Really, you should go on ahead."

Thomas frowned and shook his head. "I'll wait."

"I can get you a ride back to the start?" the attendant offered.

"No, it's okay. I can walk the rest. Thank you." Luka got to his feet and gave his legs an experimental wiggle. "I promise, I'm fine. You should keep running," he told Thomas again.

The Big Bad Wolf shrugged. "I'm tired too. I can walk with you." Thomas fell in beside him as they got back on the course. The crowd around them now was thick with dogs and strollers. They passed the four-kilometer marker in silence.

"So..." Luka said, wounds still smarting. "You run a lot."

Thomas squinted and examined the road ahead, perhaps on the lookout for more obstacles for Luka to crash headlong into. "Some."

"I don't actually run," Luka blurted.

Thomas' mouth quirked. "I suspected."

"Yeah…" His elbow throbbed. "Obviously. It's harder than I thought."

"It does take some training."

"I'm sorry I messed up your run."

Thomas shrugged again, turning his face up to the dazzling sun. "You didn't mess it up. There are worse things than a walk in the sunshine."

Well, fuck. It was clear the gorgeous man was also thoughtful and kind. He was not making it easy.

By the time they had made it back to the starting line, the closing ceremonies were underway, but they arrived just in time to see Finn and Ilona up on stage accepting the award for top corporate fundraising team. Luka and Thomas joined their group under the tent as they cheered.

"There you guys are!" Tawney chirped when she saw them. Then she noticed the bandages on Luka's knee and elbow. "Luk! Are you okay? What happened?"

"Just a mild run-in with a dog leash and my own hubris," he assured her. "I'm fine."

Tawney fussed over him as Thomas vanished for a moment, then reappeared, handing Luka a bottle of water and a banana.

"Thanks." Luka was starving, and devoured the fruit gratefully, with one eye and ear on the stage as the ceremony wrapped up. Then Finn and Ilona came back with a photographer in tow for a group photo. Thomas tried to stay out of it at first, but when Tawney wouldn't have any of that, he hid in the back row, slouching behind Finn and Rory.

There was a barbeque afterwards, so most of the crew headed off in search of food, but then Finn saw that Luka was limping. "What the fuck, Moreno?"

Luka sighed, bracing himself for the ragging he was about to take.

Thomas stepped in. "Wayward dog leash. Completely unavoidable. Congratulations on the fundraising, Finn. May I see your plaque?"

Finn passed it over and forgot about teasing Luka. "Our team has raised almost ninety grand in the last five years!"

"That's amazing. You should be very proud."

"Eh, it's a team effort. I'm proud of everyone. We were glad to have your support."

"My pleasure."

Luka shot Thomas a grateful look as Finn turned to find Rory and a hot dog. "Thanks for heading him off there. Finn shows no mercy when he senses weakness." Luka's chuckle turned into a grimace as his knee twitched.

Thomas looked worried. "You should sit down. There's a bench just over there."

"I'm fine—" Luka began, but Thomas had a hand on his elbow and was guiding him over to the park bench.

"Can I get you a hot dog?" Thomas asked once Luka was settled.

"Oh my gosh, no, you've already done so much. I'm okay."

"Hmm." Thomas looked at him steadily. "Ketchup and mustard?"

Luka examined the gleam in Thomas' eye. He was a hard man to say no to. "Just mustard, please. Thank you." A warm glow seeped through his bones, replacing the sharp pains under his bandages.

Luka's gaze lingered on the black spandex again as Thomas disappeared into the crowd. It wasn't fair how hot he was. Or sweet. The man was off getting him food, for God's sake. Luka made a mental note to pick up lunch for Thomas one day this week, as a thank you. When he reappeared a few minutes later with two hot dogs, he handed one to Luka and sat next to him on the bench. Both had just mustard on them. Thomas bit into his.

"Thank you," Luka said. "Turns out exfoliating with pavement works up quite an appetite."

Thomas nodded and swallowed his bite. "I remember my dad patching me up every time I took a tumble off my bike… He'd always make me chocolate milk and peanut butter and crackers after. Then he'd tell me to be more careful, and I'd bail again in a day or two."

"Me too!" Luka laughed. "My dad always liked to complain about all the bandages I was going through."

Thomas smiled a little wistfully at his hot dog. "Mine did too…but he kept buying the expensive superhero ones."

"Aw, that's nice. He sounds like a good guy."

There was a pause as Thomas was lost in a memory for a minute. "Yeah," he said. "The best." They finished their food in thoughtful silence, the crystal blue sky stretching on endlessly above, the chatter of the crowd fading as people started heading home.

Luka and Thomas went back to help Finn tidy up when they were done. Thomas got to work collapsing the tent with Rory, while Luka began collecting trash.

"Wanna grab a beer?" Finn asked as they tossed the last of the water bottles into the recycling. "I need some nachos or something."

"Sorry," Luka said. He hurt everywhere now, the injuries blending in with an overall baseline ache. "I'm gonna go home and lick my wounds…metaphorically speaking."

"Need a ride, babe?" Tawney asked as she shouldered her bag.

"Yeah, thanks."

He looked around at the stragglers to express his gratitude to Thomas again for all this help, but he spotted him in the distance on the other side of the park helping Rory load the tent into Finn's truck. He'd have to wait for work tomorrow.

The first thing he did at home was heave himself into a hot bath, then he spent the rest of the day on the couch, binging *The Great British Bake Off* and eating chips. This was more his style.

He did remember to thank Thomas again first thing Monday, but otherwise the rest of his thoughts were consumed by feeling quite sorry for himself for the pain he was in.

And if Luka had thought he was sore Monday, Tuesday was an entirely new plain of excruciating existence. His knee and elbow felt much better, but every other muscle screamed at him, raging against the colossally poor decision he had made on Sunday.

Luka moaned as he fell into his desk chair, doing his best not to bend his legs at all.

Thomas looked over and offered a sympathetic smile. "Day two is always the worst. You'll feel better tomorrow. Ibuprofen helps."

"There is not enough ibuprofen in the world," Luka mumbled. "It hurts to breathe."

"Maybe some gentle stretching?"

"Can I stretch without getting out of my chair? Or moving at all?"

Thomas hummed. "At least you raised a lot of money for cancer research."

Luka nodded, feeling the pull in his neck. "You're right. Worth it." Then he thought about Thomas' hand on his shoulder. That part of it had been good, too.

Chapter Five

Open Table

"Moreno!" Finn barged into Luka's office at 5:01 on Friday, shrugging on his jacket. "It's quitting time."

Luka didn't look up, in the middle of madly scribbling notes in the margins of the latest analytics. "I just have to—"

"Nope!" Finn snatched the papers out from under his pencil and held them aloft. "Everyone's going for drinks."

"Finn!" Luka reached for his work, but then paused. "Everyone?" he asked, very casually.

Finn, of course, didn't miss a thing. "Everyone," he said pointedly.

Luka chewed his lip and eyed his monitor. There was nothing he *had* to get done before the weekend. Working with Thomas was going well. While he had gotten a glimpse of the man behind the Big Bad Wolf, they had stuck almost entirely to work talk the rest of the week, and had been very productive.

That was not to say he didn't feel an insistent, pervasive and intensifying attraction whenever

Thomas was near. Which was most of the day. It was exhausting. How was he supposed to focus with someone so mind-numbingly attractive sitting a meter away from him? Maybe a drink or two was what he needed to unwind a bit. And if Thomas was also there, having a drink or two... Well, maybe they could unwind together.

"Okay." He stood and grabbed the papers back from Finn so he could tidy them away. "Where are we going? Do not say Exchange."

Finn grinned.

Luka groaned. The Bitter Exchange was a sketchy pub a few blocks away, right by the subway station, down an alley tucked in between sleek office buildings. Despite Luka's best efforts, it had become the go-to spot for after work drinks. Sticky floors and questionable washrooms aside, the owner, Kazio, who was *always* behind the bar, detested Luka. To be fair, he didn't appear to like anyone, but his sneer turned up to eleven when Luka was near. It probably didn't help that Luka had pronounced his name wrong for at least a year. It turned out it was 'Kah-zho', not 'Kah-zee-oh'. Luka was not used to working so hard to have someone like him, particularly when it seemed to make Kazio like him even less.

"Why do we have to go there?" Luka whined.

Finn clapped him on the back. "Ten-dollar pitchers and the best wings in town! What's not to like?"

"Were you wanting a list, or...?"

Finn gave him a playful shove and turned to charge out. "Last one there buys the first round!"

* * * *

Luka pushed open the door, casting a hopeful yet futile glance toward the bar as his eyes adjusted to the dim lighting. Damn it. There was Kazio. Of course. Most of the gang was gathered around their usual mismatched tables in the corner and he gave Finn a wave as he headed over to the bar. He also happened to notice there was no sign of Thomas.

Kazio narrowed his eyes as Luka approached.

Steeling himself, Luka did his best to sound cheerful. "Hello, Kazio."

Kazio curled his lip under his pointy nose. "The usual?"

Nodding, Luka handed Kazio his card. "Yes, please. And can you please put the first round on me, please?" *Fuck. Too many pleases.* He made every effort to be polite, but it didn't seem to matter.

Without a word, Kazio tossed his long, aggressively white-blond hair, and stormed off to make Luka's Bloody Mary.

Luka leaned against the bar, taking another look at their tables. The pub was busy with usual Friday evening traffic. Most of the booths with their ragged red vinyl seats were full, and lots of people clustered together, voices raised in greeting and weekend-adjacent enthusiasm. But still no Thomas.

Kazio reappeared with Luka's drink, plunking it down on the counter and slapping Luka's card next to it. "Tasha will bring out the pitchers."

"Th—" Luka started, but he was already speaking to an empty space. "God," he muttered to himself, then took his drink and headed over to his friends.

He climbed onto an empty stool next to Rory. "Hey, bud." Rory was a person of few words, thin with straight black hair that fell onto their forehead, and multiple visible piercings. Combined with the tattoos and a brilliant, analytical mind, Rory was more than a little intimidating at first. Luka remembered Rory's first staff meeting with great fondness. Ilona had paused, frowning, to shuffle through some papers looking for a particular analytic from the last quarter, and Rory had piped up.

"The downloads for the PDF were up by two hundred and five percent," they had said. Heads had snapped over. "It was one hundred and twenty percent the previous quarter."

Ilona raised an eyebrow.

Rory had looked abashed. "I'm pretty sure."

Ilona had flipped to the next page and ran her finger down some columns. "That's right." She studied Rory for a moment. "Any chance you know the click-through rate?"

Well, as a matter of fact, Rory had known. They had proceeded to rattle off any metric Ilona could ask about.

"Um." Ilona was not often at a loss for words. She had put the papers down. "Thank you, Rory."

Eidetic memory aside, Luka also knew that they were endlessly patient and gentle, always having time for a quick chat and a kind word.

Rory looked over and smiled as he sat. "Hey, Luka."

Finn would be lucky to have them. But since Rory's default mode was being the kindest person on earth to *everyone*, it was hard to say if they felt the same about Finn. Also, Luka had promised Finn he wouldn't say anything.

"How was your day?" Luka asked, taking the first delicious sip of his drink. Kazio might be a prick, but damn, could he make a Bloody Mary.

"It was great!" Rory said. "Finn and I were looking at the favorables from the new Boyer spot for most of the morning. Looks like we killed it."

"That's great! Cheers." Luka offered his glass and Rory clinked it in return.

"Yeah." Rory smiled. "Finn thinks we finally cracked our twenty-five to thirty-four target..." They continued to talk, eyes shining, as Luka tried not to let his lip twitch every time Rory dropped Finn's name. Chances looked good that they felt the same.

Luka took in a breath, ready to prod into Rory's weekend plans on Finn's behalf, when a large figure at the end of the table caught his attention. Thomas was there talking to Tawney.

He looked back at Rory, his heart speeding up. "What are you up to this weekend?" he managed to string together, rather coherently, he thought. But he couldn't resist shooting another quick glance at Thomas. His stomach jolted when Thomas looked back at him.

Thomas' sleeves were rolled up again, his tie gone. His shirt didn't have to work quite so hard to keep his bulk contained when the top three buttons were undone. A hint of chest hair peeked through. Well, that just seemed unfair. It was going to be difficult to do anything but stare.

Luka leaned a little closer to Rory to listen to their answer, swallowing hard and nodding. They chatted a while longer, but Luka was intensely aware of where Thomas was, noticing when he took a seat next to Ilona. Then Morgan arrived, making a beeline for his latest target.

Rory excused themselves to use the washroom while Luka tried not to pay attention to the blond preening and touching Thomas' arm. "Christ," Luka muttered, finishing off his first drink. He reached for the pitcher and a glass.

He got up, new drink in hand, and spotted Tawney over at the dartboard. "I fucking hate Morgan," he announced when he arrived at her side.

"That's 'cause he's a dick," she agreed. She clinked his glass. "Cheers."

"That's insulting to dicks," Luka muttered. Then he noticed what she was wearing. "Excuse me with this dress, by the way."

"This old thing?" Tawney gave him a pose, tapping a dart on her chin. The black and white plaid pencil dress was total perfection, set off against her warm acorn skin.

Luka sighed and tilted his head. "Marry me."

She rolled her eyes and held out a handful of darts. "Oh, stop. I'm still going to kick your ass."

Tawney won the first game, barely. She gloated enough that Luka demanded a rematch, which then turned into a tiebreaker, with several beers along the way. Tawney always knew how to take Luka's mind off his ex. The next time he glanced at them, Thomas was on his way to the bar, and Ilona was talking intently to Morgan.

"Time for another drink?" Tawney asked, giving Luka a meaningful look.

"I'm sure I have no idea what you're talking about." He sniffed at her. "Plus he's probably not even gay."

She smirked. "He is. Ilona told me. And single."

Well, shit. That was very, very interesting. But before he could pretend to be *un*interested for Tawney's sake, she gave him a little push toward the bar.

He glared at her as he combed his fingers through his hair and made his way over. He wasn't sure if he was wobbling a bit or if it was just a natural side effect of winding through the tables. Thomas was propped against the counter in an effortless, sexy lean.

"Hi," Luka said, trying to empty his head of the way that ass looked in those dress pants.

"Hello," Thomas replied.

"How's it going?"

"Good. You?"

"Good. Good." Luka watched Kazio at work, ignoring them on purpose probably. "This guy hates me," he said in a low voice, nodding at the bartender. He realized he was listing too close to Thomas' lips. He straightened up. "Let's see how long it takes me to place an order."

"Hmm." Thomas frowned. "Excuse me, sir?" he called in Kazio's direction.

Kazio looked up, scowling.

"Could you please add Luka's order to my pint?"

Luka smiled, ignoring the way Kazio's scowl deepened. "Thanks. Could I get a shot—" He paused and looked at Thomas. "Two? Two shots of Brawler, please."

"One minute," Kazio snapped.

"He does seem to hate you a bit," Thomas mumbled once Kazio stalked off. "What did you do to him?"

"I think it's mostly just that I exist." Luka laughed. *Am I too loud? And why am I so close to his lips again?*

"Hmm." Thomas looked at him, and Luka could swear his eyes flicked down to Luka's mouth. His tongue slipped out to moisten his lower lip. *What if we kissed right now? What? No!* He scolded himself for being ridiculous, not to mention unprofessional, and turned to watch Kazio at work. The silence stretched out as Kazio took his sweet time lining up the shot glasses.

"Sooo." Luka glanced back at Thomas. "Why do they call you the 'Big Bad Wolf'? I mean...big" — he waved a hand at Thomas' size — "I can guess." Then he realized that 'big' might refer to something much more specific than his overall size. He flushed and cleared his throat, determined to blunder on. "Badgley, bad, makes sense. But why wolf?"

Thomas raised one shoulder, face blank. "I don't know."

The buzz Luka had going was quite pleasant. "Come on! You must have some idea!"

Thomas frowned at his hands on the edge of the bar. "Something about...um, a lone wolf, slipping in silently, then gone again." He avoided Luka's eyes.

A sadness settled over Luka. "Oh." It would be a hard life, moving from office to office, town to town, never getting comfortable in any one place. He cleared his throat and searched for something else to say. "I thought maybe it was because of the way you move, sort of like prowling."

"Prowling?" Thomas quirked his eyebrow.

Shit, that's weird. "Err, you're just...graceful." *Fuck, that's even worse.* Luka flushed.

He was rescued by Finn appearing and throwing an arm around Luka. "We challenge you, Big Bad Wolf!" he bellowed, waving his beer at Thomas. He'd had a few as well.

"We challenge him to what, darling?" Luka leaned away from Finn's beer breath.

"Pool!" Finn announced with glee. He pointed his beer at the new pool table in the back room. New for the bar, that was. It had seen better days. "Me and you versus Thomas and Rory! We'll crush them."

Luka was not much of a player. He laughed. "If you say so." He looked at Thomas, who appeared skeptical. "What do you say, Thomas?"

Thomas frowned. "Probably not a good idea."

Luka deflated. He was already picturing it in his head. The laughing, teasing, casual brushes of their shoulders as they moved around the table...

"Why not?" Finn squinted at him.

"I don't want to listen to you whining when you lose," Thomas said, face stone-cold.

Finn blinked at him then burst out laughing. "Loser buys the next round, pretty boy."

"Deal."

Kazio dropped off their drinks with a sneer while Finn went to round up Rory and a pitcher.

Luka handed Thomas his shot, their fingers brushing together. They tapped glasses and tossed them back. Thomas swallowed, his tongue darting out to lick a stray drop off a plump lip.

"Are you any good?" Luka asked. "At pool, I mean." They made their way over to the table.

Thomas shrugged, straight-faced, but Luka could swear there was a twinkle in his eye as he chose a cue. "Guess you're about to find out."

"Oh hoho, is that how it is?" Luka grinned, taking one for himself.

Thomas just cocked an eyebrow and chalked his cue. "Rack 'em."

"You guys can break," Finn said, pouring himself a glass while Luka racked up the balls.

"Go ahead." Thomas gestured to Rory when the table was ready.

"Give us a good spread!" Finn called as Rory lined up their shot.

The triangle of balls exploded and clattered all around the table, but none went in. Rory groaned.

"Excellent work, Rory!" Finn purred. "Open table." He strutted around, making a show of deciding what his best shot would be. "Three, corner pocket." He sank it easily. "We're solids. Don't let me down, Moreno." He picked up his pint with smug satisfaction.

Luka eyed the table, chewing his lip. He could feel Thomas watching him. His heart rate picked up as he bent over to aim. A vision of Thomas standing behind him, grasping his hips, and thrusting into him flashed through his mind. The cue slipped off his hand and bumped a nearby ball.

"Are you kidding me right now?" Finn asked after a moment of incredulous silence.

"Sorry," Luka said sheepishly, rubbing the back of his neck, avoiding Thomas' gaze. *Jesus, I am a mess.*

Finn shook his head. "Brutal."

"I guess it's me," Thomas rumbled.

Guess so. Luka watched him prowl around the table. *Yup. Wolf.* He stared at Thomas' forearms as they tensed before his shot. With the precision of a sniper's bullet, a striped ball slammed into a pocket.

"Ah, fuck. I picked the wrong partner," Finn moaned.

"Mmm," Thomas agreed.

Luka would have been offended if Finn weren't completely right. He got one more turn, which he missed, then Thomas and Rory cleared the table.

"All right, all right," Finn muttered, signaling Tasha for another pitcher. "Rematch. Get it together, Moreno!

You're breaking. I swear to God..." He took a swig, muttering to himself.

Luka inhaled. *You can do this. No need to embarrass yourself. Again.* He didn't handle the break with Rory's power, but he did manage to sink a stripe.

"That's my boy!" Finn cried, his mood improving. He slapped Luka on the back.

"Well done, Luka." Thomas nodded. "You were bound to sink one eventually."

Luka gasped. "How dare you, sir? Just for that, we're going to destroy you!"

"Starting when?" The corner of his mouth twitched.

Luka felt the flush of his fourth — fifth? — drink in his cheeks. *Is he flirting with me?* "Just you wait!"

Finn sank another ball and Luka squirmed as he analyzed his options. Happily, an easy shot was waiting for him that he managed not to mess up.

He breathed a sigh of relief. "Scared yet?" he asked the other two as Finn hunched over the table.

"Fuck!" Finn swore as the cue ball followed the other into a pocket.

Rory grinned. "Nope. Good try, though, Finny."

"It's still early. I'm not worried." Finn pushed his curls off his forehead and reclined against the table.

"Well, I'm going to need you to move," Rory said, pointing at the shot they had in mind.

"What if I don't want to move?"

"I could make you move." Rory took a step closer, eyes glimmering with amusement.

Luka glanced between them. Electricity crackled. Maybe they were further along than he had thought.

Finn blinked first. He cleared his throat and stepped aside. "Still going to beat you," he mumbled.

Rory slammed another ball home. "We'll see."

Rory and Thomas won again. They high-fived each other while Finn pouted.

"Good game." Rory grinned at Finn, offering a hand. They shook, and Luka was sure he wasn't imagining the spark between them. He shook Rory's hand, too, then he turned to Thomas.

"Good game," he said as their hands touched. A spark flashed right up his arm to every nerve ending in his body. Their eyes met as the rest of the bar faded away. Thomas' chest rose and fell with a slow breath, a small strand of hair spilling over one eye. Luka's other hand itched to push it back. The smell of Thomas' cologne mixed with the scent of the dark ale he'd been drinking. The shake went on, Thomas' grip not loosening.

"Good game," Thomas said to him, and the rest of the pub snapped back into focus. Finn was snickering. Their hands dropped.

Thomas cleared his throat. "Thanks, everyone," he said to the three of them. "I think I'll be heading home."

Luka nodded, mouth dry. "Have a good weekend."

"You too." Thomas nodded, and headed to the bar to settle his tab before making his way out into the darkness.

Luka watched him go. He dreamed about the pool table that night.

Chapter Six

Blackmail

"Morning." Thomas' deep baritone startled him.

Luka looked up from his desk where their presentation was spread out. "Oh! Morning." He took in Thomas' sharp navy suit. It looked new. His mouth watered at the way it hugged his every bulging muscle.

"You've been here a while?" Thomas asked, nodding at Luka's near-empty coffee cup and paper-strewn desk. He set his bag down.

Luka nodded. "I was up early. Had trouble sleeping." As of about four a.m., he hadn't been able to stop going over his presentation in his mind, so he thought he might as well do that at work. Aleandro Sartini himself would be arriving with his team today for an update on their project.

"Me too," Thomas admitted. "I went for an extra-long run."

"Well, that's good. And, you know, no running for me, so..." Luka's brain started to drift as he pictured Thomas in running tights again, then he shook himself. *Have I always been this horny?* he wondered before jumping to his feet. "Coffee?" he offered. "I need a warm-up."

"Mmm."

Luka now knew that was Thomas for 'yes'. He headed down the hall and found Finn and Rory giggling together in the staffroom.

"I told you!" Rory laughed. "It goes off the rails in the second season."

Finn's grin stretched from ear to ear. "You're right. I should have listened to you. But it started off so good!"

Rory shook their head. "Think of the time we've both wasted now. Maybe if we turned it into a drinking game…"

"Moreno!" Finn announced when he saw Luka approaching the coffee maker. His eyes were sparkling and Luka knew that glow had nothing to do with him. "Ready for the big day?"

"As ready as I can be." Luka topped up his coffee and grabbed a mug for Thomas. Pure coincidence that it said 'Marketers Make the Best Lovers'.

"We've got this. Aleandro is going to love it," Finn assured him.

"'Course he will!" Rory chimed in. "You're both brilliant artists."

Luka was sure Finn was blushing as he looked down at his shoes.

"Thanks, Rory. I guess we'll find out soon!" Luka smiled and left them to their flirting.

He carried the coffee back to their office and set Thomas' down next to his laptop. He studied the big man and saw no sign of any nerves. He was the same as always—calm, quiet, sturdy. Gorgeous.

Thomas looked up at him. "What?"

"Oh." Luka swallowed hard. "Nothing. I was just—you don't look nervous at all."

Thomas shrugged one shoulder and picked up his mug. "No reason to be. Our work is solid." He took a thoughtful sip. "Are you nervous?"

Luka laughed. "Yes! Was it not obvious?"

"You don't need to be. Aleandro is a good guy, and if he doesn't like anything, we change it."

Luka took a deep breath. "Okay. Thanks." Heart-pounding beauty aside, there was something about Thomas that was very…soothing. "Still, can we go over it a few more times?"

Thomas gave him a small smile. "Sure."

Luka had been paying careful attention, and so far from Thomas he had seen only amused mouth twitches and the odd glimpse of a tiny smile like this one. He wondered what he could do to get a bigger one.

* * * *

Aleandro Sartini had an old-fashioned, dignified air to him. His black hair was heavily streaked with gray. It was swept back off of his forehead, emphasizing his widow's peak and mutton chops. Luka had seen pictures of Aleandro before, but they had not captured the man's elegant authority. A three-piece suit and a pocket watch completed the look.

Seated next to him was his wife and CFO, Penelope. She was in a crisp suit, petite and beautiful, although in a severe way, with her hair pulled back into a stern twist, mouth unsmiling. She looked like someone who didn't suffer fools. A woman with long, wavy strawberry blonde hair who Luka didn't know was sitting with them.

Jennifer Moffatt

The team gathered in the conference room, a nervous energy palpable as they settled. Ilona smoothed her hair and straightened her dress. Luka wracked his memory and decided he had never seen her so nervous before. It would have been cute, if it didn't also send his stomach swirling again.

Ilona stood and the room hushed. "Welcome to Breakpoint," she said to the guests. "Allow me to introduce you all to our team. Aleandro Sartini, CEO of Sartini Wines."

Aleandro inclined his head gracefully. "Pleasure to be here."

"Penelope Sartini, CFO."

Penelope bobbed her head but didn't speak.

"And Georgia Black, head of marketing for Sartini Wines. She'll be our main liaison," Ilona continued.

Georgia smiled and waved.

"Our team is thrilled to share their work with you. Let's get started, shall we?" Ilona lifted her chin at Luka and Thomas.

They rose, their gazes meeting. Thomas gave him a tiny nod. *You've got this.*

Luka stumbled over a few lines at the beginning, but his confidence grew as he spoke, Thomas' presence a steadying force. Penelope was hard to read, but Aleandro and Georgia looked happy, smiling and nodding. Aleandro made a few quick notes on his notepad.

As they sat back into their chairs, Thomas squeezed his arm. It was only for half a second, but he was sure the whole office would notice the heat flaring in his cheeks. Luka stared at his blazer where Thomas' hand had been, feeling the imprint on his skin. It was a pleasant distraction as Morgan began speaking.

Morgan played the music he had shared last time that was, in fact, mostly Luka's work. But there were some new pieces, too. Passable, but not as good. Apparently, Aleandro didn't like them either. His mouth turned down in the slightest frown as he scribbled at his notepad. Luka risked a glance at Morgan. He was already sulking. Luka wasn't sure whether he should feel smug or embarrassed for the firm.

Finn and the print campaign team spoke, and Rory shared some preliminary marketing analysis. When everyone was done, Aleandro stood to address them. "Great work, team. You're off to a wonderful start. The three of us will meet with Ilona and Thomas and we will talk about the next steps. I look forward to seeing where you go from here."

"Thanks, everyone," Ilona said. "Thomas or I will touch base soon."

Luka snaked out of the conference room with the rest of them. Morgan pushed past him and disappeared into his office.

"Great job, bud." Rory clapped Luka on the back.

"Thanks, you too." Luka looked down as his phone buzzed. It was a text from Thomas. "See you guys later." He waved, then headed to his office and shut the door.

Great job. You can start on the scripts. I'll be there soon.

Luka smiled as he sat at his computer.

It indeed wasn't long before Thomas came in. "Aleandro loved your work," he said, adding a few files to the stack on his desk.

"Our work," Luka corrected him.

Thomas smiled at him, the corners of his mouth curling up far enough to crinkle his eyes a bit. *The biggest smile yet.* Luka tucked the memory of this one away to think about later. The moment stretched out. "What's next?" Luka asked to break the silence.

"We're heading up the team for the commercials. Scripts, casting..."

Luka's eyes bugged out. *"We?"*

"Yes, 'we'. Aleandro said he wanted you as a lead with me."

Luka opened his mouth then closed it again. "Uh. Wow. Okay." He tried not to fidget.

Thomas was still smiling at him. "Let's get those scripts done."

They were just getting down to work when Morgan slunk by, casting a furtive glance into Luka's office. Then he walked past again a few minutes later. By the third time, it hit Luka. *He wants to ask for help, but he can't because Thomas is here.* Luka answered one of Thomas' questions and ignored the pathetic man in the hallway with great satisfaction.

When it was time for a stretch break, Luka headed down the hall to the washroom. Aleandro and Penelope were standing together outside Ilona's office. Her face was turned up, his bent down to her. They weren't touching, but they smiled at each other. Then Aleandro ran a finger down her arm as he whispered something to her. The stern lines from Penelope's face were gone. She just looked...happy.

An unexpected wave of yearning swamped him as he passed by. He wondered if they had met at work. Because being in love *and* being co-workers clearly was not a problem for them.

He continued to ponder the idea of successful workplace romance until Morgan found him while he was washing his hands. "Lukaaa." The high-pitched voice dragged out his name.

Fuck. Luka braced himself and turned, drying his hands with a paper towel. "What's up, Morgan?"

"Well..." He batted his eyelashes. "I was wondering if you had a few minutes to take a look at the changes I made to the score." It wasn't that Morgan was incompetent. He was well educated — a double major in music theory and sound design from a prestigious school — and his work was fine. It was just missing a spark...an ineffable quality that made it memorable. And it seemed like he knew it, too.

Luka clenched his jaw. "Not really. Thomas is riding me pretty hard to get the scripts finalized." Yes, he was a petty man who chose 'riding me hard' on purpose.

"Please? It will only take a second." Morgan's lower lip stuck out.

"No, Morgan. It won't. You'll have me redoing the entire thing and I don't have time."

Morgan's eyes narrowed as he dropped the act. "I wonder what Thomas would think about us secretly dating."

"I already told him," Luka replied, stomach clenching.

Morgan arched his eyebrow. "Oh, really? You told him we were fucking for *months* and didn't mention it to HR?"

Luka was paralyzed by guilt. Because no, he hadn't exactly told Thomas that. He didn't reply.

Morgan chuckled. "I don't think Ilona would be happy, either."

The words washed over him, settling in his gut. "Are you *blackmailing* me?"

Pressing a hand to his chest, Morgan gazed at Luka with wide, innocent eyes. "I would never."

This piece of absolute shit. Luka had worked so hard at this job, given it his all. The idea of Morgan fucking it all up for him, of getting him kicked right off the ladder...of never seeing Thomas again... "Fine," Luka growled through clenched teeth, hating himself almost as much as he hated Morgan. "Let me have a look."

What stung the most about Morgan, a knife twisting in his back, was that he had let his guard down. Trusted him enough that he played his guitar for him. The list of people who had heard him play since he was thirteen—since the *Say Hi* Horror—contained exactly three people outside of his family—Tawney, Finn and Morgan. The humiliation burned fresh in his mind.

Luka had been a gangly kid, always tall for his age, with huge feet. This had progressed into an awkward adolescence, all bumbling legs and arms. The easy charm and confidence he had now as an adult, when his long limbs started working for him rather than against him, was nowhere to be found at thirteen. Money was tight, and his clothes and shoes were wrong. His lunches were wrong, too. The other kids had been telling him since he could remember that the food his mom packed was weird—rich, fragrant soups and stews in his thermos. Everyone else had sandwiches, if they even bothered to eat at all. The things he liked to do at school—paint and draw and sketch—were wrong. He had no interest in playing sports. That was wrong. He was wrong, wrong, wrong.

His parents didn't understand. His mom was baffled as to why he wasn't the most popular boy in school. "Do they know you play the guitar?" she asked one day. Her five o'clock appointment had made a rare cancellation, and she appeared in the kitchen to eat dinner with the rest of them. Normally she missed it, because after school and early evening were prime piano lesson hours. She made the dinners during the day, when she just had a few housewives for clients, the ones looking to rediscover the music in their fingers that had been worn down by years of cooking, cleaning and caring for their families. She popped the meals in the oven and left them to warm so they were ready for the family when her husband got home.

"They don't care that I play the guitar, Mom," Luka mumbled into his beef stew. He knew the leftovers would be in his thermos tomorrow.

"They would care," Marta insisted. "If they knew."

"Of course they would," his dad agreed.

Well, maybe. Luka knew he was good. He could play the guitar like he'd been born doing it, could hear a melody and recreate it on the piano without even thinking. He had heard the torturous sounds made by his mom's students for as long as he could remember, and he knew he was better than just about all of them.

When his school announced they were holding a talent show, he signed up, scribbling his name down and scurrying off before anyone noticed. That night, he was doing his homework at the kitchen table when his mom joined him. She had just finished her lessons for the day. She sank down next to him, rubbing lotion into her hands.

"I signed up for the talent show," he mentioned.

"Oh, Luka, that's wonderful!" She reached over to squeeze his shoulder. "What will you play?"

"Uhhh…" He had no idea. Any song he chose would be wrong.

His mom gasped. "You should play Say Hi!*"*

"My own song?" He gaped at her. "No way!"

"Why not? It's brilliant. They'll be so impressed!"

Luka shook his head, but...it sounded like a good idea once he thought about it. Then he wouldn't have to worry about choosing the wrong song, and there was no original version to compare him to.

Maybe that had been his mistake. Maybe if he had asked Yasmin what song to play instead, it would have been fine. His sister was already in senior high, pretty, popular, her limbs all the right size. He knew she ate her lunches after school once she got home. She would have known what song to play.

But he didn't ask her. So that was how, at thirteen years old, he stood in front of the entire junior high, alone with his guitar, and played a song he had written. The crowd was a little restless by the time it was his turn. They'd already sat through three dance routines, girls gyrating their hips just a touch more than was probably appropriate. They'd seen rock bands and gymnasts and jugglers. Now, it was just Luka and his guitar.

Rehearsing in his living room, with his mom and dad cheering him on, he had felt like a rockstar. In the five seconds of silence before he struck the first chord, he summoned that feeling again. "This is called Say Hi," he said into the mic. His voice boomed around the gym, unsettling him. Then he started playing.

"I saw you across the way
Looking so good today
And I wanted to say
Now please don't be shy
Come over and say hi."

He could see the smirks appearing before he even finished the first chorus. Not from everyone, of course. Most of the students were bored or indifferent. A handful looked *embarrassed for him. He didn't know what else to do but go on. His voice shook.*

"I saw you smiling down the hall
So cute with your brown eyes and all
I wanted to say
So please don't be shy
Come on over and say hi."

Now the smirks were turning into whispering, laughing. There was a hum in the gym. He soldiered on.

"'Cause it's clear to see
That it won't be me
I guess I'm way too shy
Please come over and say hi."

Ghastly silence fell as the last chord faded. He stared at the crowd. They stared back at him. Most of them looked confused, but a few looked...eager. Predatory. The teachers began clapping, and some polite souls joined in. Luka all but ran off stage and out through the gym doors. He was supposed to stay to watch the rest, but he sensed he had to get far, far away.

It didn't matter. After school that day, he passed by a group of kids who burst out laughing when they saw him. "Hey, Luka!" one of them called after him. "Come over and say hi!" Luka put his head down and hurried to the bus, a rock in his stomach.

"How did it go?" his mother asked not long after he got home, sticking her head through his bedroom doorway.

He was lying face down on his bed. He could barely hear her over the angst rock he was blaring. "Don't you have a lesson right now?" he mumbled.

"Pardon?" She took a step into the room.

Luka lifted his head and glared at her. "I said, don't you have a lesson right now?"

"I told her I had to use the washroom." Marta pinched her eyebrows together. "Luka…is everything okay?"

"Fine," he said flatly, flopping his face back onto his pillow. "It was fine." He waited for her to reply, but when he looked up again, she was gone.

It was an hour later when his sister appeared at his door. "Hey."

He hadn't moved from his spot on the bed. The album was on its third play. "What?" he demanded. She never talked to him unless she wanted something, like to borrow money or try to get him to switch chores.

She shuffled into the room, then poked at the wolf figurine sitting on his dresser. "Nicki saw the talent show." Nicki lived across the street and hung out with Yasmin a lot, even though she was a year behind Yasmin and still went to Luka's school.

"So?" he snapped at her, his insides clenching.

"She said you were really good, but, uh…"

Luka willed himself not to cry. "Just say it. I'm a huge loser."

"No, it's… She said you were really good. That's all."

Luka scowled at her, deciding on the quickest way to get her out of his room, before the tears came. "I'm not trading you for the dishes again. Last time you didn't even do them and Mom got pissed at me."

Yasmin shook her head. "Just ignore the assholes, okay? And…and can you please play something else, for God's sake?" Then she left, closing the door behind her.

Ignoring the assholes was easier said than done. He'd been on the bus for five minutes the next morning when the kids at the back started calling his name. "Luka! Come over and say hi!" And the same thing continued all day at school, from *just about everyone. He tried to ignore them – he did. But the mocking laughter got under his skin and stayed there.*

"Brown eyes, hey?" Stephen Mercer said, appearing next to Luka at his locker after lunch. "Who's got brown eyes? Oh, wait, I do!" Stephen's cronies erupted into hoots of laughter. "You got a crush on me, Luka?"

Luka's heart fell. The brown eyes referred to Patrick Taggart, in fact, a sweet, quiet kid in his English class who also happened to be one of the stars of the basketball team. He admittedly had not thought about anyone grabbing onto the brown eyes thing, because the majority of people had brown eyes. That didn't matter to this crowd, of course. If anything, it just encouraged them.

"Cooper has brown eyes!" Stephan announced, nodding at his main henchman, who snickered. "You like Cooper?" He pointed to a group of girls passing by. "How about the fat one there? She's got brown eyes."

Luka slammed his locker shut, an acrid taste in his mouth.

"Hey, Luka, don't be shy, come over and say hi!" Stephen cooed in falsetto as Luka turned to make his way to math class. He could hear them howling the whole way down the hall.

His mom was taken aback when Luka told her he didn't want to perform in her recitals anymore. There was a big one coming up and Luka was supposed to close the show. "I'm too old for recitals, Mom."

"What do you mean, 'too old'? Lucy and Rita are older than you."

"Lucy and Rita are like fifty."

"They're in their forties!"

"It's just…not my thing anymore." Drawing and painting was a much safer way to express himself. No one made fun of his art. No one harassed him every day because of it.

Marta was crushed, but she didn't push it. She seemed happy that Luka still played in his bedroom. His parents never stopped encouraging him, and he never stopped playing. He even started writing songs again. But he never performed in front of a crowd. And the longer he went, the larger his fear of it grew until it became insurmountable. Even allowing his best friends to see him play was a huge, huge scary step.

Letting Morgan in had been a mistake. One he was still paying for.

* * * *

"Where were you?" Thomas looked up from his laptop and frowned as Luka tiptoed back into his office.

"Oh." Luka's mind raced. "Morgan wanted to show me what he'd been working on."

"You were gone for a while."

"Yeah, we...got to chatting. I had a few suggestions."

Thomas looked skeptical. "Really. That's generous of you."

"Mmhmm," Luka squeaked, busying himself checking his email. A minute later he snuck a look at Thomas. He was typing away, brow furrowed. Luka cursed himself, because now he had tried to fix a half-truth by outright lying.

If he thought hard, he could remember moments with Morgan that were happy. The way he kissed, lips nimble and eager to please. The soft sounds he made when Luka touched him just right... It was hard to reconcile those warm moments with the conniving, selfish asshole who was now blackmailing him.

He vowed that next time he would just say no to Morgan, no matter the consequences.

Chapter Seven

I'll Give You a Hint

Thomas peeled off his shirt, his muscles rippling in the soft light. He prowled toward Luka, who sat naked on the edge of his bed. Thomas splayed one hand on Luka's chest and pushed him back, flat onto the mattress. Quivering with anticipation, Luka watched Thomas slide his pants and underwear off. He licked his lips as Thomas' hard length sprang free. Thomas climbed onto him, straddling his hips.

"You want me?" Thomas asked, his voice impossibly deep and sexy. His brown hair was loose, brushing his shoulders. He pushed it back with one hand, biceps flexing.

Luka couldn't speak. He nodded frantically.

Thomas ground down onto him, rubbing them together. "I said, do you want me?"

Luka's lips wouldn't open. He met Thomas' eyes, trying to make the yearning plain on his face.

"If you want me" — Thomas leaned down, his lips ever so slightly brushing Luka's — "you just have to tell me, Luka. Just tell me."

Luka tried to make his mouth form the words, but nothing would come out. He wanted to cry in frustration. He gave one last final, straining effort, then jolted awake, panting. "Oh, God," he moaned, scrubbing a hand over his face.

The sex dreams would not stop. He had woken up achingly hard, heart pounding, almost every day the past week. He looked over at his clock. Just past six o'clock in the morning. Too early for a Sunday.

The dream came back to him in the shower. He let his soapy hand drift downward, touching himself slowly at first, then faster, imagining what might have happened next in the dream. It provided some relief, but not enough. He did a load of laundry, vacuumed and made a half-hearted attempt at cleaning off his desk, but filing old mortgage papers wasn't helping pass the time. He was too jittery to play his guitar. After rattling around his condo for another hour, moving things then moving them back, he felt like screaming. He grabbed his keys, phone, earbuds and a sweater, then headed out the door, not sure where he was going.

He decided to head left out of his front door, and joined the usual Sunday morning foot traffic, mostly consisting of parents with strollers and crowds heading out for brunch. Turning off the main road, he wandered through his neighborhood, noticing the pumpkins dotting front steps here and there. His feet took him to his favorite park and kicked at the fading red leaves as they blew past him.

The houses and buildings around him grew less familiar the farther he walked, but he spotted a coffee shop he used to visit sometimes when Tawney had lived nearby. He hadn't been since she'd moved last spring. It was called Jitters and he remembered why he loved it the moment he pushed open the door and the smell of roasting beans flooded his nostrils.

It was a funky old place, with a long, irregular shape and exposed brick along the back wall, crammed with fading, comfortable armchairs and vintage wooden furniture. The baristas were the best part though, lots of blue and purple hair and colorful socks, and they changed the quote on the chalkboard every few hours. Right now it read, *Pilates? I thought you said pie and lattes.*

Sitting down with a steaming mug in a creaky chair by the window, he slipped his earbuds back in and caught up on his latest podcast obsession. It took a deep dive into the craft of a different music legend every week, and the details in those interviews fed Luka's very soul. The time drifted by as he managed to get his mind off Thomas, when suddenly he was aware of a large figure standing in front of him.

His head snapped up.

It was Thomas.

Holy fuck. His stomach bottomed out. "Hi."

Thomas was wearing black running tights and a dry-fit shirt. His hair was back in a messy knot, curls escaping down the sides of his face, and he was sweaty. Very sweaty. A day's growth of dark stubble somehow helped him reach a new, catastrophic level of brain-melting hotness. He was carrying two cups of coffee. Luka's insides turned to jelly.

"May I join you?" Thomas asked.

"Of course," Luka stammered, attempting to act like he was still in one solid piece.

"I got you a refill." Thomas eased his heavy frame into the chair and pushed one of the cups over to him. "Two cream, two sugar?"

"That's right. Thank you. Out for a run?" Luka tried not to stare at the way the sleeves of Thomas' shirt strained around his arms. *Poor shirt.*

"Yup. I usually grab a coffee here when I'm done."

"You live close?"

"Renting just across the street." He pointed to the new condo tower. "Do you come here often?"

I do now. "Sometimes. Tawney used to live nearby. But... Well, it was a bit of a walk this morning, to be honest. I was feeling a little stir crazy. Normally it would be two stops on the train."

Thomas nodded and took a drink.

"So...you're liking our office? Feeling settled in?" Luka asked, noticing a bead of perspiration on Thomas' temple and wanting very much to wipe it off for him. Warrior vibes were coming off him in sweat-soaked waves. He imagined Thomas on a battlefield, armor gleaming, sword aloft, striking down manipulative, blond jackasses.

"Yes, it's been nice. Everyone has been very welcoming."

"Do you have any idea how long you'll stay?" he tried to ask casually.

Thomas shrugged a shoulder. "It depends how the campaign goes, and if Aleandro extends our contract." He studied his coffee cup. "Might be nice to stay in one place for a while."

"Would you rather stay in one place permanently?" He regretted asking the question. He didn't know Thomas well enough to grill him about his life choices.

Thomas shook his head. "No, I like my lifestyle. It's...easier like this. Simple." The corners of his mouth stretched out. "Nothing weighing me down."

Luka nodded and blew at the steam coming off his cup, relieved Thomas didn't seem to mind the question. "Well, we're happy you're here."

"Thank you."

The silence settled over the table as Luka searched for a new topic. "Are you going to go to Finn's Halloween party?" It was coming up soon. Finn hosted the office party every year.

"I don't know… I don't usually like to bother with costumes."

"Are you kidding me?" Luka blurted, eyeing Thomas' chest. "If I was built like you, I'd go as a superhero every single year. You wouldn't even need a padded suit." *Oh, God. That was too much.*

Thomas looked down. Luka thought he detected a slight flush to his cheeks.

"I don't know about anything in a cape, but yeah, maybe I'll come."

"Super." Luka grinned and took a sip of his coffee. The party just got a whole lot more interesting. Maybe there would be more to do than just watch Finn and Rory flirt.

Thomas' eyes crinkled. "What are you dressing up as?"

"Tawney and I are doing a couple's costume! It's a surprise." Luka wiggled in anticipation. He loved dressing up. "But, I'll give you a hint. It'll give you *chills.*"

"Interesting." Thomas gave him an amused look. "Elsa and Anna?"

Luka burst out laughing. "Good guess! But no."

"Mr. Freeze and Poison Ivy?"

He laughed again. "No. Perhaps my hint was misleading."

A Hard Sell

Warmth flickered in his chest as a full smile reached the corners of Thomas' face. Fuck, he was beautiful. What he wouldn't give to look at that smile every day for the rest of his life.

"I guess I'll have to wait and see." Thomas leaned back in his chair, shoulders relaxing.

"What would you go as?"

"Hmm...I'll need to dig through some boxes. I don't take much with me from place to place."

"I'm sure you could rent a Superman costume if you hurry." Luka winked at him.

Thomas fiddled with his cup and smiled. "I'll keep that in mind."

"What else do you get up to on weekends?" Luka asked.

The conversation drifted from there, Thomas sharing what he'd discovered in Oakport so far, Luka nodding along eagerly.

"Have you eaten at Montecalvo yet?"

Thomas shook his head.

"Oh, you have to try it. It's the next town over, a bit of a drive, but it's worth it. They hand-make the most incredible pork-stuffed pastries. It's like you've died and gone to heaven."

"Sounds delicious."

"We should go sometime." Luka wanted to bite back the words as soon as they escaped. *Holy shit, did I just ask him on a date? Chrissake, Luka!* He scrambled. "Sometimes Tawney and I will make a day trip of it. You could come with us."

Thomas shifted in his seat. "Sure."

"Okay, great."

There was an awkward pause while they each took another drink. "So, what made you get into advertising?" Thomas asked, filling the silence.

"Well...I've always loved to create things," Luka said, a little shy. "Things that will touch people, connect with them, speak to them. Maybe make them laugh, or feel inspired. And seeing the ideas that were in my head, fully realized on a screen?" He shook his head. "I remember the first time I saw my work out there... I was folding laundry, watching a rerun of *Friends*—had my hands on an old Harry Styles tank top, to be exact—and then there it was—an ad for the Oakport Mountain Lodge. I made that, you know? There's nothing like it."

Thomas stared at him for a moment, coffee forgotten in his hand. "Yeah. That's...that's exactly it." He cleared his throat. "But I also enjoy the administrative side—coordinating departments, providing support where it's needed, helping pull the whole vision together..."

Luka nodded. "You're very good at it."

It was Thomas' turn to look shy. "Thanks," he said, eyes on the table.

"What do you think you'd do if you weren't in advertising?"

"Hmm." Thomas frowned. "Well, I wanted to be a lawyer when I was a kid. I went into Business Admin thinking I'd go to law school once I had my degree. But I spent a few summers working at a law firm and...it wasn't for me. Too regimented, too structured. Then in second year I took an elective in marketing and fell in love with it."

Luka pictured Thomas storming around a courtroom or glaring at opposing counsel across a conference table. He would be scary. "Ah, so that's where you got your sense of style, then?" He grinned. "Lawyers."

Thomas raised his eyebrows a little before he chuckled. "I feel like that's a shot, but you're right."

"Not a shot! I love your suits."

"Thanks." A corner of his mouth lifted. "What about you? What else would you do?"

The answer to that one beat through Luka's blood like a drum, but he couldn't say it out loud. "Not sure, something to do with art, I suppose. Like a cartoonist, or, ooh, maybe an art gallery director."

"That sounds nice. Are there any good art galleries in town?"

They chatted for another while about the local gallery scene and their favorite artists until Thomas looked at his watch. "Oh, wow, it's gotten late. I'd better head home and take care of a few things."

"Okay. Thank you for the coffee." Luka swallowed hard as Thomas stood. His gaze flicked to the bulge in the man's tights, his face turning bright red as he realized what he'd done.

He risked a glance up at Thomas, who was watching him. *Fuck. He saw that.* How could he blame him, though? It was very…noticeable.

"Enjoy the rest of your day." Thomas nodded. A hint of a smile ghosted his lips.

"You, too." Luka watched him walk away. Speaking of noticeable…

Luka wrenched his eyes back up as Thomas turned and waved before he pushed open the door.

Luka stared after him through the window, the sunlight glinting off the black spandex. He stifled a moan as last night's dream came back to him. He suspected there would be spandex in his dream tonight. And just like that, he was right back where he started.

* * * *

"I'm gonna do it." Finn threw himself into the chair in Luka's office.

"Do what?"

"I'm gonna ask Rory to wear a couples costume with me."

Luka tried not to laugh. "That's a great idea. Or, you could just ask them out."

Finn sucked in a breath, shaking his head. "No, this is okay. This is good. This is a step."

"If you say so," Luka said. "What costumes were you thinking?"

Finn rubbed his face. "I have no idea. Maybe crayons?"

"Good God, please, no." Luka thought for a minute. "Daenerys and Jon Snow? You'd rock the blond wig, and Rory would look sexy in that cloak."

"Fuck, no! Too coupley! And I can't support that show after what they did to Dany... The Mandalorian and Grogu?"

Luka wrinkled his nose. "I'm thinking maybe no to the parent–child vibe? Plus those costumes would be crazy expensive if you're going to get good ones. How about a classic — Batman and Robin?"

"No tights." Finn shook his head.

"What about *Dirty Dancing*! Baby and Johnny?"

Finn raised an eyebrow. "And who's going to want to wear those tiny shorts, me or Rory?"

"Good point," Luka mused. "Goose and Maverick?"

Finn blinked at him, then a slow smile spread over his face. "You are a fucking genius! Flight suits are sexy, the inherent homoeroticism of *Top Gun*... I love it!"

Luka grinned. "At your service."

"Okay." Finn stood and took a deep breath. "Now I gotta go ask them."

"You can do it, Finn. You're just suggesting costumes, not proposing," Luka reminded him. "Oh, and hey, if something does happen, make sure you go to HR right away."

"Well, of course." Finn rolled his eyes. "I'm not an idiot."

Ouch.

Finn took another breath, too caught up in his own turmoil to notice Luka flinching. "You're right, I can do it. Okay, here I go." He didn't move.

"Finn?"

"Yeah?"

"You're still here."

"Fuck." He shook himself and strode out, passing Thomas on his way in.

"He's in here a lot," Thomas commented as he settled in his chair.

"Yeah," Luka agreed. "He can come across as a bit...loud, but he's a really good guy."

"Hmm."

Oh, shit. Does he think I like Finn? "He was just — well, he's trying to plan a couple's costume. With Rory." *Fuck, did I just give away that he likes Rory? Change the subject, Luka.* "So...any ideas for your costume?"

"I think I've figured something out. But I'll keep mine a surprise, too."

"Do I get a hint?"

"Well..." Thomas tilted his head. "I'm a time-traveler."

"Um...Marty?"

Thomas frowned. "Who?"

Luka gasped. "Hello? Marty McFly? *Back to the Future*?"

"Oh, right. Never seen it."

"What?" Luka lurched forward in his chair. "*Any* of them?"

Thomas shook his head, having the decency to appear remorseful at least.

"Okay, this is just unacceptable. We are having a marathon."

"All right." Now Thomas looked amused.

Luka shook his head, muttering, "Never seen *Back to the Future*, I mean honestly…"

"Well, my spotty movie-viewing history aside, how do you feel about those casting options I sent you?"

Oh, right. Work. "I had a look and I mostly agree with you, but I was thinking about making one change." They got down to it, flipping through head shots, but a large part of Luka's brain simmered with excitement. He couldn't wait for the party.

Chapter Eight

We Go Together

Luka turned to examine himself in the mirror. Skintight black pants and a clinging black off-shoulder top. He adjusted the curly blond wig and stepped into a pair of red pumps he'd borrowed from Tawney's roommate. The perfect Sandy. He just had to ignore the way she'd changed everything about herself for a guy, even one as cute as young John Travolta.

He hummed along to the *Grease* soundtrack as he clipped on hoop earrings and applied his makeup. "Tell me about it, stud," he cooed into the mirror when he was done.

He was snapping a selfie when his phone buzzed. It was Tawney. He grinned. She was Danny and he couldn't wait to show up at the party with her. Then he read her message.

Omg, Luk. I'm so sick. I can't make it tonight.

Oh no! Are you okay??

My stomach's been hurting all day and I just threw up. I'm in bed. I'm so sorry.

It's okay, babe. Take care of yourself. Stay hydrated. xo

Poor Tawney. He was disappointed his other half wouldn't be there. Sandy would have to be cute on her own.

He hopped onto the subway, giving the oglers a little extra wiggle in his walk on the way by. Fortunately, Finn's place wasn't far from the station. Luka wasn't used to getting around in heels.

Finn lived in an old but meticulously maintained bright yellow bungalow, the front walk lined with crude jack-o'-lanterns in compromising positions. The inside of the house was all redone, but retained its funky, vintage vibe with wood paneling, an avocado-green couch and smooth, ceramic lamps. Large paintings adorned most walls, abstract with hints of skin and hands and lips. Luka knew that Finn had painted them all. A hallway on the right led to a bathroom and bedrooms, and the living room was to the left.

Luka made his way in, smiling and complimenting costumes. A decent crowd was already there, mostly from accounting and IT, people he didn't know as well. The kitchen was toward the back, partially visible through a pass-through window. A bar was set up on the counter on this side of the sill, and a table of snacks and candy was along the far wall.

Luka took in his surroundings, very much aware that he was looking for Thomas and Thomas was not there yet. He sighed and was about to find Finn, when

Thomas appeared from the hallway. Every cell in Luka's body curled up and died.

"Oh, my fucking God," Luka moaned under his breath. "Is he *kidding?*"

Thomas was all in black—tight jeans, fitted T-shirt and an impossibly sexy leather motorcycle jacket. His hair was pulled back into his usual knot, with heavy black sunglasses completing the look.

Luka's insides quivered as Thomas scanned the room. His face relaxed when he saw Luka and began to make his way over.

Luka took a deep breath, trying to get his heart under control.

"Wow," Thomas murmured as he approached. "Your costume is...amazing." He took off his sunglasses, his eyes sliding up and down Luka's body.

Goosebumps prickled all over Luka's skin. He laughed, cheeks flushing. "Do you have chills?" *Or is it just me?*

Understanding dawned on Thomas' face in response to Luka's hint, then he offered a tiny smile. "They're multiplying."

"Nice." Luka grinned. "Tawney was supposed to be Danny, but she's sick."

"That's too bad."

"And you're...a time-traveler?" Luka frowned and took the opportunity to study Thomas' costume. *Shit, apparently I have a thing for biker boys.*

"I'll give you another hint. 'I need your clothes, your boots and your motorcycle'."

"You're the Terminator!" *Explains why I'm dying.* "Great costume!"

Thomas shrugged. "I had it in my closet."

Holy fuck, that's his jacket. "You have a motorcycle?" Luka resisted the urge to fan his face.

"Mmm. I take it out on weekends, mostly."

Luka bobbed his head, speechless.

"So…" Thomas cleared his throat. "Are you and Tawney…?"

Luka waited, not sure what he was asking.

"…together?" Thomas finished.

"What? No! Oh…no, no, no. No. I am single…and very gay. No, she's just my friend." Luka shook his head emphatically as his mind replayed their conversation in the coffee shop. *Couples costumes… 'Tawney and I will make a day trip of it'… Fuck, I'm dumb.*

"Oh. Okay. I wasn't sure. Me too." Thomas tucked his sunglasses into the inside pocket of his jacket.

Luka's mind raced, but he couldn't come up with anything to say better than *I already knew you were gay because Tawney and I were talking about you.* So he bobbed his head. "Cool." Then they stood there in excruciating silence until Finn swooped in, to the rescue once again.

"You crazy kids!" He clapped them on the shoulders. "Welcome! First question—why don't you have a drink yet?"

Rory followed behind. "Danny and Sandy!" they exclaimed. "You guys look great!"

Luka and Thomas looked at each other in surprise.

"Holy shit," Luka laughed, realizing that Thomas could in fact very easily be Danny. Something promising fluttered in his chest. "Actually, Tawney was supposed to be Danny, but she's sick."

"And I'm the Terminator," Thomas added.

"Oh," Rory chuckled. "That's funny. You go together like rama-lama-lama."

Luka's heart thudded as they all laughed. "Yeah, I guess that works out for me, then. You two look great, too!" he said to Rory and Finn, changing the subject.

The patch on Rory's flight suit said 'Goose' and Finn was 'Maverick.' They grinned at each other.

"I feel the need…" Finn began.

"The need…for speed!" Rory joined in. They high-fived each other, cackling.

"Adorable." Luka shook his head and bit his tongue.

"Not adorable. Badass," Finn corrected, popping his aviators on. "Bar's over there. Get on it." Finn pointed at Luka. "And there's karaoke later. I'd better see your ass up there, Sandy."

A rock dropped into Luka's stomach. He smiled in what he hoped was a pleasant, non-committal way, and was relieved when Finn moved on to greet the next group of revelers. *Karaoke. Fuck no.*

"Shall we?" Luka asked Thomas, waving an arm toward the bar. They made their way over, greeting Ilona's assistant Sabrina as she darted by, dressed, appropriately enough, like a witch. She was followed by a giggling black cat and a tipsy dragon, whose cardboard wings Luka had to dodge as it stumbled by. When they arrived at the bar, Thomas fished in the tub of ice and handed a beer over to Luka. They popped the tops and clinked bottles.

Georgia, Aleandro's head of marketing, was pouring herself a glass of wine when they caught her attention. She was dressed as a princess in a sweet lavender dress with a long blonde braid winding down her back. "Oh, cute!" she exclaimed. "You're Danny and Sandy!"

"Actually" — Luka chuckled — "Thomas is the Terminator. Tawney was supposed to be Danny but she's sick."

"Really?" Georgia giggled. "No way. You match perfectly."

They looked at each other. "Yeah," Luka agreed. Thomas took a sip.

"Can I get a picture of you two?" Georgia asked.

"Uh...sure?" Luka glanced at Thomas. He nodded.

He put a hand on his hip in his best Sandy pose while Thomas shuffled closer. There was a tingle where Thomas' shoulder touched Luka's back.

"Thanks!" Georgia said, snapping a few photos on her phone. "I'll text it to you."

Then Morgan strutted in.

"Oh, God," Luka muttered when he saw him. Morgan was wearing pale blue jeans, a white tank top and a black studded leather belt with a matching armband. His hair was slicked back and sprayed black, complete with a ratty-looking mustache stuck precariously to his upper lip.

"What?" Thomas glanced over his shoulder. "Oh, nice, I love Queen."

Luka sighed. "Just wait." Of course Morgan was dressed like Freddie Mercury. Of course. He probably thought he was better than one of the biggest music icons in the history of the world.

"Hello, gentlemen," Morgan drawled as he approached.

"Morgan," Luka nodded. "And who are you?" he asked, pretending he didn't know, just to be an ass.

"Freddie Mercury, of course." Morgan smirked and tossed his head. "I thought it was fitting."

I'm sure you did. Luka couldn't help himself and took the bait. "How's that?"

"Well, I don't know if you know, but I'm starting a band, so..."

"'Course you are." Luka tried not to sneer.

"Ah," Thomas said politely. "What kind of music?"

"Sort of pop slash arena rock, you know." Morgan plunged ahead, oblivious to Luka's curled lip. "I'm the lead singer and lead guitarist. I'm still working on a name, and I just need to find a decent drummer and bassist. Honestly, the people out there who call themselves drummers..." He rolled his eyes. "My dishwasher keeps better time than most of them." He sighed, then his eyes flicked back and forth between them. "And who are you supposed to be? Oh. *Grease.* Cute."

"Actually—" Luka started, reluctant to have to explain to Morgan that it was just an accident.

"Thanks," Thomas interrupted. "Turns out Luka and I are both big fans."

Luka raised a subtle eyebrow at Thomas as he covered a grin with his bottle.

Thomas shrugged at him, corner of his mouth twitching. A little bubble of happiness fizzed up Luka's throat. Morgan managed a half-hearted nod before he wandered off into the kitchen, saying something about needing fresh ice.

"It just seems easier than explaining all night," Thomas leaned over to murmur into Luka's ear.

Luka shivered. "Yeah, totally."

"Happy Halloween," a smooth voice said from behind them. They turned to see Aleandro and Penelope smiling at them.

Aleandro was a vampire, his costume immaculate — an expensive-looking tuxedo underneath a thick cloak with a red satin lining. He had pointed nails to go with his sharp teeth, and his face was pale. Luka noticed for the first time that Aleandro had perfect vampire hair, swept dramatically back off his forehead. Penelope was a sorceress, wearing a glamorous blood-red dress with peaked shoulders and high collar. A medallion glinted around her neck.

"Aleandro, Penelope! I didn't know you were coming." He and Thomas shook their hands. "Wow, your costumes are gorgeous."

"Thank you. Penelope and I take Halloween quite seriously," Aleandro replied. "It's our favorite holiday. After our anniversary."

Penelope gave him a soft look, then linked her arm in his. "I love *Grease*," she said to them.

"Who doesn't?" Luka agreed, casting another glance at Thomas. His eyes were on Luka.

They chatted a while longer before Penelope and Aleandro excused themselves to circulate. Luka was in need of a new drink. "You ready for another?" he offered.

"Thanks. I'm just going to use the restroom."

Luka was digging through the ice again when Finn appeared and threw his arm around Luka's shoulders. "Luka!" he hissed.

"Buddy. What's up?" he asked. The redhead seemed a little tipsy.

"Umm…" Finn looked around furtively, then leaned in to whisper into Luka's ear, which was unnecessary given the volume of the room around them. "I think Rory might like me."

A Hard Sell

"You don't say?" Luka tried not to laugh. "What happened?"

"Well, we were in the kitchen talking, and they asked me out of nowhere if I thought Maverick and Goose ever hooked up."

"And what did you say?"

"I said for sure, and then they asked which one I thought would have made the first move." Finn fiddled with the zipper on his flight suit.

"Goose, obviously."

"Right."

"So? What did they say to that?"

"Well, then I came out here."

Luka blinked at him. "And they're just waiting in there still?

"Yeah."

"Get back in there, you absolute moron. Go fucking kiss them." Luka shoved Finn in the direction of the kitchen. "Now," he added before Finn could protest.

He couldn't resist peeking in as Finn shyly shuffled in and said something to Rory. A slow smile spread across Rory's face, then Finn kissed them.

Luka felt a little thrill of happiness as their arms slid around each other. The kiss deepened when Finn leaned Rory back onto the counter. Luka smiled and turned to go get a beer for Thomas.

Chapter Nine

Losing Control

Luka handed Thomas his beer when he came back from the washroom.

"Thanks. What are you smiling about?" Thomas asked with an arched eyebrow.

Luka grinned. "Oh, nothing. Finn just got some good news."

"Hmm." Thomas twisted the cap off and took a drink. "Does it have to do with Rory?"

Luka guffawed. "It's so obvious, right?" He nodded his head in the direction of the kitchen.

Thomas leaned over to peer through the window, then turned back to Luka. He smiled softly. "Good for them."

"Excuse me." They were interrupted by Morgan's voice blasting from a speaker. The entire room of people cringed and covered their ears.

"Whoa, let me just turn that down a bit." Morgan giggled into the microphone.

They turned to see him in the corner where the karaoke machine was set up, fiddling with the knob on the amp. He seemed a little unsteady on his feet.

"It's time to kick things off," Morgan announced as he righted himself, "with a little *Somebody to Love*."

"Oh, fuck," Luka said, more loudly than he should have. "He's about to butcher one of the greatest songs in history."

"Let's do this," Morgan yelled, holding up a shot of tequila. He threw it back, then coughed a few times before wrenching the mic off the stand. He wailed the first note in a pitchy falsetto, then the backing track kicked in, and he somehow went even higher.

Luka looked at Thomas with wide eyes, 'Help me' written across his face.

Thomas shrugged. "Maybe he'll be good?" it looked like he said, but Luka couldn't hear.

It was too loud to engage in any conversation, so Luka suffered in silence as Morgan insulted every Queen fan that had ever existed, and those still to come.

Luka tried not to grimace too obviously. Morgan's voice wasn't *awful*, to be fair. He'd heard worse. The problem was he was oblivious to his limitations, and the higher the notes got, the more off-key he was. He was no Freddie fucking Mercury, that was for sure.

When the song was over and Morgan was done strutting and posing, he took a dramatic bow.

Georgia took the mic stand next. "Wow, thanks, Morgan!" she said, turning down the volume a bit more. "That's a tough act to follow. I haven't done this in a while, so wish me luck!" She launched into a lovely, soft folk-rock song, which allowed for conversation again.

Or, rather, it would have, if Morgan hadn't made his way over. He mopped his brow with a napkin. "I don't know how Freddie could do an entire concert with that much energy."

The smell of tequila rolled off him. Luka bit his tongue before an insult spilled out.

"I suppose I'd better get in better shape before my band starts performing," Morgan said with a put-upon sigh. He eyed Thomas. "Any pointers?"

Thomas shifted. "I used a personal trainer when I got started."

"Hmm, that doesn't sound like much fun, so impersonal." Morgan pushed out his lower lip.

"Yes, personal trainers are famously impersonal," Luka said.

Morgan glared at him but continued talking to Thomas. "I was thinking I could maybe join you for a workout or two, pick up some tips from someone who knows what he's doing." His gaze swept up and down Thomas' frame. Luka wanted to puke.

"Uh." Thomas blinked at him.

"Thomas was actually just saying to me"—Luka broke in, seeing Thomas was uncomfortable—"how he hardly has time to work out at all these days. He fits it in at five a.m." Luka knew that Morgan refused to get out of bed before seven for any reason, and before noon only for work.

"Oh." Morgan frowned. "That's a little early for me…"

"You should check out that new gym that just opened up by the office. I'm sure you could meet with a trainer after work," Luka suggested.

"Yeah, maybe."

"Great idea, Morgan," Luka said, nodding.

"Thanks." Morgan looked confused.

"And what are you going to sing, Luka?" Thomas asked, so smoothly that Morgan couldn't even be sure how the conversation ended up not on him anymore.

"Oh, no, I don't sing," he said, hoping that was that.

"Sure you do," Morgan piped up.

Shut uuuuup, Luka thought, glowering at Morgan.

"I thought you might want to do a duet with me," Thomas said to Luka. He waved his hand at their costumes. "There's the obvious one..."

Luka swallowed hard. "I don't think I can."

Morgan rolled his eyes. "Well, if Luka is going to be weird about it, I'll sing with you, Thomas."

The hell you will, Luka thought. His eyes swept the room. It was all people he knew, and they were all laughing, smiling, drinking, having a good time. They'd barely even notice he was up there. He could either suck it up and go for it, or let Morgan sing with Thomas. "Okay. Okay, let's do it."

Morgan huffed while Thomas smiled. "Great." Luka could have sworn for a second that one of Thomas' eyelids fluttered in a wink. He replayed the moment in his mind as they made their way over to the karaoke machine.

Luka hummed under his breath as Thomas flipped through the tablet to find the song. *Holy shit, am I really doing this?* He picked up a mic. For a split second, he was in front of the junior high audience again, but then he looked over at Thomas who gave him an encouraging nod. He took a breath and relaxed. Just a small crowd with a few friends paying attention. Well, a few friends and Morgan.

The music for *Summer Nights* began. He tried to let the tension out of his shoulders. He'd been singing this song his entire life and could do Sandy's part in his sleep.

Thomas started, his voice smooth and nice to listen to. Luka sucked in a breath and sang when it was his turn. The back-and-forth nature of the song meant he didn't have a chance to get into his head about it, and all he could see around the room were people happy and having a good time. Lots of them were smiling at him and Thomas.

Morgan got bored, flouncing off to the bar to down another shot. But Thomas... Thomas' gaze was on him almost the whole time. Luka's heart thudded against his ribcage whenever their eyes locked, until he had to look away.

Luka's breath left him in whoosh as the song finished. There were a few scattered applauses that he barely noticed.

"That was..." Thomas swallowed. "You are...really good." They put their mics down and shuffled away to make room for the next performers.

"Thanks." Luka tucked a stray piece of hair back under his wig. His face was so hot. "You were good, too."

"No, but like...you're a singer."

Luka's face grew hotter. "Not really."

Thomas looked skeptical. "If you say so."

Luka searched for words but the blood pounding in his head was making it hard to latch onto any of them. All he could think was that he had done it. *Thanks to Thomas*.

"Can I get you another drink?" Thomas offered.

"Sure, thanks." Luka saw a glimmer of amusement cross Thomas' face. He suddenly knew what was coming.

"Don't—" he started, right as Thomas said, "I'll be back," terrible Arnold accent and all.

Luka laughed, then gave a dramatic groan. "Okay, but that's the only one you're allowed tonight."

Thomas smiled back, holding his gaze longer than necessary. "Deal."

Luka licked his lips, mouth very dry, then Thomas turned and melted into the crowd.

Did someone crank up the heat? Luka wondered as he pulled his wig off and fanned his face. He was pretty sure he wasn't imagining the tension tonight. A small part of him was starting to wonder if perhaps Thomas was also interested. He exhaled. Maybe he should ask Thomas what he was up to tomorrow. Maybe they could meet for coffee again, just as friends...for now.

He plopped his wig back on, tugging it into place with resolve. Yes, he could do this. It was just coffee. No big deal. A noisy group of accountants took to the mic for an off-key *Ghostbusters*, so Luka retreated to the snack table for a few pigs-in-a-blanket and a handful of veggies.

Ilona came over and selected a lollipop from the giant bowl of candy. "Evening, Luka," she said, pulling the wrapper off.

"Ilona!" Luka gasped. "Wow, look at you!" She was dressed in a skintight latex bodysuit and tall black boots, with her hair loose about her face. She looked ready to kill. "You might pull that off better than Kate Beckinsale herself."

Ilona slid the lollipop into her mouth and gave him a pleased look, then popped the candy out again. "Officially, how dare you."

Luka snickered. "We won't tell Kate."

"Mmm." She gave it another lick. "So. You and Thomas are getting along well." It was not a question. "Your duet was fantastic."

Luka's cheeks flushed again, damn them. "Thanks. And yes. He's—it's been great working with him." He stuffed a carrot into his mouth to avoid saying anything else.

She sucked on her candy as she appraised him for a moment. "Yes, he thinks the same about you."

Luka almost choked on his carrot. "He does? Did he say that to you? I mean…good to know."

Ilona smiled, shoving the pop to the side of her cheek with her tongue. "Have a nice night, Luka." She vanished again.

Hope bubbled up in his chest. *I'm fucking doing this.* Luka scanned the room. Still no Thomas. He checked the kitchen, then headed into the foyer toward the bathroom. He frowned when he saw a long line waiting.

He was debating whether he should knock on the door to see if everything was okay in there, not sure where else Thomas could be, when it opened. Thomas came out holding onto Morgan with an arm around his waist.

Luka froze. *What the hell?*

Morgan's head lolled to the side, mustache gone, face green.

Thomas looked grim. Then he saw Luka. "Too much tequila for this one."

Morgan groaned.

Finn and Rory appeared, both glowing. "Everything all right?" Finn asked when he saw Morgan slumped against Thomas.

"Morgan needs to go home," Thomas grumbled. "I can take him, make sure he gets there okay."

Luka's mind raced. He wondered if Morgan could just crash here, but then he saw Finn watching Rory, his pinkie finger brushing the back of Rory's hand. He couldn't do that to those two, dumping a drunken fool on them to babysit tonight.

"That's nice of you," Luka said helplessly to Thomas.

Thomas shifted his grip as Morgan groaned again. "Do you have a plastic bag or two we can take with us?" he asked Finn.

Finn rushed to the kitchen and came back with a handful of grocery bags and two bottles of water. "Here. Make him drink these before he passes out."

"Thanks." Thomas collected the items and hefted Morgan upright as he began to list. "Well..." He looked at Luka. "I guess I'll see you Monday."

"Yeah." He thought about mentioning the coffee shop, then Morgan's cheeks bulged.

"Air!" He gulped, lurching toward the front door.

"Have a good night," Thomas mumbled, and they left.

Luka watched the door close, then turned to his friends.

"Sorry, man. That sucks," Finn said to Luka.

Luka forced a smile onto his face. "Yeah. But..." He looked at Finn and Rory's fingers now laced together. "Let's enjoy the party."

"Has she lost that loving feeling?" Rory asked Finn, nodding toward the microphone.

"Fuck, no. That song's too sad. I have a better idea." Finn pulled Rory over to the karaoke machine, the touch lingering as they flipped through the song choices. Luka watched them giggling. He wanted to be happy for his friends, and he was, but…

Then the music kicked in as they crowded together at the mic. "Are they serious right now?" Luka whispered to himself when he heard the song they had chosen—*You're the One That I Want*, Danny's and Sandy's happy ending song.

Finn began, badly singing Danny's opening line. Rory sang Sandy's line back, a little more in tune.

They flirted and shimmied, nothing but lightness and joy, and all Luka could see in his mind was Thomas. He sighed. There was no point denying it.

He's the one that I want.

Chapter Ten

Sharing a Drink

Luka cracked an eye open Sunday morning. Correction—afternoon. He moved his head an inch to look at his clock, then groaned when the vice clamped down on his skull. His stomach lurched in protest.

"Fuuuuck," he moaned, burying his head under the pillow and blindly groping at his bedside table for a water bottle. No luck. He peeked out to glare at his bathroom door. So far away. Too far. He burrowed back under the pillow to block out the afternoon sun.

Sifting through the foggy memories from last night, Luka wondered at which point things had gone horribly wrong. He remembered watching Thomas' broad back draped in the world's sexiest leather jacket leaving the party early because Morgan was the literal worst. Then Georgia had offered him a Jell-O shot. Right. The *tray* of Jell-O shots. His stomach heaved again.

He had a vague recollection of singing *Bennie and the Jets* with Georgia, then leading a *Sweet Home Alabama* singalong with the accountants. After that it was much hazier. He might have done a solo of *Toxic*, complete with Britney's choreography, which he had mastered in his bedroom when he was about fifteen. At least Thomas hadn't seen that.

Thomas.

In the stone-cold-sober light of morning, through the nausea and pounding headache, he wondered if he had imagined the whole thing. The tension, the flirting, the lingering gaze... Was that just Thomas enjoying himself at a party?

When the need to relieve himself became even more urgent than his desire for water, he stumbled out of bed. He felt much better after taking care of both issues and letting himself soak in a long hot shower.

He found his phone on the kitchen counter next to an empty container of potato salad. Ah yes, he remembered polishing that off before he caromed into bed. He saw that Finn had sent him a series of GIFs around one a.m. — mostly Britney, then a few stop signs and finally SpongeBob burying himself in the sand. Luka sniffed. His Britney was spot-on, as a matter of fact.

Then he saw a message from Georgia...and the picture of him and Thomas. Luka thought that he looked a bit ridiculous, smiling brightly under his Sandy wig, but then — Thomas. Dear Lord, Thomas. 'Smolder' didn't even begin to cover it. He stared directly into the camera, a little Travolta smirk playing at his lips. Raw sexuality oozed from every pore, chin tilted down, hip cocked, thumb hooked in his pocket, just a solid mass of black leather and muscle and... *Fuck.* A low moan escaped from his lips as he wiped at the sweat beading on his brow. His stomach swirled, then heaved again.

Thinking some fresh air might clear the last of the lingering hangover, he scrambled to grab his keys. It was a chilly, damp day, but he set out at a brisk pace and somehow found himself at Jitters, the café where he had met Thomas last time. This time the chalkboard said *If you were looking for a sign to have a muffin, this is it.* He sat with his coffee and chocolate chip muffin, eyes shooting to the door each time it opened. But no six-foot-two Greek god with warm brown eyes came through.

He looked at the picture from Georgia again, then opened his text thread with Thomas and stared at the keyboard. Should he? What if he had come on too strong last night? Had he embarrassed himself? What if Thomas had *wanted* to take Morgan home? Maybe Thomas had stayed the night to make sure he was okay. Oh God, what if he and Morgan were still together right now? Luka put his phone away. He'd see what Thomas was like at work tomorrow.

Then his phone buzzed and he wrenched it back out of his pocket. Tawney.

Hey Sandy, how was the party?

Luka sent her the selfie he had taken.

Good…mostly. How are you feeling?

Way better. Just a twenty-four-hour thing. What do you mean, "mostly"?

Are you free for coffee?

* * * *

Thirty minutes later, Tawney was sitting across from him. He told her everything.

When he was done, she reached across the table to squeeze his hand. "Oh, Luk. I noticed some chemistry between you two, but wow. You're really gone on him, huh?"

Luka covered his eyes with his other hand, nodding. "Apparently. What do I do?"

"Sweetie...I hate to say it, but I don't think it's the best idea. He's basically your boss, he's only here for few months, and, to be honest, you don't have the best record. You got lucky with Finn, because look what happened the next time you dated someone from work."

Luka bristled. "Thomas is no Morgan."

"I know, babe." She squeezed his hand again. "I'm sorry. It just doesn't seem like it would end well."

He blew out a breath. "You're right. I just.... Fuck, I can't stop thinking about him."

Tawney looked at him with a crooked, sympathetic smile. "Well, shit."

"Pretty much."

* * * *

Luka's condo had never been cleaner. The kitchen gleamed, every brown and beige pillow fluffed and placed perfectly on the cream-colored couch. He dedicated all his brain power to convincing himself that he did not have a massive all-consuming crush on Thomas, and even if he did, he was not doing anything about it. He was just going to admire him from afar. Well, not that afar since they were sharing a desk. But he was a grown up, and he didn't have to act on every little feeling. It was fine. *Minor* crush, if anything. Moving on.

He arrived at work Monday resolved to act like it. He wore a new blue and red floral shirt with fitted navy trousers, hoping the snappy outfit would give him that little extra boost. Then he saw Morgan waiting at the elevator. *Fuck.*

"Morgan," Luka said as he joined him, only because there was no avoiding it. "Feeling better?"

Morgan glanced over. "Yeah, I think I had some sort of stomach bug."

Luka held back a bark of incredulity. "Is it not exhausting being so delusional?" slipped out anyway.

Morgan's lip curled, his eyes glinting as he ignored Luka's question. "It was so sweet of Thomas to make sure I got home okay, wasn't it?" The elevator dinged open and the two of them entered.

Luka tightened his jaw. "Sure." *I will not take the bait.*

"He even put me to bed."

"That's great, Morgan."

"I stripped off all my clothes in front of him, so *embarrassing!*" He was not even the tiniest bit embarrassed.

"Mmhmm." Luka stared hard at the climbing number display.

"Anyway, it's a bit of a blur after that…"

Luka blinked. Was Morgan implying something else had happened? *Surely not.* He eyed Morgan. The asshole was examining his cuticles.

They arrived at their floor and the door slid open. *I will not take the bait.* "Have a good day, Morgan." Luka strode away.

His mind raced as he made his way to his office, replaying the conversation. He slumped into his chair,

but before he could draw any conclusions, Finn appeared in his doorway, a smile like the sun stretching across his face.

Luka had to smile back. "And how was the rest of your weekend?"

"Good. So fucking good, Luka." He collapsed in the other chair, glowing with happiness.

"Look at you," Luka mused. "You're…completely in love."

He expected bluster back, but Finn just softened further. "Maybe."

"That's great, Finn. I'm so happy for you two."

"Thanks. We already made our appointment with HR." He sighed. "Rory is amazing. And the sex… God."

Luka shook his head and laughed. *That's more like it.* "Congratulations."

"Right? All weekend, man, like—"

Just then Thomas walked in, his face a thundercloud. He saw Finn and his scowl deepened.

Finn did his best to tone down his grin, but couldn't quite manage to erase it completely as he got to his feet. "Morning, Wolf. Did you get Morgan's drunk ass home okay the other night?"

"Yes," Thomas said, dumping his briefcase on his desk with considerable force.

The room was silent as they waited for Thomas to say more. He did not.

"Well, okay, then. See you guys later." Finn shot Luka a look and eased out of the door. No doubt heading straight back to Rory's office.

Luka watched Thomas silently powering up his laptop. "Morning," he said.

"Morning."

Again, Luka waited for him to say more, but he did not. "How are you?"

"Fine."

"Are you, though? You seem a little...not fine." He wondered what Thomas could be mad about. Had he done something? Had Morgan? Then blind panic hit him for a moment—what if Morgan had told Thomas some crazy story about how they had broken up and turned Thomas against him? What if he was mad at the way Luka had acted at the party, rolling his eyes at Morgan's costume and singing? His heartbeat picked up as his mind raced.

Thomas paused, his shoulders slumping. "Sorry. I just—" He blew out the rest of his breath. "I think I got up on the wrong side of the bed this morning."

"Okay." Luka tried to relax a little. "If you want to talk about anything, I'm here."

Thomas looked at him. "I... Thanks."

Luka nodded and opened up his email. They had a lot of details to hammer out for the upcoming commercial shoots, so he started sorting through the relevant messages. Or rather, that was the plan, but his brain was spinning. What had happened between Thomas and Morgan?

He didn't need to wait long to find out more. He was on his way back to his office after lunch when he heard Morgan's voice coming from inside. He paused just out of sight.

"...the rest of your weekend?" Morgan was saying.

"Good," Thomas answered shortly.

"Thanks again for putting me to bed. I just feel so silly." Morgan gave an affected giggle.

"You're welcome."

"I would have liked to thank you properly, but you ran out of there so fast."

Luka relaxed a bit. That absolute dick, acting like he couldn't remember what happened.

Thomas didn't reply, so Morgan continued. "Perhaps I could thank you this week sometime? Buy you a drink after work?"

Luka held his breath, heart pounding.

"Thank you for the offer, but I don't date people I work with," Thomas said.

"Who said anything about a date? I didn't even know you were interested in men. And we all know how Breakpoint feels about employees dating! No, just thought we could get to know each other a little better."

There was a long pause. "Okay," Thomas replied.

Luka leaned against the wall, his stomach dropping into his shoes. *What the fuck.*

"Great. I'll text you." The satisfaction in Morgan's tone made Luka's skin crawl.

"You don't need to—how about today?" Thomas asked.

"Amazing idea. I'll meet you here at five? My favorite bar is just one stop away, on your way home."

Luka rolled his eyes. He knew which bar Morgan was talking about. Stuck-up servers and heinously overpriced drinks. Morgan loved it.

"Sure." At least Thomas didn't sound too excited about it.

"Can't wait," Morgan purred.

Luka hurried away down the hall a few steps, then turned to walk back toward his office right as Morgan came out.

He saw Luka and the vilest smirk crossed his face. "See you later."

Luka couldn't even bring himself to acknowledge the man as he strode past him and entered his office. Thomas was frowning at his laptop.

"Hey," Luka said as he scooted up to his desk. "I was thinking about that email from the director and I'm not sure he's quite getting the vision."

They got right back to work, but his brain continued to pick at it, until it was a festering sore on his consciousness. *Oh my God, a date. They're going on a date. Thomas took him home and now they're going on a date.* He tried to swallow it down, but it burst out of him in the afternoon after a long, silent stretch. "So. Any plans for later today?" he asked, punching a few things into a spreadsheet.

"I'm, uh…going for a drink. With Morgan." Thomas mumbled the last part.

"Oh."

"It's not a date or anything. He said he wanted to get to know me better."

"Okay." *Not a date.* Luka moved some papers around, then stopped and folded his hands. The sore was still festering. "It's just, Morgan is…not a very nice person." He nearly shook with the effort of not using a more colorful description.

Thomas leveled his heavy gaze at him. "I'll keep that in mind."

Luka nodded and left it at that. Thomas was a grown up, entitled to go for a drink with a colleague. But he made sure to clear out of his office at 4:55, not wanting to risk being there for the moment Morgan arrived to 'pick up' Thomas.

"Have a good time," he said to Thomas, watching him pack his bag. "I'll see you tomorrow."

"Yeah." Thomas looked uncertain. "Thanks."

Luka took his water bottle with him and wandered into the staffroom to fill it up. He found Aleandro there, sipping tea and flipping through a stack of papers.

"Luka," Aleandro said with a kind smile. "How are you this afternoon?"

"Uh." Luka searched for an appropriate word. "Fine. I guess."

Aleandro frowned. "Is everything okay?"

Luka remembered being near terrified of Aleandro at first, but not a single thing he had done since was the least bit terrifying. An idea occurred to him. "Yes, but I was thinking about going for a drink. Are you free?"

"As a matter of fact, I am! Penelope is having dinner with Ilona tonight. Thank you for the invitation. Oh!" Aleandro said, sitting up straight. "Finn keeps telling me I should go check out the Bitter Exchange. This is the perfect opportunity."

Luka sighed. *Of course.* Oh well, maybe it was a good idea. Perhaps Kazio's derision and dirty looks would distract him from thinking about what Thomas and Morgan were up to. "Sounds great."

* * * *

"May I see a wine list, my good man?" Aleandro asked as he settled onto a stool at the bar next to Luka.

Kazio appraised him. "What are you in the mood for?"

"Hmmm…a red. Something rich and oaky."

Kazio nodded. "I have the Sartini Baschet, or the Tricchonne Demi-Sac."

A twinkle appeared in Aleandro's eyes. "Which do you recommend?"

"The Baschet," Kazio said without hesitation.

Aleandro smiled. "Haven't had that one in a while." He turned to Luka. "Would you care for a glass?"

Luka grinned. "Sure, thank you."

Aleandro watched Kazio pour. "Do you recommend the Baschet often?"

Kazio sniffed. "Most people around here don't appreciate it. But yes, I do. Elegant, reasonable price point and pairs well with almost everything on the menu."

"For me, it's the old-world character." Aleandro swirled his glass then stuck his nose over it, breathing deeply.

Kazio looked confused. "Yes, exactly."

"Tell me, what do you think about the Sartini Courbis?"

"Excellent as well, not as rich. But this year's vintage is a little off."

"It's smoky, isn't it? It was the forest fires." Aleandro took a small sip of the Baschet and let it roll around in his mouth before he swallowed.

Kazio's gaze flicked back and forth between Aleandro and Luka, obviously thinking. Then Aleandro put him out of his misery and extended his hand. "Aleandro Sartini. CEO of Sartini Wines. Pleasure to meet you."

The corner of Kazio's mouth curled up in the barest hint of a smile. "Kazimierz Arkadiusz Złotowski. Proprietor of this fine establishment." They shook hands, and launched into the most intense discussion of wine Luka had ever heard. He tried to keep up at first, but after about a minute of baffling lingo his eyes glazed over. He sipped his elegant, old-world Baschet and let his mind wander. He wondered if Morgan would try to impress Thomas with his knowledge of wine. God knew he had tried with Luka, to no avail.

"I'd better get back to work," Kazio finally said, examining the crowd gathering at the bar with disdain. "It was an honor to meet you, Mr. Sartini."

"Please, call me Aleandro." They shook hands again.

Luka watched Kazio take the next order with a scowl, then he turned back to Aleandro. "Well. You'll have to teach me more about wine so I can win him over, too."

"Where would you like to start?" Aleandro asked with a wink.

They sipped their wine leisurely, then took their second glasses over to a table to order dinner. Luka had a great time listening to Aleandro's stories. Fresh out of school, a young Aleandro had taught English in China for two years, before he saw the devastating effects of an earthquake firsthand and spent some years volunteering for the Red Cross. Then he had worked his way around Europe, learning about the restaurant industry in some of the best kitchens in the world, before coming back home, where he had trained as a horticulturist in Camarillo. That was where he purchased his first vineyard. The man had done so much and traveled so extensively that it seemed like he had already lived several lifetimes before he had hired Penelope, fallen in love and built a successful winery with her.

Aleandro was also very kind, and quick to laugh at Luka's jokes. He was having such a good time that he almost forgot about Thomas. Almost.

After their third and fourth glasses were finished, Aleandro glanced at his phone. "Well, my goodness.

Would you look at how late it is! I should be on my way."

He signaled to their server for the bill, which he insisted on paying despite Luka's protests. The matter settled, Aleandro punched a few buttons on his phone. "I've called a cab. Can I offer you a ride?"

"No, thank you. I think I'll stay for a nightcap." Luka wasn't quite ready to be home alone with his thoughts. "Thank you again for dinner and the company."

"It was my pleasure, Luka. Let's do it again."

The pub was starting to thin out by the time Aleandro left. Luka wandered back to the bar and plopped himself onto a stool. Kazio came over and stared at him.

"I'll have a scotch for the road, please, Kazio."

"Label?"

"You choose. Nothing *too* expensive, though," he added, careful not to give Kazio the opportunity to slap him with a three-digit bill.

"Hmm," Kazio replied, taking a page from Thomas' book of noises. Luka wondered if Thomas and Morgan were still at the bar. Or maybe they'd gone back to Morgan's place again.

"Can I ask you something, Kazio?" Luka blurted as the bartender placed a tumbler in front of him. The plunge he had taken with Aleandro had paid off, and since then the wine had only emboldened him further.

Kazio looked around as if needing a reason to escape. "If you must."

"Why don't you like me?"

His eyebrows rose a hair. "I don't like anyone."

Luka nodded, bobbing his head. "Fair...except you liked Aleandro. And you seem to not like me...a little bit extra."

Kazio eyed him for a moment, considering. "I despise making Bloody Marys."

A shocked laugh burst from Luka's throat.

Kazio glared at him.

"Sorry! God, I'm so sorry. I didn't mean to laugh. I was just surprised."

"That drink has *ten* ingredients."

Luka started to count in his head but then gave up, taking a thoughtful sip of his scotch. He managed to wheeze only slightly as it burned down his throat. "So good," he said in a strangled gasp.

The corner of Kazio's mouth curled. "Beats the hell out of a Bloody Mary, doesn't it?"

* * * *

Luka had another dream, blurred by the wine and scotch, perhaps. At first, it was just images, sensations. Thomas climbing on top of him, his hair tickling Luka's cheek. The delicious weight of Thomas' bulk, the heat pressing inside him, exquisite pleasure curling his toes... Then he was standing beside the bed watching Thomas at work, hips rolling, ass clenching with each thrust. Luka licked his lips and reached down to squeeze himself, wishing he was still under Thomas. He frowned and looked to see who the lucky man was, feeling a sense of relief when he saw it was himself, eyes closed in bliss. Then those eyes snapped open, and they were gray instead of his own blue. And they were staring from Morgan's face.

Luka gasped as Morgan's mouth twisted in a cruel smile.

"Yes, Thomas," he cooed, without taking his eyes off Luka. "Ooh, yes. Just like that."

"Stop," Luka forced out.

"No, don't stop. Don't stop, Thomas!" Morgan's hands clutched Thomas' ass. Thomas sped up, and Morgan tipped his head back and moaned. "Oh, yes, harder, Thomas, harder. Yes, yes, yes!"

Luka woke up with a start. He covered his face with his hand. "Noooo."

* * * *

The next morning Thomas was on a call when Luka arrived in their office. Thomas nodded at him before replying to the person on the phone. "We finalized those contracts on Thursday… Yes, I'm looking at them right now." He picked up a handful of papers and rolled his eyes at Luka.

He replied with a wan smile as he opened his email and began to click through the stack of messages, listening to Thomas insist that the contracts in his hand existed. *How it went with Morgan last night is none of my business* played in his head on a loop.

When Thomas got off the phone they dove into their list of tasks for the day. The first commercial shoot was tomorrow. There was a lot to do, and if Thomas wasn't going to mention Morgan, neither was he.

The dream meant nothing. It was fine.

Right?

Chapter Eleven

First Date

"Morning," Thomas mumbled as he slid into Luka's car, two coffees in hand. He popped one of them into the cupholder in the middle.

"Thanks, I'll need that." Luka rubbed his eyes as Thomas buckled in. It was five a.m. and they were headed to a studio across town for day one of their commercial shoot.

"You're welcome." Thomas shivered as he wrapped his fingers around his cup.

"Getting so cold in the mornings," Luka said. "I'm thankful for underground parking. Just saw some poor bastards scraping their windshields." He signaled and pulled back onto the road. Not much traffic so early. "Do you still run outside when it's this cold?"

"Year round."

"You do?"

Thomas nodded and took a drink. "Yeah."

"You just run through the snow?"

Thomas chuckled. "Mmm."

"Isn't it freezing? And slippery?"

"I have special shoes for snow and ice, and I warm up quick once I get going. And I take a long, hot shower afterwards."

Luka pictured Thomas wet and soapy for the tiniest, completely respectable amount of time. "If you say so. I prefer spending chilly winter mornings drinking coffee on the couch."

"Mmm. That's nice, too," Thomas said, looking out of the window.

Luka's stomach fizzed as he imagined Thomas curled up next to him one cozy morning. The silence hung, a little thick for a moment, when Thomas' phone buzzed.

"And so it begins," he muttered after he read the message.

"What?" Luka reached for his coffee.

"Hanna says the heat isn't working. It's just above freezing on set."

"Oh, God. Can they fix it?"

Thomas' fingers flew as he answered the text. "Let's hope so."

When they got there, they found Hanna, the AD, on the phone, pacing in the hallway. "I don't care what time it is, if you're not here in twenty minutes, I will be at your door to drag you out here *myself*." She hung up, then she saw Thomas and Luka and smiled sweetly. "The building manager is on his way."

"Great," Luka said, making a mental note to not piss her off at any point.

The crew was arriving by the handful and the first delivery truck pulled up with the furniture for the restaurant set. Thomas got busy directing the setup while Luka fielded phone calls and checked in with the various department heads. It was still freezing, so everyone had left their coats on.

"The building manager is here!" Hanna called down the hall when she saw Luka. He crossed his fingers for heat. Or he would have, if his fingers weren't frozen solid.

When the extras began to arrive, he herded them into wardrobe and makeup. He frowned at the room, checking his clipboard and counting them twice. They were short two.

He went out into the hall and saw Thomas striding toward him. "We have another problem," they said at the same time.

"What's your problem?" Luka asked as Thomas turned to lead him back to the set.

Thomas waved a hand when they rounded the corner.

Luka stopped short when he saw. "Ummm…"

"I know."

An elegant 'restaurant' was laid out before them, dark wood paneling, tables draped in crisp white linens, bold art on the walls. Except…

"White folding chairs?" Luka exclaimed.

"Yup."

They stood staring at the set together.

"It's half fancy restaurant, half summer garden wedding," Luka said.

"Yup."

Luka ran a hand through his hair. "What the hell! Where are our chairs?"

"Some sort of mix-up. I already called the rental place, and they said they don't have anything else."

"Okay… Where do we get forty brown leather chairs at the last minute?"

Thomas sighed and pulled his phone out. "I'm on it. Wait, what was your problem?"

"We seem to be short two extras."

"Great."

"I'll deal with this one."

Thomas nodded, already typing.

"Hanna!" Luka called. She was across the room talking to the set decorators as they unpacked the china.

"What's up?" Her breath was a puff of white in the air.

"How are we doing with the heat?"

"He said he needs a new part. He's calling around."

"Speaking of calling around, did the agency contact you at all about being short extras today?"

"What? No. How many are we missing?"

"Two. I'll call, you keep doing what you're doing."

It was a short phone call. "They said they can't get anyone," he told Hanna after he hung up.

Thomas walked up to join them and grunted in annoyance. "I'm working on the chairs. I got a hold of Aleandro, and he knows a few restaurant owners in the area. We might be able to borrow some chairs from one of them."

Luka nodded, his anxiety spiking. Current score — three problems, zero fixed.

Hanna eyed them, chewing her lip. "How about you two?"

"How about us for what?" Luka asked.

Hanna sighed. "As extras!"

"Us?" Luka and Thomas looked at each other, before turning back to Hanna, wide-eyed.

"Yeah. You're both gorgeous, and all you have to do is sit at the table and pretend to enjoy the shit out of your meal. Maybe a fake laugh or two."

"Uh…" Luka looked at Thomas again.

"I don't—" Thomas started, confused.

"Great, let's get you into costume." Hanna hauled them down the hallway and into the hands of their wardrobe and makeup team.

"Don't you need us to help with setup?" Thomas tried.

"Nah, I've got your designs. You can still approve before we begin shooting. Here you go, Darlene! Two more diners for you!" She patted their shoulders and darted out again.

That room was a little warmer, due to being smaller and packed with bodies. Someone had found an ancient space heater that was grinding away in the corner. They hung up their overcoats and turned to face Darlene.

"Hmm…" She had a solid frame and two measuring tapes around her neck. She eyed Thomas skeptically and tugged at the seam on his shoulder. "I don't think we have a suit jacket that fits you, honey. Are you okay wearing yours?"

"Sure." He still looked uncertain. A little corner of Luka's heart melted. He was used to seeing Thomas so sure-footed and confident at work.

"And you." She turned to appraise Luka. "I have just the thing for you. Forty-four long?"

Without even waiting for his response, she left to dig through a rack and came back carrying a gorgeous light gray suit and cerulean tie. "This'll bring out those baby blues."

He nodded and took the clothes from her, still a little bewildered. Darlene waved him over to a changing curtain and shooed Thomas into a makeup chair.

The suit clung to him like silk and felt amazing. He inched out and caught Thomas' gaze in the mirror through all the hustle and bustle of the room. Thomas' jaw dropped a hair. Darlene swooped down on Luka

127

and guided him to a chair a few seats away, so he didn't get a chance to talk to Thomas again until the extras were herded into the hall on their way to a holding room.

Luka tugged at the tie. "I don't normally wear these things," he said when Thomas approached him.

"Mmm. Too bad, it looks good on you."

"Thanks," Luka mumbled, staring down as he pretended to fuss with his cuffs.

Then Hanna appeared. "The heat's back on!" she crowed. "And...come with me." She beckoned them down the hall to the set. "Ta da!" All the folding white chairs were gone, replaced with brown leather. "Aleandro came through!"

Luka sagged with relief. "Looks great."

"Come check out the table settings."

They perused the setup, thrilled with everything, right down to the food that no one would be eating. They helped with a few finishing touches, ensuring the bottles of Sartini wine were displayed prominently on every table, and conferenced with Hanna and the director, Yuan, before the extras were brought in.

"All right, let's get you seated here." Hanna placed them at an intimate table for two. "You're on background all morning, so all you need to do is act like you're on a date. You can whisper-talk to each other, smile a lot, bat your eyes, pretend you're eating... Just have fun!"

They watched while Hanna directed the rest of the extras around the set, then she gathered up the ones playing the servers.

"So...come here often?" Luka cracked quietly to fill the silence as they waited.

"Hmm." Thomas laughed in a low chuckle. "First time."

"I think I've forgotten how to do awkward first date chit-chat. It's been a while."

"Why?"

"Why what?"

"I mean…" The faintest hint of a blush dusted Thomas' cheeks. "You must have offers."

"Um, not really!" *Well, this is embarrassing.* Luka fiddled with the silverware. "I don't know… I work a lot. I don't go out to meet people much."

Thomas looked like he wanted to say something, but he just nodded, the silence stretching out again.

One of the set dressers appeared with two plates. "Don't touch the food," was all he said in a bored voice as he plunked the meals down in front of them.

They looked at each other.

"Terrible service," Thomas said.

Luka shook his head. "This is going in my review online."

And so for the next three hours, they sat at their table holding forks and knives, smiling and pretending to eat.

"What's the worst first date you've ever been on?" Luka asked at one point when the director had paused to adjust the lighting.

"Hmm…" Thomas frowned. "Probably this guy who had just broken up with someone. He got drunk, borrowed my phone to call his ex right in front of me and then he threw my phone into the ice bucket after he hung up."

Luka laughed. "Wow. That's bad."

Thomas nodded. "Dodged a bullet with that one. What about you?"

"One time, fresh out of college, the guy took me back to his house, only it was his parents' house. We had to sneak into his room in the basement. And it was filthy.

Cereal bowls, empty chip bags, bread crusts…" He shuddered. "But I tried to get over it because he was brutally hot. Then when we were completely naked and, you know, *engaged*, his mom came into his room to put his laundry away."

Thomas pressed a hand over his mouth, trying to hold back a laugh.

Luka ducked his head and laughed too. "It's funny now, but I left my shoes behind running out of there!"

Thomas snorted through his fingers.

"They were my favorites," Luka said wistfully.

"Quiet on set!" Hanna called. They choked their giggles down.

When they paused for lunch, they were delighted to open their boxes to find chicken sandwiches on thick, nutty bread, with caramelized onions and provolone cheese.

"Wait, I chose the caterer, didn't I?" Luka said, a memory stirring.

"Amazing work," Thomas said. "I trust you for all my food and beverage decisions from now on."

"As you should," Luka agreed. He basked in the sparkle from Thomas' eyes.

Then it was back onto the set for two more hours of their fake date. Hanna appeared at their table after a break. "You two have amazing chemistry. Wanna try some acting?"

"Um." Luka shot a look at Thomas, who stared back wide-eyed and shrugged. "Okay?"

"Great!" Hanna steamrolled ahead. "We thought we could get a few closer shots of you in date mode. Just chatting, smiling… Then as the camera pans over your table, I want you to reach for his hand, Thomas, and squeeze it. Give me, like, third-date, head-over-heels energy. And then pull back and pick up your wine glass."

"Got it." Thomas nodded, avoiding Luka's gaze.

"Places," Hanna called as she retreated back behind the camera with Yuan. "Background... And, action!"

Thomas looked at him, and Luka's stomach swirled like it was the first time meeting those eyes. *Oh God.* Stomachs didn't do that for no reason. Stomachs did that when people were suffering from excruciating, all-consuming infatuation. He wanted to laugh at his futile attempt to pretend he was over it after the party. He was not over it. He was under it. Deep.

"What's your favorite thing to do on a date?" Thomas whispered with a gentle smile.

"What?" Luka's heart was racing.

"Just making fake conversation."

"Oh. Oh!" Luka laughed. The camera began to pan over.

Thomas reached for his hand. Thomas' hand was large, bigger than Luka's. It covered his completely.

"Um..." Luka said, his mind blank.

"Cut!" Yuan barked.

Hanna conferred with him, then hustled over. "Uh, Luka. You looked, maybe confused, when he touched you? Can you look like you're in love? There are no confused people at Aleandro's."

"Right, yup." Luka bobbed his head. "Got it. Sorry."

"Places," Hanna ordered again. The servers reset. "Action!"

"Well?" Thomas said. "Whenever you're ready." He tilted his head and looked at Luka with soft eyes. Every thought flew from Luka's head again. Thomas was a good actor. *Imagine if he was actually in love with me, looking at me like this.* His chest ached.

He placed his hand on Luka's again, rubbing his thumb in small circles.

"I...I don't know," Luka stammered. *Am I dying?*

"Cut!"

"Shit, sorry." Luka rubbed his face and looked at Hanna. "Sorry."

"In love, Luka."

"Got it." *Jesus. Pretty sure I can act like I'm in love with the sexiest man on earth.* He looked at Thomas again and let himself do what he was always trying not to — stare. Really stare. The hair stylist had redone his bun, but after a long day, a few hairs were starting to escape, frizzing around his temples. His eyes were as molten as ever, lashes thick, nose sharp, jaw that could cut granite. And those lips...pink and plump, a soft arch, begging to be sucked on... *Fuck.*

"My favorite date is just hanging out," Luka said, the words suddenly coming easily. "Like eating and watching a good show." That's all he did with Morgan of course, but... "And just...laughing. Enjoying each other's company. Feeling safe with that person, like you can be yourself. And knowing they feel the same."

Thomas stared back, unblinking.

"Cut!"

"Thomas," Hanna said, a hint of exasperation creeping into her voice. "You forgot to touch his hand. Look guys, I can get someone else."

"No! No. No, we've got this." Thomas shook his head at Hanna then looked at Luka. "Right?"

"Hell yeah."

"One more time."

They got it perfect the next time, and the time after that. Thomas touched his hand again, and again. And again.

Luka was crushed when Yuan called, "Cut! We got it."

* * * *

"Well, that was quite a day," Luka announced as they got into his car close to ten o'clock. He knew he should be tired, but he still felt like the tingles he got when Thomas had touched him could launch him into space.

"Mmm," Thomas agreed.

He wasn't ready for the day to end. The words 'Do you want to pick up some food?' were on Luka's tongue when Thomas yawned, his head thunking back onto the headrest.

"And we have to do it all again tomorrow. Can't wait to crawl into bed," he mumbled.

Right. It was late. "Totally," Luka agreed. "So tired." They drove straight back to Thomas' place. Luka consoled himself with the fact that he would be back here picking up Thomas in less than seven hours.

The next day went much more according to plan. No surprises, no no-shows, no need to be in front of the camera again, and they were out of there by eight this time.

They were almost back at Thomas' condo when an impulse hit. Luka turned into a drive-through.

Thomas looked at him with an eyebrow raised.

"You said I can make your food decisions, and I need some ice cream." Luka grinned as he pulled up to wait for the car ahead of them. "We're celebrating finishing the shoot. What can I get you?"

"Hmm." Thomas strained to look at the menu board, but he didn't have a clear view. "I hardly ever have ice cream. Just…a vanilla cone, please."

"A vanilla cone?" Luka made a face as they pulled up to the speaker. "We'll need a minute, please!" he announced to the invisible employee. He turned back to Thomas. "Okay, I feel like you should take your time. If you want a vanilla cone, by all means, but" — he waved a hand at the menu — "take a look." They had at least twenty flavors to choose from, and would mix them with just about any topping imaginable.

Thomas blinked. "Yeah, okay. I do need a minute."

Five minutes later they pulled away, bowls of chocolate chip cookie dough ice cream swirled with peanut butter cups for both of them.

Thomas dug in right away. "Oh my God." He groaned.

Luka felt a twitch in his nether regions. "Good?" he squeaked, gripping the steering wheel as they pulled back into traffic.

"This is…" Thomas swallowed another spoonful, groaning again.

"You're making me hungry." *And thirsty.*

"Oh, sorry, it's rude that I'm eating mine." He licked his spoon clean.

"No, please. Don't stop. Eat." A sweat broke out along his hairline. Listening to the sounds of Thomas enjoying ice cream was a whole new experience. Luka shifted in his seat, thankful for the darkness.

As soon as they pulled up in front of Thomas' condo, he tore the lid off his own ice cream. He let out a groan himself when he had his first taste. "Excellent choice," he told Thomas, sucking on his spoon. "This is orgasmic."

Thomas made a strangled noise on the spoonful he was swallowing.

"Oh my God, are you okay?" Luka stuck his spoon back in the ice cream and reached to pat Thomas on the back.

Thomas coughed and nodded. "Yeah, just swallowed wrong." He cleared his throat and took another bite.

"Well, be careful. I'm not driving you to the hospital till I finish this." Luka grinned and shoveled in a huge scoop.

Thomas swallowed another spoonful. "This is the best ice cream I've ever had. Not skipping my run tomorrow, though."

Luka side-eyed him. "I think you can afford to miss a day."

"I missed yesterday and today. I do better sticking to routines, not letting the bad habits creep back in."

"That's why I prefer to not let them creep out in the first place."

Thomas smiled. "Glad that works for you."

"I don't know if it works. It's just how I've always done it."

"I would say it does."

Luka flushed as he swallowed his next bite.

They sat chatting until they were finished, laughing about Hanna terrifying the building manager and the near disaster with the wedding chairs, which seemed funny now with some distance and a bellyful of ice cream. Thomas thanked Luka for dessert again, Luka noticing that he even scraped the liquid from the bottom of his cup and licked it off his spoon.

Luka was staring at Thomas' mouth again.

"Good work today," Thomas said, reaching to collect Luka's empty cup from him.

Luka shook himself. "You too. We did good."

"We sure did. See you tomorrow."

"Night."

He watched Thomas climb out of his car, waiting until he vanished through the front doors of his building.

He could still taste the ice cream. Good day.

Really good day.

Chapter Twelve

Thanks

Later that week, they were huddled around Luka's computer, watching some rough cuts of the commercial. It was a bit strange, editing footage of themselves on their 'date'. It was only about a two-second shot in the current version, but damn, they looked good together.

Finn stuck his head in the door as Luka was clicking 'send' on the update for Ilona. "Moreno! What are you up to for Thanksgiving?"

Luka leaned back in his chair. "My mom's trying to get me to come for the weekend, but I'd love to have a good reason not to." He had put in an appearance last year, and felt like he had earned a year off from another visit consisting of relentless questions about why he was still single and refereeing spats between his mom and sister.

"Then you're in luck! Come to my place for dinner on Saturday. You too, Wolf. Rory and I are cooking."

"Lovely! I'm in. Thank you." Luka was already composing the text to his mother in his head. She'd get over it...by Christmas, hopefully.

"Thomas?" Finn lifted an eyebrow.

Thomas nodded once. "What can I bring?"

* * * *

Luka climbed out of the cab with great care, an apple pie balanced in his hands and a bag of rolls tucked under his arm. He had made three separate trips to the grocery store and spent the entire day making this pie *from scratch*. He was not risking it on a subway ride.

Another cab pulled up right behind him. His heart gave a flutter when Thomas' broad shoulders emerged. Thomas held a pumpkin pie with one splayed hand and a small potted plant with the other. He smiled when he saw Luka. He was wearing dark gray trousers and a black polo under a matching blazer, and Luka was having trouble deciding where to look first — the way the soft-looking fabric was melting across his pecs, or the long swath of neck and chest visible where the buttons were not done up.

"Hi," he said as Thomas approached him. "I like your shirt."

"Thanks. It's new."

"It's very nice. Looks soft."

"Thanks." Thomas cleared his throat. "I like yours, too."

Luka was wearing one of his old stand-bys — a long-sleeved white button-down with tiny black specks swirling around, which always reminded him of tadpoles. And he might have left quite a few buttons undone as well. *If you've got it, flaunt it,* he had encouraged himself in the mirror as he was getting ready.

"Thanks." His heart skittered again.

They made their way up the walkway to Finn's yellow house. The door flung open before they could knock, the frame filled with a beaming redhead.

"Happy Thanksgiving!" Finn declared. He took the rolls from Luka. "Get in here, you two. Help me convince Rory the gravy isn't too thin."

"This is for you," Thomas said, handing the pot over to Finn. "I noticed you don't have any plants."

Finn eyed it skeptically. "Yeah, I always kill them. But"—he brightened up—"it might have more of a chance now that Rory is around. Thanks, Wolf."

Finn bustled them into the kitchen where they deposited the food they had brought. Rory was stirring gravy in a 'Kiss the Cook' apron.

"Luka, Thomas," they said warmly, giving each of them a hug. "Thank you for coming."

"Thank you for having us," Luka replied, blushing when he realized he had answered for Thomas. "Wow, this all looks amazing. Especially the gravy."

Rory tisked at Finn and swatted him with a dish towel. "You told them."

"No, I... Yeah, I may have mentioned something. But the gravy is perfect, love."

Luka smiled at the pet name. They could not be any more adorable. Then the dining room caught his attention through the doorway. It was beautifully set, warm colors accented in gold, shimming in candlelight.

"Just the four of us?" Luka asked when he saw how...*cozy* it looked.

"Yup," Finn said. "I asked Ilona, but Aleandro and Penelope had already invited her to Camarillo. Everyone else had plans."

Thomas' face was unreadable. Luka did his best to keep his impassive, too, as his brain chattered away about how this felt *very much* like a double date.

"Dinner is almost ready!" Rory announced, turning off the burner. "Why don't you two have a seat? Finn will get you a drink."

"Aleandro dropped off a whole case!" Finn grinned. "Is the Chéreau okay?" They made their way into the dining room.

"Sounds great." Luka pulled a chair out and sat. "The table is beautiful."

"That's all Rory," Finn said. "For a numbers guru, they fold a mean napkin." He pointed proudly at the swans.

Rory followed them in, dropping off a dish of potatoes. "Thanks, hon."

Finn smiled at him, eyes shining. He slid his arm around Rory's waist and planted a kiss on their cheek.

Once every spare inch of the table was covered with food, Finn and Rory settled across from Thomas and Luka, all soft touches and lingering glances. At one point Finn refilled Rory's glass, and Rory leaned over to kiss him.

Luka could sense Thomas shifting in his seat beside him.

"So, Thomas," Luka started, turning to face him. "I've been meaning to ask you, what was it like working in Fullerton before you came here? You can tell us." The Fullerton branch was known for their outlandish ideas that were sometimes hits, sometimes catastrophic misses.

"Fullerton?" That got Finn's attention. "That crew is crazy."

"Mmm," Thomas agreed, taking a sip of his water. "You'd fit right in."

Rory and Luka snickered while Finn pointed his fork at Thomas with an amused smirk. "Watch it, Wolf. I'm not above taking you down a peg or two."

Thomas cocked an eyebrow at him. "You can try."

"Yes, yes, you're both very tough," Luka appeased them. "Tell us about working for Harvey. You must have some stories!"

Thomas told them about Harvey's famous temper, and the time he had fired nearly the entire branch over a bungled farming equipment campaign. "If you even so much as *mention* a thresher around him now..." Thomas shook his head. "Watch out."

"Ilona is a little intimidating, but at least you know she's not going to snap and fire you on the spot," Rory said.

Finn laughed. "I don't know about that. Luka, remember that copy editor who was messing around with half the assistants?"

"What? No." Luka frowned, trying to recall.

"It must have been before you came. Yeah, it turned out this guy had slept with like five different women in the span of two months and none of them knew about the others. He got fired the second Ilona found out, officially for not disclosing any of the relationships."

"Oh." Luka gulped. Finn didn't know he had spent several months fucking Morgan. He could feel Thomas' eyes sliding over to look at him.

"Speaking of sleeping around" — Finn took another slice of turkey — "you seeing anyone these days, Luka?"

Oh, that smirk of his… The heat crept up Luka's face again. *Damn it, why do I blush so easily?* "Nope."

"I don't want to be that person, but you know what? My cousin Dimitri just broke up with his boyfriend. I think you'd like him," Rory piped up.

"Uh…" Luka swallowed hard. "No, thanks. I'm good."

"He's cute, too!" Rory added. "I promise. He grew up in Paris, has an accent and everything. He also has like four dogs, but who doesn't like dogs, right?"

"No, it's just… Thanks, but I…" *Oh God. Help.* Luka floundered.

"You have your eye on someone else?" Finn finished.

Luka gave Finn his best murder eyes. "No," he said with gritted teeth. "I'm just not…interested in dating anyone right now." *Ah, fuck.*

"Oh. Okay." Rory smiled over at Thomas. "What about you?"

Thomas froze, eyes wide. "Um…I don't date much…since I move around so often."

"Don't you get lonely?" Rory asked.

"Well… I— No. I mean, yes, but…"

Rory chuckled. "It's okay. You can let me know if you change your mind." They scooped up a forkful of stuffing. "Either of you." Then they caught Finn giving them a tiny head shake. A glimmer of understanding crossed their face. "Or not," they added.

Luka was torn between relief that Thomas hadn't said anything about Morgan—he still hadn't mentioned their night out together—but also disappointment that he said he didn't date. Not that he *wanted* to date Thomas, because that would be a bad idea. Terrible. Obviously.

When they finished their meal, Rory brought out the dessert. "Apple or pumpkin?" they asked.

"Both, please," Luka and Thomas replied at the same time. They smiled at each other.

Rory cut them a generous slice of each while Finn added whipped cream. The room was quiet as they dug in.

"Did you make this, Luka?" Rory asked after a few bites of the apple pie. "The crust is amazing."

"I did, actually," Luka said.

"Remember the time you made potato salad for the staff picnic?" Finn asked.

"No!" Luka shook his head hard. "No, I do not. Moving on."

Thomas looked at Finn with interest. "What happened?"

"He gave us all food poisoning." Finn snickered.

Thomas froze with the fork halfway to his mouth. Luka covered his face with his hand. "Fuck."

Thomas laughed.

He actually *laughed,* full-throated, head thrown back, shoulders relaxed, eyes crinkled with mirth.

Luka moved his hand away to watch that beautiful face light up.

"Oh, sure, laugh now." Finn shook his head. "You didn't have to use those porta-potties."

"Shut up, Finn!" Luka demanded through giggles. "I did my best."

"Well, so did my large intestine."

Rory burst out laughing, too. Before Luka knew it, the four of them were roaring, dessert forgotten. Luka wiped at his tears and looked over at Thomas. He was looking back, eyes shining.

His stomach twisted. *Fuck. I need him.*

* * * *

"Well, thank you for an amazing meal," Luka said when they had collected themselves and finished their pie. He leaned back to pat his stomach. "I won't be eating again for at least a week."

"It was our pleasure." Rory went to stand, but both Thomas and Luka jumped to their feet and began grabbing dishes.

"Oh, no no no. You two just relax and finish your wine," Luka ordered. "We will clean up." *Stop with the 'we'. There is no 'we'*, he reminded himself.

Finn and Rory retired to the living room while Thomas and Luka cleared the table. Then Luka eyed the kitchen. It was heaped with dirty dishes, crusted pans and empty boxes, all topped with a generous garnish of gravy splatters and greasy fingerprints. He puffed out his cheeks. "Well. Let's slay this beast, shall we?"

It turned out they were as smooth and efficient in a kitchen together as they were at work. Thomas started by attacking the stack of plates next to the sink, scraping them into the garbage. He handed them to Luka who rinsed and loaded them into the dishwasher.

When the dishwasher was full, Thomas began to fill the sink with soapy water. Their shoulders bumped as Luka reached for the first pan to dry.

They chatted about work a bit, but Luka wondered if he could poke around for any mentions of Morgan. "So what are you up to for the rest of the weekend? Any plans?" In all this time he'd been at their office, Thomas had never mentioned spending time with anyone outside of work.

"The usual." Thomas shrugged, scrubbing a stubborn pot. "Go for a run, work out, get some coffee. If the weather holds, I'll take the bike out."

"Sounds nice." Luka felt like he was going to burst. *Fuck it.* "So…you never mentioned." He studied the wooden bowl he was drying. "How was your date with Morgan?"

"Not a date."

"Right. Sorry. How was your 'getting a drink' with Morgan?"

Thomas pursed his lips, considering. "It was… Well…" He put the sponge down and turned to look at Luka. "He's a little arrogant, isn't he?"

Luka sagged against the counter in relief. "The actual worst."

"He was waiting at the elevator when I arrived that morning after the party and was buzzing around me all day. I felt like I had to say yes. And then, at that awful bar, he wouldn't stop talking about wine and his band." Thomas put the word 'band' in air quotes, and Luka's heart swelled. "He barely let me get a word in edgewise. I don't think he asked me a single question. Never again," Thomas finished, shaking his head.

"I'm relieved to hear you say that." Luka reached for the pot from Thomas. Their fingers brushed.

"Are you?" Thomas' molten eyes were on him again.

Luka squirmed. "I mean, Morgan is manipulative, too. I didn't want him getting his claws into you." He took a steadying breath.

"Don't worry." Thomas grunted, turning his attention back to the greasy water. "He won't."

"Good."

* * * *

The beast slain, Luka and Thomas made their way back into the living room. Luka topped up their wine glasses and took a seat next to Thomas on the couch. Finn and Rory were making good use of the appropriately named loveseat, Finn's arm around Rory, ankles woven together. A fire danced behind the grate, casting the room in a soft glow.

"Where are you staying, Thomas?" Rory asked, breaking the companionable silence that had settled.

"I'm renting in Sunset Towers. The new condo on Gwenllech?"

"You like it?"

"Yeah, it's fine, except they're doing some work on the ventilation and heating next month and I need to stay somewhere else for a few days."

"Hmm. You don't say?" Finn swiveled his head over to Luka. "You have lots of room, don't you, Moreno?"

"Uh. Yes. Yup." Luka's mind raced at the implications. *Thomas sleeping with just a wall between us.* "You can stay with me, if you'd like. If you need to. I have an extra bed. In an extra bedroom." *Wow.*

"I can just stay in a hotel."

"No, it's no trouble." *Thomas naked in my shower.* He forced that thought out of his head. "We have that *Back to the Future* marathon to get to, after all."

Thomas hummed. "All right. Thank you."

Luka ignored Finn's smirk. Instead he nodded at the guitar resting on a stand in the corner, a handy topic change. "How's that coming along for you?"

"Oh, I know, like, three chords." Finn waved a dismissive hand. "Will you play us something?"

"You play the guitar, too?" Thomas asked Luka.

"Uh—"

"Finn says you're amazing," Rory interrupted. "Please, Luka? How about the Beatles?"

Luka's stomach swirled with a spike of adrenaline. He blinked away the sea of junior high faces that instantly popped up. Rory and Finn were so relaxed as they watched him, lazy smiles, nothing but kindness on their faces. He looked over at Thomas. His face was a little tenser, but it was...admiration, maybe? Tinged with hope, perhaps. Luka took a sip of wine and put his glass down. Deep breath. He wanted to play for Thomas.

"Sure. If you'll sing with me." He collected the guitar and a pick and gave it a quick tune before warming up with a few chords. He took one more sip of wine, very aware that Thomas' eyes had not left him.

"Let's see..." He strummed another chord, letting the sound linger in the air. The fireplace cracked. Words that had been running through his head since he met Thomas came to him. "Do you have a capo?" he asked Finn.

Finn dug the bar out of a drawer and handed it over. Luka slid it onto the second fret to put the guitar into the proper key. He gave it a few more strums and made a tiny tuning adjustment before he began the complicated finger pick intro to *I've Just Seen a Face*. Then he started to sing. He wasn't sure if it was some combination of the full stomach with the wine and the warmth from the fire, but it came out a little slower than the song's usual rhythm. Rory and Finn smiled and joined in.

Luka watched Thomas. The firelight glinted in his eyes. His face was lit up, like he was gazing upon the most beautiful thing he had ever seen. Something so beautiful he could barely contain it. Playing for him felt easy. Comfortable. He sang with all his heart, the words pouring out of him.

When he finished, silence fell. He was sure the others could hear the pounding of his heart. He closed his eyes for a moment, sucking in another breath through his nose. He felt giddy with relief and... something else. He opened his eyes as his friends began applauding.

Thomas was shaking his head. "You're... incredible."

Luka ran a hand through his hair. His tongue was tangled up. "Thanks," was all he could say.

Thomas looked like he wanted to say more, but he stood to refill their wine glasses instead.

Luka watched him. *Yes, I am falling.*

Chapter Thirteen

Roommates

"Thomas is...staying with you?" Tawney's eyebrows reached an impossibly high point on her forehead.

"Er, yeah. Just for a few days while his manager repairs the heating."

"Okay." Tawney laughed. "Good luck, my friend."

"What? It'll be fine. We'll just...hang out. Get to know each other some more."

"Mmhmm."

"It'll be fine."

"Right. So you mentioned."

"Totally...fine."

* * * *

There was a knock on Luka's door. He almost jolted right out of his skin even though he was sitting there, waiting. He took one more look at his immaculate condo, then smoothed his hair and tugged at his shirt before he swung the door wide.

Thomas was wearing jeans, boots and a peacoat, all black, with a thick gray scarf wrapped around his neck. The temperatures had plummeted after Thanksgiving, and it was now a chilly December. He looked warm and cuddly…and amazing.

"Hi." Luka swallowed hard. "Come on in."

"Thanks." Thomas seemed extra-large as he stepped into the narrow entryway next to Luka, bundled up, holding a garment bag and a duffel.

"Let me take those for you," Luka said, holding out his hands. "You can hang your coat in the closet there."

He waited for Thomas, then led him down the hallway to the extra bedroom.

"Here we go, this is for you. And my room's just there if you need anything." *Oh, my God.* "You have the hallway bathroom all to yourself. I left out some fresh towels for you, and there's more in the linen cupboard."

He set Thomas' bags down on his bed then stood awkwardly, not sure what to do with his hands. He had done his best to make the room cozy and inviting, adding another thick blanket to the foot of the bed, and even picking up some flowers at the corner store on a whim. He eyed them on the bureau now, regretting it. It was too much. The sunflowers mocked him. *It's adorable how hard you're trying*, their smug faces said.

Thomas nodded once. "Thank you."

They stared at each other.

"I like the flowers," Thomas blurted.

"Oh." Now they both stared at the flowers. "You're welcome. I mean…glad you like them. I just saw them outside the store on my way home."

"You didn't have to go to any trouble."

"Oh, no, I didn't. I like flowers."

"Okay. Good."

"Okay," Luka said, aware that his voice was too loud again. "I'll just leave you to…settle." He turned to go, then stopped. "Um, you're welcome to come, uh, hang out, if you want."

"Okay."

"Okay." *Jesus.* Luka ducked into the kitchen to pour himself a glass of water to quell the heat in his cheeks. His kitchen was open to the rest of the main space, a large island separating it from the living room. Tall windows on the other side provided a view of the city. The lights were twinkling, with a few stars visible in the inky black sky.

He heard the closet door open and close, and got a glimpse of Thomas heading into the bathroom. Then Thomas joined him in the kitchen, looking shy and beautiful. "Hi." Luka clutched his glass.

"Hi."

Fuck. Are we just going to repeat words back and forth for four days? "Did you want to get started on that *Back to the Future* marathon?"

"Sure," Thomas replied.

"Can I get you a drink?"

"Water, thank you."

They settled on opposite ends of the couch. Thomas was so…large and black in his light-colored space. Even his socks were black. He looked uncomfortable, sitting tall and straight, hands resting on his thighs. Luka wondered if Thomas was as nervous as he was.

He took a breath, deciding to focus on the movie. It was no small thing to share a formative experience with someone. What if Thomas didn't laugh at the funny parts? What if he thought it was just okay? What if he wished he had never come here at all?

Luka hit play, trying to keep his leg from bouncing. Thomas focused on the screen. Luka told himself that if Thomas didn't like *Back to the Future*, they could still work together. Not a big deal. It would be fine. Then Luka held his breath as Marty began his audition, watching Thomas out of the corner of his eye.

Thomas frowned and leaned forward. "Is that Huey Lewis?"

"Yes!" Luka breathed with relief, wiggling in his seat. "Isn't he great? Sometimes musicians can't act for shit, but he's flawless."

Thomas nodded, looking a little pleased with himself, and settled back into his seat. Luka let himself relax.

And as the movie went on, the little ball of hope Luka had tucked away unfurled. He had begged friends to watch his favorite classic movies before, and it almost always ended in disappointment. They'd talk during the important parts, or be on their phone half the time. But not Thomas. Thomas was riveted, chuckling at all the right moments. He got goosebumps at the same triumphant swell of *Earth Angel* as Luka did. He even clutched the armrest during the clocktower climax. He was perfect.

When it was over, Luka turned the TV off and faced Thomas. "So. What did you think?" He tried to keep his voice casual.

Thomas smiled. "It was great."

"Really? You're not just saying it because you know I love it?"

Thomas tilted his head. "I *wanted* to love it because you love it, but I actually did."

Luka let out a breath, his heart pounding from the intensity of Thomas' gaze. "So you're up for part two?"

Thomas chuckled and looked at his watch. "Maybe not tonight."

"Oh, no! No, definitely not tonight. I can't stay up that late on a work night anymore. But...tomorrow?"

"Tomorrow."

* * * *

Bedtime was fraught. Luka was unable to forget that Thomas was so *close* and in varying states of undress through just one thin wall. It would be inappropriate to get himself off with Thomas right there, so he lay on his back, arms frozen at his sides, staring into the darkness, wondering if he could hear Thomas tossing and turning or if he was just imagining it.

After what felt like not very much sleep at all, his alarm woke him at six. Luka got out of bed to turn on the coffee maker before he showered, then paused when he caught a glimpse of himself in his mirror. He was wearing pajama bottoms. Only pajama bottoms. The chances of running into Thomas out there were small, but not zero. But...no big deal, right? He probably wouldn't, and, well, if Thomas *did* see him...

He stepped into the hallway at the exact moment his roommate came out of the bathroom. Wet. With nothing but a towel around his waist.

Luka made an audible wheeze as the blood rushed out of his head. Thomas was...beyond words. He didn't know where to look first. Pecs he could sink his teeth into. Deltoids that deserved to be memorialized in marble. Chest hair dusted over a devastating torso. A water droplet slid down the groove between his ab muscles. How was he real? The way his obliques disappeared where his towel was starting to dip... He was art.

Thomas saw him and paused. His gaze flicked over Luka's chest. A hint of a smile danced on the corner of his mouth. "Morning," he rumbled.

"Morning," Luka gasped, placing a hand on the doorframe in what he hoped was a casual manner. "Did you sleep well?"

"Uh...yes. You?"

"Yup." It came out too high-pitched. "Well, I was just going to"—his mind groped for what he was doing—"put on the coffee!" he finished triumphantly.

"Great, thanks. I'll go...get dressed." Thomas pointed at his door.

"Brilliant." Again, they stared at each other, until Thomas turned and disappeared into the bedroom, closing the door behind him. The way his back tapered...

Luka slumped against the wall. *Fuck.* How could he be expected to be normal with a fucking *god* just walking around almost naked? Through the miracle of muscle memory, he got the coffee going, then scooted back to his room and into the shower. He let the water cascade over him, and when Thomas' ridiculous body flashed into his brain again, his dick twitched. He resolutely turned the temperature down a notch before it got any further ideas. "Sorry, buddy. Not right now."

It was easier to function once Thomas was in his suit, although Luka had to try to forget what he looked like underneath it. Otherwise it was kind of fun with Thomas around, pouring him a travel mug and having him along for the subway ride. They talked about their tasks for the day as the train rattled around them, knees bumping together. Their first commercial had aired in ten major markets the previous week, and Rory would have the preliminary numbers for them today. By the time they got to the office, they were ready to dive in.

"What do you feel like for dinner?" Luka asked at the end of the day as he collected their coats from the closet. *Wait, shit. I just assumed he wants to eat dinner with me.*

"Hmm." Thomas frowned as he bundled up. "Is that Thai place down the road from you any good?"

Luka breathed a sigh of relief that Thomas didn't seem to find his question weird. Then he shuddered, picturing Morgan inhaling their noodles. "No. But there's a new Japanese place just around the corner?" They stopped to wait at the elevator.

"Sounds great."

A bubble of happiness welled up in his chest. *Imagine this every day, deciding what we want for dinner as we head home after work. To our home.* The idea was so warming that when Luka caught a glimpse of Morgan watching them from the reception desk, face in a scowl, he didn't care one fucking bit.

* * * *

Part two of the trilogy went just as well as part one, but now that he could relax knowing Thomas liked them, he was much more distracted by the thick, solid presence at the other end of the couch. After a bathroom break, he swore Thomas was sitting a little closer to him.

When Thomas grunted approvingly at a fun plot reveal, Luka reached over and squeezed his arm without even thinking about it. His forearm was like a small tree trunk. He got a whiff of Thomas' cologne as he pulled his hand away, which never failed to send his stomach whirling.

When the movie was over, they cleaned up their dishes and tidied the kitchen together, settling into their usual easy rhythm. When they went back to the living room, Thomas eyed Luka's guitar propped on its stand. "I remember you mentioning a while ago that you write down songs sometimes when they come to you."

"Uh." Luka's heart skipped a beat. "Yes. But I don't—I haven't played them for anyone."

"Oh. Well, if you feel comfortable, I'd love to hear one."

Thomas was studying him like he was something special. Like he deserved to be listened to. He swallowed hard and remembered how it felt to sing to Thomas on Thanksgiving, warm in front of the fireplace with his friends. The way Thomas had looked at him that night. He wanted that again.

"I guess I could." Luka picked up his guitar and settled on the couch, heart pounding. "There's this. It's called *Could I*." It was his latest song. He cleared his throat and strummed a chord or two. *Deep breath*. Then he began.

> *"Could I be here*
> *With you?*
> *Could I have you*
> *For a day*
> *Could I touch you*
> *Hold your hand*
> *Could I smile at you*
> *Is there a way?*
> *Is there a way*

For us to be…
Could I love you?
Kiss you, hold you
What will it take
For you to say…
Is there a way
For us to be…
Be the one
Be your love
Be forever yours
Be the one
Be your love
Be forever yours."

Luka couldn't even look at the beautiful man sitting next to him on the couch while he sang. It was too much. He sang to the floor, the heat building in his cheeks, his heart thudding the bassline. The song was so obviously about Thomas. He wasn't sure what had possessed him to sing it at this moment, but, well, he was.

When the last note faded, Thomas swallowed. "Wow."

Luka risked raising his eyes. "You liked it?" The room was so silent around them now.

There was a brightness in Thomas' gaze he hadn't seen before. "I'm just worried."

"Worried? For what?" *Shit. The song was too much. He thinks I'm in love with him. He's freaking out.*

"You may be in the wrong career. I mean, you're amazing at your job, but…" He gestured at Luka and his guitar.

"Oh." Luka chuckled in relief and looked down again. "Nah. Music's something just for me." He wiped his sweaty palms on his pants.

Thomas watched him still. "I'm honored you shared it with me. Thank you."

"You're welcome." Sitting next to Thomas was starting to feel very difficult, so he stood to put his guitar away. "Well. I think I'll head to bed."

"Me too." Thomas stood too, smoothing his shirt. Luka's gaze was drawn to the way his sweatpants sat on his hips, hugging his thigh muscles.

He had trouble falling asleep again, but when he finally did, his brain betrayed him with another dream about Thomas. He was performing for him again, singing the same song, but when it ended, Thomas took the guitar from him, and climbed onto his lap. The sweatpants slid right off like silk on silk.

When he woke up, the dream stayed with him, how Thomas had felt under his hands, hard and hot. The softness of his lips, his wet tongue. Luka shook his head and sat up, scrubbing at his face. Best if he didn't dwell on it…too much.

* * * *

"The thing to know about part three," Luka explained as they settled on the couch with their tacos the next night, "is it's a bit…wackier."

"The first two weren't wacky?"

Luka laughed and swatted Thomas' shoulder. *Granite.* "Okay, fair point, but they go back to the Wild West in this one."

"I know."

"You know?"

"I did some googling to see what I was getting into."

"Oooookay," Luka said in a sing-song, eyebrows raised. "I don't think you're ready, though."

Thomas chuckled. "Try me."

They weren't too far in when Thomas hit pause. Luka fucking *loved* that he paused it whenever he had something to say so they didn't miss anything.

"Wait, why does his great-great-grandmother on the McFly side look like his mom? Does that mean his parents are...?"

Luka grinned. "I warned you. Don't overthink it."

Thomas shook his head. "Of course. My bad." He smiled back. "You have a little something—" He pointed at one side of his lip.

"Oh." Luka flushed. *Of course.* He wiped at his face. "Did I get it?"

"No."

He tried again on the other side. "Now?"

"Here, let me." Thomas leaned over and brushed his finger along the underside of Luka's lip. "There. Just a crumb." Their eyes met.

Luka's heart was pounding so hard he was sure Thomas could hear it. "Thanks." For a fraction of a second, his instincts screamed at him to toss his tacos and throw himself at Thomas.

But Thomas cleared his throat and turned the movie back on.

Luka took a steadying breath and focused on not getting any more of his dinner on his face.

* * * *

"You're right, there was a *Back-to-the-Future*-shaped void in my life. I feel whole now."

Luka giggled. "I sense you're mocking me, but I'm okay with it."

"No, really." Thomas leaned an elbow on the back of the couch and propped his head on his hand. "I loved it."

"Favorite character, besides Marty and Doc?"

"Hmmm." Thomas looked thoughtful, and Luka loved how seriously he took the question. "Biff."

"Me too. Ooh!" Luka lunged for his phone. "Okay, sorry, but you have to watch this. So the actor, Tom Wilson, actually did stand-up for a while, and he has this song he sings called *The Question Song*. It makes fun of all the people who ask him the same things over and over. You know, 'What's Michael J. Fox like?' I've watched it a hundred times and it never stops being funny. Here…" He scooted over to Thomas and held his phone so they could both watch.

He was delighted that Thomas seemed to find the song as funny as he did. When it was over, both of them giggling, Thomas pointed at one of the suggestions. "Look, there's a newer version from a con. Can we watch that?"

"Yeah, we can." Luka clicked with relish and settled back, their shoulders touching.

Before they knew it, they had watched every version of the song that existed, then they were on to *Back to the Future* trivia, retrospectives and anniversary talk show appearances. Luka had folded a leg under himself, and his knee was pressed against Thomas' thigh. When Thomas put his arm along the back of the couch as he leaned in to see better, Luka swallowed hard and let himself slump a little closer. He prayed to the YouTube gods that they never ran out of videos to watch.

Until his eyes started to burn and he realized it was almost one a.m. "Shit," Luka rubbed his face. "What did we do?"

Thomas yawned and stretched, and Luka eyed the strip of rippling stomach revealed above his waistband. "Wow. I lost track of time."

"Was that a *Back to the Future* joke?"

Another yawn turned into a laugh. "No…regretfully."

Luka smiled at him. "Thanks for watching them with me. It was really fun."

"It was."

* * * *

"You skipped your run this morning?" Luka leaned on the counter and took a gulp of his coffee, ignoring the fact that it was too hot for gulping. He knew he looked like shit, hair sticking up, bathrobe old and faded.

Thomas was in his slacks and dress shirt, but hair was still loose and wet and he looked adorably bleary as he fumbled for a mug in the cupboard. "Yeah, I overslept. I had all these crazy dreams about time travel."

"Oh, that's too bad."

"It's fine… It's all in the past." He paused to look at Luka, eyes crinkling with amusement.

It took Luka a second, then he snorted a laugh. "Wow. How long were you waiting to tell me that one?"

Thomas poured himself some coffee. "For a good twenty minutes now. I thought of it in the shower."

"What a waste of time."

Thomas rolled his eyes with a chuckle. "We could do this all day."

"You started it!"

Thomas hummed as he leaned against the counter across from Luka. "I got an email that I can go back home today. Thanks for letting me stay here."

"Anytime."

Thomas took a sip of coffee, then frowned as he studied Luka.

"What?" Luka shifted, self-consciously trying to smooth his hair.

Then Thomas smiled. "Nothing, just...how old is your robe?"

Luka gasped. "Are you judging my robe?"

"Not at all. It looks...very comfortable."

"Hmm," Luka sniffed, mollified to a degree. "My sister gave it to me when I left for university."

"Ah. Well, I love it."

"Thanks." They drank their coffee in silence.

"So did you go to university fifty years ago, or...?"

Luka leaned forward to poke Thomas' gray shoulder. "Pretty bold for a man who only wears shades instead of actual colors."

Thomas' eyes crinkled again. "Fair."

Thomas' scent hit him, fresh and clean from the shower. His stomach swooped. "Well." Luka cleared his throat. "I'd better get dressed." His mind spun as he went back into his room. He didn't want him to leave. Having another big, warm body around was comforting. He liked seeing Thomas in his kitchen, on his couch. Washing dishes, folding the tea towel and putting it back so neatly. He could smell him everywhere he went and Luka just wanted more. He fell back onto his bed, stifling a groan of despair. On the other hand...maybe what he needed was some space. This obsession was not good. It was hard to think about anything else when he was just *right there all the time.*

They took turns refilling their coffees all day at work, humming bits of *The Question Song* at each other when things got too quiet. Luka's shoulders were shaking at another time travel joke when he realized that they were friends. Good friends. Even if nothing could ever happen with Thomas romantically, he had that to hold on to, and it was pretty great by itself.

As the end of the day approached, they finally got the track from Morgan to add to their third and final commercial. Luka hit play and they watched it with the music.

Thomas rubbed his forehead as it ended.

Luka sighed. "I know."

"It's not awful, but..."

"It's missing...depth."

"Exactly."

"What if we added a few more layers of the vocals right before the logo, and maybe hit the tag a little harder?" Luka suggested.

"I like that."

They scribbled a few more notes, and Luka went to go catch Morgan in his office before he left for the day.

"Hey, thanks for the track—" Luka started.

"But?" Morgan interrupted.

"Well, we had a few suggestions—"

"Why don't you just do it, then?" Morgan said, keeping his eyes on his screen.

Luka paused, biting back the retort that came.

"I don't have any time, anyway," Morgan muttered, giving a few angry clicks on his mouse. "I have, like, ten other projects on the go right now."

"Morgan." Luka sighed. "You know it's not my job."

Morgan turned to look at him. "Things going good with Thomas?" he asked. The threat hung in the air for a moment. Then his shoulders drooped. "What if... Could you—maybe you could come by my place tonight and we could both work on it?"

Luka narrowed his eyes and took in Morgan's appearance. There were dark circles under his eyes, and he was overdue for a haircut. Normally Morgan was meticulous about going every five weeks, and he had clearly worked his way well past that. His shoes were off, one socked foot tucked up under his leg.

Ugh. Maybe this was the fastest way to get it done. "Fine. After dinner. Eight o'clock?"

"Sure." Morgan looked back at his screen and didn't say anything else. Luka slipped away.

* * * *

He knocked on Morgan's door right at eight and it opened instantly.

"Come in," Morgan said, waving an arm. He had changed into slim but comfortable-looking gray sweatpants and a thin white T-shirt. Luka was still wearing his work clothes.

He stepped into Morgan's apartment, looking around, and the last time he had been there came rushing back to him. It had been about a month before they broke up, a long, lazy Sunday. He remembered being stretched out in Morgan's bed, naked under the sheet, although it was hard to say what time of day it had been. They'd already ordered food once, but hadn't been up and dressed yet.

Morgan had been curled next to him, his usually freezing-cold feet warm for once where they were pressed up against Luka's calf.

Jennifer Moffatt

"Do you think you'll stay in advertising forever?" Morgan had asked out of nowhere, idly running his fingers through Luka's chest hair.

"Yeah," Luka had said, turning his head to look at Morgan. "I mean, it's kind of my dream job. You?"

Morgan had been staring past him, out of the window, eyes unfocused. "No. I'm not even sure how I ended up here." Then he had blinked and shaken himself, snapping back into focus. He had given Luka a loaded smile. "You good to go?"

"Again?" Luka had laughed, but Morgan had already been climbing on top of him, hungry lips pressed to his.

He looked around the apartment now, noticing the changes. The art was all different—bigger, brighter— and the throw pillows had gone from beige to azure. It just seemed...more lived in, the clean lines from his memory of Morgan's apartment now fuzzy in front of him. A stray sock peeked out from under the couch, and a lone cereal bowl sat on the coffee table, a few sad flakes clinging to the rim.

"Drink?" Morgan asked, retreating into the kitchen. More cereal bowls were stacked in the sink, an empty milk carton abandoned on the counter.

Luka followed him. His instinct was to say no, but he thought it might make the night go down a little easier. "Sure." Morgan poured two rum and Cokes that were mostly rum.

Morgan handed him a glass. "This way," he said, disappearing down the hallway, even though Luka knew where to go. The second bedroom in Morgan's place was more like a music studio, a twin bed pushed up against the wall, but otherwise dominated by a huge desk covered with all kinds of computers and other

165

sound-mixing and recording equipment. Morgan wheeled an extra chair over from the corner for Luka.

"All right. Gimme a second to load it." He clicked a few buttons. "So, you fucked Thomas yet?" he asked nonchalantly, taking a sip of his drink.

"What?"

"It's okay, I won't tell anyone."

"Morgan. No. I have not."

"Too bad. I tried, a couple times. He shut me down."

Luka shook his head. "No. Definitely not. He's my boss."

Morgan shrugged. "Bosses fuck too."

Luka's stomach turned. He changed the topic as the software interface popped up. "Show me the strings track?"

Despite everything, they worked well together. Morgan was adept at adding the musical elements Luka suggested, and it was only a couple hours until Luka was both happy with the track and pleasantly buzzed from the rum.

"What about this?" Morgan said, clicking a few buttons before he hit play. The track played at twice the speed with honking noises added in.

Despite himself, Luka laughed. "It reminds me of you."

"Hmmm." Morgan gave an exaggerated frown. "I wouldn't have described it as 'devastatingly sexy' but okay."

"Nah, I meant more 'short and clown-like'."

This time Morgan laughed and gave him a playful shove. "Fuck off."

For a moment it was like the old days, when Morgan's banter made him feel cute and clever. They were giving it one final listen, for real this time, when

Jennifer Moffatt

he realized Morgan had grown very still. He looked over to find gray eyes watching him. Morgan shifted closer in his chair and licked his lips.

It would be so easy to kiss him right now. He was a good kisser. He clearly wanted to be kissed. Luka contemplated it for one brief moment. Then he remembered why he was there. Pictured Morgan hitting on Thomas. Imagined Thomas seeing them sitting here together.

Luka stood. "Okay, this is done. See you tomorrow."

For a split second, it looked like Morgan's face was about to crumple, then it hardened. "Glad you're finally satisfied." His voice was cold.

"You'll upload it to the server?"

"Yeah."

Luka didn't say anything else. He let himself out.

* * * *

Luka came in a little early the next morning, wanting to have the new version ready for Thomas. He downloaded the updated track and synced it with the commercial. "Yes," he said after he watched it. "That's more like it."

When Thomas came in, Luka took a moment to enjoy the usual butterflies in his stomach at his appearance, but then he couldn't wait. "Morgan redid the music!"

"Already?"

"Yup. I gave him our suggestions and he...worked on it last night."

"He did? It must have been a late night."

Luka gulped. "Yeah, I think so."

"Well, let's hear it."

He hit play. He watched Thomas' face move from skeptical to pleased. "Wow. That's exactly what we talked about. He took our notes to the letter. I guess Morgan can come through sometimes."

"Yup. I guess." Luka was lying again, and it didn't feel good.

Chapter Fourteen

Secret Santa

"What do I get Rory for Christmas?" Finn tumbled into his chair in his usual carefree manner. The difference was that he didn't wait until Luka was alone anymore. Thomas was now privy to the ins and outs of Finn's relationship with Rory.

Luka tapped his chin. "I mean, technically, nothing, unless you draw their name."

Finn stared at him. "You're joking, right?"

"What? These are the rules! You're only supposed to get a gift for someone at work if you have them for Secret Santa."

Finn blinked a couple times, then turned to Thomas. "What do you think I should get them, Wolf?"

Thomas froze, eyes flicking between Luka and Finn. "Uh, do they need a new wallet?"

Luka sniffed. He would tell Tawney he at least *tried* to make them follow the rules if she asked.

Later that day, the Secret Santa Queen herself popped in carrying a Santa hat. "Ho, ho, ho, boys! Time to pick your name. And remember, do not tell anyone who you got!" Tawney shook the hat and held it out for Luka.

"Yes, ma'am." Luka reached in, breath held. *Thomas, Thomas, Thomas...* He grabbed the first paper he touched, but when he pulled it out, Tawney tsked.

"Oops! You've got two there." She plucked one from between his fingers and put it back in the hat. She shook it again, then held it out for Thomas.

As Thomas was pulling his slip out, Luka took a peek at the paper crumpled in his palm. *Morgan Di Meo.* "Are you f—" he started to say, but Tawney shushed him.

"No hints, Luk!"

"Can I have that other one, though?"

She gave him a stern look and an admonishment about the Christmas spirit before she bustled off again.

Thomas looked at his paper, his face remaining blank.

"How do you do that?" Luka asked.

"Do what?"

"Never mind." He peeked down the hall to make sure Tawney was gone then turned back to Thomas. "Who did you get?"

Thomas furrowed his brow. "Tawney said not to tell."

"Oh, sure, *now* you're a rule follower."

* * * *

As Luka was tidying up at the end of the day, he ran his shopping list through his head. "All your Christmas shopping done?" he asked Thomas.

Thomas clenched his jaw as he pulled his coat on. "I don't have many gifts to buy. Lone wolf, remember?"

"Oh." Luka's heart broke a little more. "Oh. I'm sorry."

"It's fine. I just need to get this Secret Santa gift."

"I was going to head out for a bit of shopping right now. Do you want to come?"

Thomas pondered a moment. "Sure."

They wandered down Main Street in the gently swirling snow. The streetlamps were on, reflecting the flakes in Thomas' hair. His whole head shimmered when he stepped into a circle of light. *How can he be so beautiful?* Luka wondered, crunching along the sidewalk next to him. He imagined looping his arm under Thomas', feeling the warmth of their bodies pressed together in the cold evening.

"Who do you need to shop for?" Thomas asked as they paused to take in a window display. A model train wound through a snowy village, lush-looking gifts displayed throughout. There was a wicker picnic basket resting on a thick plaid blanket, a pottery tea set with smooth blue and gray cups just begging to be cradled and a few jars of bath salts that gave Luka the urge to sink into a steaming tub.

"Well, let's see. My parents and sister, her kids, something small for the aunts and uncles, and, as luck would have it, fucking Morgan."

Thomas flinched. "You weren't supposed to tell me!"

Luka eyed Thomas. "I have poor self-control."

"Hmm. I'm still not telling you who I got."

"Thomas!"

"No."

Luka pouted. "Fine. Then will you at least please tell me what the fuck I'm supposed to get Morgan?"

"Let's look in here." Thomas nodded at the shop.

"It's too nice for him."

Thomas rumbled a low laugh, his breath white. "Don't make me repeat Tawney's lecture about the Christmas spirit."

Luka gave a begrudging grin. "Okay, fine."

The bell tinkled when they pushed their way in, stamping the snow from their boots. The shopkeeper greeted them as they began to poke around.

"Do you think they sell humility?" Luka wondered, running his hand over a stack of blankets. "Self-awareness? A fucking clue?"

Thomas smiled, shaking his head. "You might need to settle for one of these nice candles instead. Look." He held one up. Its label read 'Not My Problem'.

"Ooh. He actually does like candles. He thinks the lighting is flattering." Luka perused the shelf. There was also 'Breathe', 'Do It Tomorrow', and 'LOL No.' "Is there one that says 'I'm a Narcissist'?"

"Hmm." Thomas pointed. "I think this is the clear winner." The label said 'No One Cares'.

"Perfection. Done." Luka picked it up. "Okay, what if I get him this and a fancy bottle of wine? Nice enough?"

"Tawney would be proud."

"Brilliant. Cross that one off the list." Luka tucked the candle under his arm and moved onto the next display. "Oh, look at this bathrobe," he breathed, running his hands over the soft white flannel. "You have to feel this, Thomas."

Thomas touched the sleeve. "Definitely a step up from yours."

Luka gasped. "How dare you. Mine is...well-loved."

"Literally hanging by a thread, more like."

Luka looked at the price and grimaced. "Well, maybe not just now. Need some time to say goodbye to the old one." He gave it a wistful pat, then went to look at the tea sets with his sister in mind.

A few shops later, Luka had done quite well. He had also found a necklace for his mom and toy guitars for his nieces. "My sister will kill me, but I'm the fun uncle," he explained as he paid, glancing at Thomas' empty hands. "Nothing caught your eye for your Secret Santa?"

Thomas shook his head. "Not yet. You hungry?"

Right on cue, Luka's stomach growled. "Like the wolf."

They found a little bistro with a small table open in a corner by the window. They wedged themselves in, coats and scarves heaped over the backs of the chairs, Luka's bags piled next to him, their knees pressed together under the table.

They warmed their hands around mugs of coffee — decaf for Luka or he'd never sleep — and both ordered the soup of the day. A silence fell over the table as they sipped.

"So, your parents aren't around?" Luka wanted to know more about Thomas' life, but so far he had shared almost nothing. "If you want to talk about it."

Thomas shifted in his chair and regarded Luka across the table for a long moment. "I was adopted when I was four. My father, the man who adopted me, passed away five years ago. Pancreatic cancer. It was just the two of us. He didn't have any family, either. That was when I started traveling around."

Luka reached across the table and squeezed Thomas' hand. "I'm so sorry."

Thomas shrugged. "I'm used to it."

Luka looked at the hand under his, so strong and solid, and imagined how small it must have been when four-year-old Thomas had clung to his new father like his life depended on it. Then he met Thomas' gaze. "I'm glad you're here now, though."

Thomas tilted his head, his eyes soft. "Me too."

"What was he like?" Luka asked, pulling back, although he wanted to keep Thomas' warm skin under his.

A faraway smile ghosted his face. "No one has asked me about him in a while."

"Tell me."

The server bustled up with their soup—butternut squash with warm, crusty bread. They ate while Thomas spoke about his father, a house painter by trade, passionate fisherman and inventor of exotic grilled cheese variations, with a scratchy beard and booming laugh. The bistro was loud around them, but they didn't notice. Snow drifted down outside the foggy windows.

* * * *

Finally, it was the day of the office Christmas party. With four days of holiday looming, there was an air of festivity to the goings-on, Santa hats and candy canes popping up everywhere, the need to get any work done significantly diminished. Finn was once again stretched out in his chair in Luka and Thomas' office.

"So what did you end up getting Rory?" Luka asked, looking up from the mock-up magazine spread Finn had come to show them.

"Oh, yeah, I did get them a new wallet, a really nice leather one that they had pointed out while we were shopping. And, well…something else." Finn wiggled his eyebrows.

"Stop, I do not need to know more." Luka laughed, holding up a hand.

"I'll let you know how it goes. I might have a suggestion for you." Finn's eyes danced back and forth between the two of them.

Warmth flared on Luka's face and he stared hard at the layout on his desk. "Thanks," he said through a clenched jaw.

Finn left, chortling.

The room was painfully silent for a minute until Thomas made a show of looking at his phone. "Well, I think I'm going to head home to change. I'll see you at the restaurant?"

Luka nodded while visions of Finn's sex toys danced in his head. "You bet."

The party was at a swanky upscale restaurant where Aleandro knew the owner. Luka gave a low whistle when he arrived. His co-workers had stepped up their game a few notches, the room awash with dapper suits and shimmering fabrics. Luka was wearing a burgundy suit over a sleek black T-shirt, his hair combed back off his forehead in carefully tousled waves.

Then Thomas came in.

Luka saw Thomas in suits every day, of course, but somehow he was not prepared for this one. He looked like James fucking Bond in a slim-fitting black three-piece with a crisp white shirt and black tie. When he paused at the entrance and straightened his cuffs, Luka forgot how to breathe.

Thomas' gaze swept across the room, and he came straight over to Luka when he saw him.

"You look…unbelievable," Luka choked out.

Thomas lifted his heavy eyebrows. "Thank you." He pointed at his tie. "Is it crooked, though, do you think?"

"Hmm." Luka stepped closer. Freshly applied cologne wafted over him while he gave the knot a little tug. His gaze traveled up to Thomas' lips, his knees quivering as he forced himself to step back again. "Looks perfect."

"Thanks." Thomas took in Luka's long frame. "You look good, too."

The lighting was low enough that he was sure Thomas couldn't tell he was blushing. "Thank you. Shall we find a drink?" He waved Thomas ahead of him, taking a long look at his beautiful round ass in those tight pants. "Because I really fucking need one," he muttered to himself as he followed.

After a delectable roast beef dinner, the whole group settled into a large circle, while Tawney, dressed like an elf, buzzed around the table of gifts. They sipped their drinks as she began calling names.

Thomas got a fancy insulated water bottle, and a black tank top with *I flexed and the sleeves fell off* written on it. Luka lost it when Thomas held it up, an expression of polite incredulity on his face.

"Who do you think got me this?" Thomas whispered to Luka when Tawney handed out the next present.

A fresh wave of giggles hit Luka. "I don't know, but can you please wear it to work one day?"

"Shut up." But Thomas was suppressing a laugh too.

Morgan peered suspiciously around the circle after he read the candle, while Luka maintained a neutral expression with a herculean effort. But Morgan seemed quite pleased with the wine, which Luka had selected by asking the shopkeeper for something a wine snob would like at an affordable price point.

Finally, it was Luka's turn. Tawney handed him a large brown paper gift bag. Luka pulled out the tissue and gasped. The bathrobe. His head snapped up. Thomas was watching him with a smile.

"Thomas! You had me? I can't believe you!" Luka lifted it out and buried his face in the soft material. It smelled like him. "Thank you so much!"

"You're welcome."

Thomas had spent far too much, but Luka had visions of curling up in his new robe on lazy Sunday mornings, a mug of coffee in hand, Thomas next to him... *Ah, fuck. Stop.* He kept it on his lap as they finished up the remaining few gifts, running his hand over the plush fabric.

Once the gift exchange was complete, the music was turned up, and a line formed at the bar.

"Moreno!" Finn was on him in a second, dragging him out onto the dance floor with Rory and Tawney. It didn't take long until Luka was sweaty and out of breath from trying to keep up with Finn's ridiculous moves. Thomas watched as he chatted with Aleandro and Penelope, but made no move to join them.

"Wolf!" Finn called as the next song began. "Get out here!"

Thomas' eyes widened as he gave a tight shake of his head.

"Let's go get him," Finn yelled at Luka over the music. He took Luka's hand and began to shimmy over to the painfully sexy man smoldering on the edge of the dance floor. Luka was just drunk enough to go with the plan.

"Come on, Wolf. Let's see your moves." Finn reached a hand out toward Thomas.

"I don't dance."

"Don't you wanna dance with us?" Finn pouted. He threw an arm around Luka and pressed their faces together. "Look how cute we are."

Thomas shifted his weight. Something like a smile played at the corner of his mouth. "I'm not saying you're not cute…"

Luka's stomach twisted as Thomas' eyes met his.

"…I just can't dance."

That just made Finn smile wider. "I have good news for you—everyone can dance! Luka here is proof of that."

Luka laughed. "I feel like I should take offense, but he's not wrong." He stuck his lower lip out and made his eyes nice and wide. "Please dance with us, Thomas."

Thomas sighed and drained the rest of his drink. "Okay." He plunked the empty glass down on the nearest table. "Don't judge me." He took Finn's still outstretched hand. Finn whooped as he hauled them all back onto the dance floor where Rory and Tawney were still going strong.

Luka thought his heart might burst with how adorably uncertain Thomas looked, starting to bounce a little to the latest Top Forty club banger.

Luka moved a little closer. "It's in the hips," he told Thomas. "See?"

Thomas watched him dance, his eyes heavy. He nodded and bent his knees more, letting his hips slide back and forth.

Luka grinned and nodded. "Perfect."

Once he settled in, it was clear Thomas was a very good dancer, which wasn't a surprise to Luka at all, given how smoothly and gracefully he moved day-to-day. As the night went on, they danced closer and closer, hips and fingers brushing together, lips parted, a thin sheen of sweat shining on their foreheads.

The beat echoed through Luka's chest, simmering in his groin while Thomas' torso rippled. "I need a break," he leaned over to tell Thomas when he felt the blood gathering down low.

He took a moment to drink some water and mop the sweat off his brow, but when he glanced at his phone, he realized the night was drawing to a close. There was something he had to do still. He approached Thomas who had followed him off the dance floor for some water. "Hey," he leaned over to say into his ear. "Do you want to get some air for a second? I have something for you."

Thomas looked puzzled, but he grabbed his jacket and nodded, following Luka out through the sliding door onto the patio.

Luka shivered in the cold as he pulled his blazer on. It was a clear night, the stars dotting the sky above. He turned to face Thomas, leaning back on the railing. "That was a fun night."

Thomas smiled, tilting his head. "Really fun. Thank you for dragging me out there."

Luka nodded. "And thank you again so much for the gift. I love it. You spent way more than the price limit!"

Thomas shrugged. "Fuck the rules. I'm glad you like it."

"I, uh, got you something too." He pulled a small box out of his pocket.

"You did? I thought the rule was…?"

Luka smiled. "A wise man once said 'fuck the rules'." He handed it to Thomas, heart pounding. *It's too much.*

Thomas unwrapped the white paper and lifted the lid. A pair of silver wolf cufflinks were nestled in the tissue.

"There's two wolves," Luka said, unable to look at Thomas, "because you're not alone."

Thomas inhaled sharply, then a silence hung over them. He risked a glance up. The warm brown gaze of the other man threatened to light him on fire.

"Luka, I..." Thomas shook his head, his voice strangled. "Thank you."

Luka swayed forward. "You're welcome."

Then the door slid open and Georgia stuck her head out. "There you guys are! We were looking for you. Ilona and Aleandro want to say a few words before everyone leaves."

"Okay," Luka said, straightening up. "Great. Yup. Be right there."

He looked at Thomas. Thomas was looking back. Georgia stood waiting at the open door. "After you," he said.

They gathered back with the crowd inside as Ilona and Aleandro thanked them for their work and wished them a happy holiday. Luka's heart raced as he considered the moment they had had. *Almost* had.

The party wrapped up after that, the air filled with wishes for a merry Christmas and happy holidays as people said their goodbyes.

"Well, I'm leaving for my parents' place in the morning," Luka said, when he couldn't avoid saying goodbye to Thomas any longer.

Thomas nodded. "Drive safely."

"I will." Then he slipped in for a hug. Thomas tensed for a second, then his arms slid around Luka in return.

It was hard to explain, the dizzying feeling that swept over him as Thomas held him. He was warm, weak, safe and so very turned on all at once.

"Merry Christmas, Thomas," he scratched out as he pulled away, letting his fingers linger on Thomas' arm.

"Merry Christmas, Luka."

It hurt to walk away.

Luka left for Andchester early, bracing himself for four days of invasive questions about his personal life and the high-level acrobatics required to stay out of his mom's and sister's sparring. He'd play in the snow with the kids, watch whatever sporting event his dad had on, eat and drink his way through his mom's stockpile and absolutely, definitely not obsess about Thomas every second.

"Great plan," he told himself as he drove. "Fuck."

Chapter Fifteen

You Couldn't Even Wait Till Breakfast?

Waking up in his parents' house, in the room he slept in for eighteen years, was always strange. It was a guest room now, his old belongings long gone, but it still had the same feel. The same light creeping in and falling across his pillow. The same air.

Luka rolled over and stretched, listening to see if anyone else was up. When he heard the clink of the coffee pot sliding into its place, he sat up and reached for his new robe. It didn't smell like Thomas anymore, but putting it on still made him feel closer to that sweet, gorgeous man. He sighed and checked the time. *Made it till 6:08 without pining.*

"Morning, Dad," Luka said as he shuffled into the kitchen.

His dad looked up over his reading glasses. "Morning, Luk. Sleep well?"

Luka blew out a breath. Not especially, being haunted by the memory of that hug. "Sure. Fine."

His dad shook out the paper. Luka looked at him fondly. Oscar still insisted on reading an actual physical newspaper every morning.

Luka went to pull two mugs out of the cupboard, adding milk and sugar to his as the coffee brewed. He poured for the two of them and sat across the table. His dad had been called out last night for a burst pipe and Luka hadn't had much of a chance to talk to him yet.

"Did you get their water back on okay?"

"Oh, sure." Oscar shrugged. "Just a small one."

"Not all plumbers would drop everything to run out for a house call after dinner on December twenty-third." Oscar owned the business now, but still made house calls in emergencies.

His dad shrugged again. "Part of the job." He took a gulp of coffee and eyed Luka over the rim. "How are things for you?"

"Good. Work's been great. Busy."

"Good to hear." His dad pursed his lips, obviously debating whether or not to say anything. "Your mother's got another one for you."

Luka scrunched up his face and groaned. "Christ, Dad."

"I know, I know. I told her to mind her business."

Luka blew out a breath. Every time he arrived back home still single, his mother grew increasingly offended. She took it as a personal mission to rectify the problem, as she saw it. He had forbidden her from setting him up, but that hadn't stopped her yet.

Speaking of the devil, Marta came scurrying into the kitchen, already dressed and made up. She was about five feet tall and resembled a Christmas tree, all green and covered in baubles.

"Morning, my heart," she said, planting a kiss on Luka's cheek.

"Morning, Mom."

She busied herself pulling eggs out of the fridge and whisking a few up in a bowl. "So, Luka. Cynthia's son—"

"Oh, God, Mom. No, thanks."

She sighed and turned to face him, setting down the whisk. "Luka, you are thirty-two years old—"

"I'm aware." He attempted to push the irritation down that was scratching its way up his throat.

"—and I had two kids by the time I was twenty-eight!"

"I also know this. Jesus, you couldn't even wait until we've had breakfast?

Marta sighed again as if the weight of the world was upon her shoulders. "His name is Travis—"

"Mom, what? You want me to be in a long-distance relationship with Cynthia's son Travis?"

"Well, Cynthia said he's thinking about moving to the city."

Luka looked at his dad. "Will you tell her?"

Oscar just held his paper up higher, sinking behind it.

Luka seethed. "I'm seeing someone at work, okay?" *Well, fuck.*

"You are?" Marta's face lit up, jaw dropping wide. "What's his name? How old is he? What's his position?"

He pinched the bridge of his nose. "His name is...Thomas. He's maybe thirty-eight or so."

"You don't know how old he is?" She peered at him suspiciously.

"We haven't been dating long, Mom. It doesn't matter how old he is."

"Do you have a picture?"

Luka sighed and flipped through his camera roll to the shot of them on Halloween. "Here." He held it up to show her.

She leaned over to squint at it. Even Oscar waved Luka's hand over to have a look.

"Oh, my. He's awfully handsome. Very…large." Her face melted into a smile. "You said he works with you?"

"He's a VP."

"Your boss?" She looked concerned.

"Mom, I assure you, I am a full-grown adult, and the situation is under control." *Does it count as lying if I'm lying about a lie?*

"And where is he for Christmas? Where is his family?"

Ah, shit. Luka could see where this one was going. Well, at this point, what did it matter? "His family is in Solano." He picked a small town not too far away, but far enough.

"Hmm." He could see her wheels turning. "Are you sure he doesn't want to come for a quick visit? He could pop down the day after Christmas?"

"Mother." Luka drew the word out. "It's a four-hour drive. There is no 'popping'. And besides, we have been dating for only a few weeks. Just let me breathe, okay? You'll get to meet him at some point if things work out."

"Well." She wasn't entirely convinced. "Easter, maybe."

Luka stifled a groan. He and Thomas would have to 'break up' before Easter.

"Be nice if your kids were close in age to Yasmin's," she muttered as she picked up the whisk again.

Luka shared a glance with his dad. Oscar shrugged.

Luka went for a shower.

* * * *

Merry Christmas, Luka typed.

He stared at the words for a second, then hit send. Thomas replied right away.

Merry Christmas.

Luka tapped the edge of his phone for a minute.

Hope you're having a good day.

"Yes, brilliant," he said out loud to himself as soon as the message sent. "Hope you're super happy alone on Christmas."

Yeah, it's fine.

Luka replied.

So, funny story. My mom was trying to set me up with her friend's random son and I might have told her I was dating you.

He stared at the three dots as Thomas read the message. They disappeared, then came back. Then disappeared again. *Oh God, that is not a funny story. That is a fucking awkward story. What have I done?*
So Luka added more in a panic.

Of course now I'm in trouble because I didn't bring you with me. Can't win!

Three dots. Three dots. Then… *Oh, fuck. I should have brought him with me,* he realized. *Right? Yes. No! No, he's my boss. That would have been super weird. But…he's also my friend. And he's alone.*

Luka sagged. He had gotten so caught up in his own feelings that he had left his friend alone on Christmas. *I am a jerk.*

Then a message came through.

That's funny. Glad I could help.

Um…I feel like an asshole. I should have invited you to come with me. I'm so sorry.

This reply came quickly.

No, you don't need to be sorry. It's a lot to join someone's family for the holidays.

Still. I should have asked.

It's okay. It's important family time for you. You don't need me in the way.

Of course Thomas would be kind and forgiving about it.

Are you kidding? I'm sure my mom would prefer you. She would have thrown a parade in your honor.

Well, maybe I can meet her another time.

Are you free for Easter? She's already booked you in.

Luka fired off another message.

I'm kidding. We'll have to 'break up' before then.

Thomas' response came in just as Luka hit 'send.'

I could come with you for Easter. If you want.

Luka's heart thudded.

You say that now. You'll regret it when my mom makes you hunt for Easter eggs wearing bunny ears.

She wouldn't really do that?

In reply Luka sent a picture of himself from last Easter, holding a basket and wearing the damn ears. He was not smiling.

Show anyone and I kill you.

You make a cute bunny.

Luka's heart pounded harder. *That's the second time he's called me cute this week.* He wiggled his fingers.

Well, I'm sure you'll be cuter.

Guess we'll see… Thanks for checking in. Enjoy the rest of your day.

You too.

He left his phone on his bedside table and went down to join the family.

* * * *

"Uncle Luka!"

He was reclined on the couch, willing his stomach to digest the twelve pounds of sugar cookies and butter tarts he had consumed since lunch. He swallowed a grumble when his nieces called his name from the back door. Then they were in front of him, two almost unrecognizable winter-gear sausages.

"Come play with us!" Zara demanded, reaching a stubby mittened hand for Luka's. She was a very wise, very opinionated six-year-old.

"Please," added Jade, the quieter nine-year-old.

Luka let Zara haul him up to a seated position. "I couldn't possibly."

"Why?" whined Zara. "Mom said you would."

"Did she now?" Luka asked.

Then Yasmin appeared around the corner. "Your boots! You're getting snow everywhere. Out!" She shooed them back into the kitchen. "Sorry, girls. Your Uncle Luka would rather lie here like a blob than play with his nieces." She gave him a pointed look before she disappeared back into the kitchen with them.

"Of course I'd rather play with them." He clambered to his feet, fighting against the sugar cookie mass in his stomach. "Uncle Luka is coming."

* * * *

Building snowmen turned into building snow forts, which turned into a snowball fight, which, mercifully, turned into snow angels.

This was more Luka's speed, although admittedly, he was certain he had burned off all of the treats and then some during the snowball fight. He was lying back now, watching the white sky above, feeling tiny prickles on his face where sharp flakes landed.

Zara was chattering away, telling Luka about all the new presents she got, even though he had been there when she had opened them.

They fell into silence as Zara debated which present was her very favorite — probably the guitar — when Jade sat up.

"Do you have a boyfriend?" she asked Luka, brushing the snow from her head.

Luka sat up too, cringing. Somehow it felt worse to lie to little humans who trusted him implicitly. "I like a man named Thomas." True at least.

"What do you like about him?" Zara asked. She scooped up a handful of snow and began licking it off her mitt.

"Ew, Zara, that's gross!" Jade scolded.

Zara gave her a long-suffering look. "It's fresh, Jade. Mom says it's allowed."

"But dogs could have peed on it."

"Not if it's white!"

"Uncle Luka, should she be eating that snow?" Jade asked.

Luka tried not to laugh. "I think it's safe if it's freshly fallen, Jade. But you're right, you definitely want to avoid the yellow snow."

"Hmph." Jade glared at Zara, who grinned and resumed licking her mitt. Then she turned back to Luka. "Well?"

"Well what?"

"Why do you like Thomas?"

"Oh." Luka flopped onto his back again. "He's very smart. Decisive. Creative. He's a good leader, people follow him. But he's also very, very sweet once you get to know him. And we like a lot of the same things. And he's funny, in a cheesy sort of way. He makes me laugh, anyway." The flakes tickled his face. They were getting bigger and fluffier.

"Is he handsome?" Jade asked.

"Extremely."

"Can we meet him?" Zara piped up.

"Oh. I don't know, hon. Maybe."

"But I want to!"

"I would love for you to meet him. We'll have to see how things go." He chewed the insides of his cheeks as two wide pairs of eyes stared at him. "Who wants some hot chocolate?"

"Me!" they both shrieked. *Ah, the power of hot chocolate.*

They opened the back door into the kitchen only to find Yasmin and Marta facing off. Marta was holding a box of fruit snacks.

"Do you have any idea how much refined sugar is in those things?" Yasmin snapped.

"It's sugar, Yasmin, not heroin."

Yasmin sucked in an outraged gasp.

Luka inched the kids back out. "How about one more snowman?"

* * * *

After dinner, they all piled into the den with the kids, blankets and bowls of popcorn in hand, to watch *The Muppet Christmas Carol*. About halfway through, Luka crept out to use the restroom, when a movement caught his eye in the living room. His mom was sitting at the piano, picking out a quiet melody with one hand. Luka paused at the door. It was the theme from Mozart's *Piano Sonata No. 11*. She glanced up as he approached and slid onto the bench next to her, adding the left hand. They finished the first variation, then a silence settled over them as the last note faded.

She leaned her head on his shoulder. "I just want the best for you both. You know that, right?"

He kissed the top of her head. "I know, Mom."

Chapter Sixteen

Unexpected

The first day back to work after the holidays, Luka woke up even earlier than normal. When his eyes snapped open, Thomas was his first thought, as usual.

He let himself sink into the memories. The feeling he'd had wrapped in Thomas' arms. The way Thomas had looked at him when he'd opened the cufflinks. The flirty texting. The way-too-expensive gift that Thomas had gone back to get for him. Luka's gaze wandered over to where the luxurious white robe was draped over his armchair. He'd worn it almost the entire time at his parents' house, even when his sister had started calling him Grandma and asking where his fuzzy slippers were. When he got dressed, he chose the tadpole shirt Thomas had complimented at Thanksgiving.

Luka was at his desk, wading through four days' worth of email—did people not stop even for Christmas?—when Thomas walked in. His heart swelled, threatened to burst, squeezing the very air out of his lungs. *Goddamnit, how is he so perfect, so insanely beautiful?* Then Luka saw he was wearing the wolf cufflinks.

His eyes shot back up to Thomas'. His throat seized. He didn't know what to say. Any greeting he could think of was not enough.

Thomas held his gaze for a long moment, then another. Then he spoke. "Good morning, Luka."

Luka wheezed out a reply. "Morning."

"How was your holiday?"

"Oh, you know." *I missed you.* "My mom is relentlessly invasive and my sister thinks she's right about everything all of the time. Her kids are pretty adorable, though, and I ate my weight in baked goods. So overall, a success."

Thomas nodded and pulled out his laptop. "That's good."

"How were your days off?"

"They were fine," Thomas said, typing in his login. "I missed...work, a bit. Having something to do." He shrugged.

Luka's heart tried to take a leap out of his mouth. "Yeah. I missed work too."

Thomas' eyes slid over and held his. Luka's heart thudded. Then Thomas turned back to his laptop. "Did you see this email from Aleandro?"

"Yeah," he replied, his voice rough. "Yes. It's a great suggestion."

They bounced a few ideas back and forth before they divided up the tasks for the day and got to work. They had another commercial to prep, so Luka was reviewing headshots and contacting agencies, while Thomas was confirming details with the director, set designer and other assorted departments.

It was a pleasant day, and they fell back into their groove easily. Luka told Thomas a funny story about Zara—she had sworn she had a classmate named 'Internet' but he was able to determine that it was, in fact, 'Antoinette'—and wrapped himself up in the warm, smooth sound of Thomas laughing. Then Morgan appeared in the doorway after lunch. Luka sighed.

"Hello, boys," the blond oozed, leaning against the frame. "Everyone have a good holiday?"

"Mmm," Luka replied, knowing that Morgan didn't really care. "You?"

"The *best*. I went up to my cousin's ski chalet in Piedmont," he gushed, not so casually dropping the name of the swanky ski resort. "Spent every second out on the slopes. You wouldn't believe the pow we got on Christmas day. It was *epic*."

"The pow?" Thomas asked, but Luka could tell he regretted it instantly.

"Oh, oops." Morgan giggled. "That's short for 'powder'."

"Hmm," Thomas replied.

Luka swallowed a giggle. He was well-versed in all the nuances of Thomas' noises by now, and that one in particular meant '*God*, you're pretentious'.

"Anyhoo, Luka, I was wondering if you had a few minutes to give something a listen for me? I've been working on Aleandro's radio spots and I would love to get your opinion."

Luka's heart sank. *Here we go again.* Morgan was getting bolder, too, asking in front of Thomas, like he knew he couldn't say no.

"Ummm, we're really busy," Luka hedged.

"That's too bad." Morgan stuck out his lower lip. "I swear you were saying earlier that you would have time today." He tapped his chin in an exaggerated show of confusion. "Hmm. Well, I suppose I could go run it by Ilona instead."

Thomas narrowed his eyes. "We actually do have some time right now. I'd love to hear it, too."

"Oh!" Morgan's voice shot up an octave. "Great! Yeah, that would be *so* great, but you know what? I just remembered that, uh, yeah, there's actually one little bit I should finish first. But I'll definitely run it by you both when it's done."

"See that you do." Thomas turned back to his laptop.

A warm glow washed over Luka. "Bye, Morgan. You have a great day."

Morgan did not run it by them later.

* * * *

"Where did you learn to play?" They were eating lunch in their office the first week back. Thomas said it casually in between bites of soup.

"Um, the piano and violin was my mom. She taught—teaches—lessons out of the house. The guitar was, uh, me."

"You taught yourself how to play the guitar?" He gave Luka a sideways look, one eyebrow cocked high.

Luka shrugged, studying his salad. "Music's just always come easy to me, same as my mom."

"Wow. Were you ever in a band or anything?"

"No." Luka knew he said it too fast to go unnoticed. He held his breath, bracing himself for what was coming next.

But instead of asking 'Why not?' Thomas just said, "Oh. Well, I know people would enjoy your music."

Luka's heart rate climbed as that school gymnasium appeared around him again. Thomas continued speaking, but Luka heard his voice echoing in the gym. "Did you know Jitters has started doing open mic nights once a month? Acoustic folk and rock type stuff."

"Oh?" Luka put his fork down, stomach wound too tight to eat.

"Yeah, I checked it out last night. Small crowd, but enthusiastic. Wondered if you might be interested in trying it out sometime."

One heartbeat. Another, louder. "What?"

"Just if you were ever thinking about it."

"Oh. No. I...don't perform."

"Okay. But you played for me, and Finn and Rory. And you sang karaoke in front of the whole office." Thomas smiled, eyes crinkling. "A lot of it, from what I hear."

Luka's face burned. The opening chord of *Say Hi* jangled in his brain. "That's different. That's just singing a few songs that everyone loves in front of my friends. And I'd been drinking."

"We could get you good and liquored up first."

Luka didn't smile at his gentle teasing, the coils tightening inside him.

"I'm kidding," Thomas said carefully. "I just thought you might be interested."

"Well, I'm not," Luka said, realizing how snippy his voice sounded.

"Okay." Thomas studied him, eyes curious. "I'm sorry." It wasn't defensive, just kind.

Luka squirmed. "No, I'm sorry, I didn't mean to snap at you. I'm…I'm kind of terrified of performing for real." There. He'd never said it out loud before.

"It's fine. I didn't mean to push you. It's… You're very talented. Just something to think about."

Luka blushed and changed the subject. Thomas let him.

When he was in bed that night, staring at the ceiling, Thomas' words echoed through his head. "*You're very talented. Just something to think about.*" So he thought.

What *if* he performed again? What if the idea of standing in front of a crowd with a guitar didn't make him break out into a cold sweat? What if he got to share this art with the world, too? The more he thought about it, the more he realized that this was exactly what he loved about his job — the chance to make something that connected with other people on a primal level. What was more primal than music? Then the magnitude of what he had been suppressing for almost twenty years hit him. He was letting the memory of a handful of children dictate his behavior. He was letting *them* — bullies who likely didn't even remember him at all, hadn't thought about him in years — determine what he did with his art. *Fuck them.*

He grabbed his phone and navigated to Jitters' webpage. He clicked 'Open Mic Night', then 'Sign up'.

* * * *

"I signed up." The words burst out of him the second he saw Thomas the next morning.

Thomas knew what he was talking about right away. "You did? Luka, that's incredible!"

"Thanks. They were pretty full, though—not until March fourth." He ran a hand through his hair. He had stared at the 'Submit' button for a good twenty minutes before clicking it. Then he had spent half the night wondering how hard it would be to unsubmit. It was probably going to be a disaster, but he had done it. Because fuck them.

"I can't wait!" Thomas pulled out his phone.

Luka realized he was adding it to his calendar. "I, uh... God, I'm so sorry, but...is it okay if you don't come?" He knew he would be a hot mess his first time and he couldn't bear the thought of Thomas seeing him go down in flames.

"Oh." He put his phone down. "Yeah, I mean, of course. If you don't want me there, I won't come."

Luka didn't think he was imagining the hurt look in Thomas' eyes. "It's just that I'm scared I'll mess up, and I don't want you to see that. Let me just get a couple under my belt before you come to watch."

"Yeah, of course. I understand."

Of course he did. "Thanks."

* * * *

If signing up was the first step, the second was deciding what he was going to play. They only let performers do two songs for their first time. Luka scribbled down the titles on a sticky note. Seeing them in writing made it a little more real. He chose covers, of course. Crowd pleasers. Some Fleetwood Mac and, his favorite, the Beatles. One step at a time. Now, practicing.

He gripped his guitar and stood in his living room. Closing his eyes, he imagined a room full of faces staring at him. His stomach curled into a ball. Then he imagined the faces were all Thomas, watching him with bright eyes, cheering him on. He strummed a few chords and ran through the set for Thomas.

* * * *

As January rushed by, they shot their new commercial and began the editing slog. One morning, as they were putting on the finishing touches, Thomas was restless and fidgety. His leg jittered as he typed. He tugged at his wolf cufflinks anytime he paused to frown at the screen.

"I talked to Ilona," Thomas blurted. Then he kept typing, watching his screen intently.

Luka stopped and looked at him. "Is everything okay?"

"Yes. I just… My last day will be March first."

"Oh." It hit him like a ton of bricks. He felt sick, the panic rising in his throat. "That's…really soon."

"Yeah."

Luka was alarmed to feel tears stinging his eyes. He had always known that Thomas would be leaving at some point in the near future, but having an actual date, and one so soon… He cleared his throat and uselessly clicked a few buttons on his screen, blinking.

"I'll miss your show," Thomas said, his voice rough. "I mean, I know I wasn't coming, but I wanted to be here for you, wish you luck beforehand."

Luka hadn't even thought of that, but it was the least of his problems. "Right. That's okay. I'll text you when I'm on my way."

"It's not the same."

"It'll be okay." Except nothing was okay. *This is it,* Luka thought. *This is the end. He's leaving.*

"I'm sorry." The room was silent.

"Well. Time is ticking. Guess we'd better get at it, then." His chest hurt, a sharp, pinching feeling.

Thomas glanced over at him. Luka gave him a weak smile. They got back to work.

* * * *

Thomas' departure loomed ahead, a dark cloud over their every interaction. As the end of February drew nearer, Luka could feel Thomas slipping away, and was helpless to do anything about it. He stopped eating lunch with Luka, dropping in at the gym instead for a quick workout. Luka also noticed that Thomas looked at him less. Normally he felt that golden gaze on him half the day, Thomas always giving him his full attention, but not anymore. He only managed glimpses when Thomas' eyes flicked up to his for half a second while they hammered out color choices and sorted through demographic numbers. A knot of dread sat in his stomach, growing and growing with each clipped sentence and quiet lunch hour alone in his office.

But, despite all this, he was still a professional. Luka did his best to keep it together, to pretend everything was fine. Pretend he wasn't bracing himself for the moment when Thomas would walk out of his life forever.

Apparently he wasn't pretending well.

"Are we going to talk about it?" Finn asked one day a week or so into February when he found Luka alone in his office. He closed the door behind him.

Luka sighed and pushed back from his desk. "Talk about what?"

Finn shook his head. "Gonna make me say it?"

"I don't know what you're talking about, Finn."

"Your undying love for Thomas." Finn gave him half of a mischievous smirk, his eyes still gentle.

Luka closed his eyes as his chest squeezed. "I don't... We're not— It's not..."

"Yeah, except you do, you are and it is."

"Fuck." Luka slumped in his chair. "Am I that obvious?"

"Yes, but if it makes you feel any better, Thomas is into you, and it is equally as obvious."

"What?" Luka shook his head to clear it. "He is?"

Finn groaned and pinched the bridge of his nose. "Jesus. I knew you were thick. Rory tried to warn me. Look. It's clear as day that he likes you back, just as much as you like him. You gotta say something. You're killing us."

Luka's heart leaped, but it crashed back to the bottom of his rib cage as reality set in. He shook his head. "He's leaving in less than three weeks, and in the meantime, he's still my boss. I can't. Now would be the worst time ever."

"Well, you don't gotta marry the guy. Looks like he'd be good in bed."

Luka flushed as his latest dream flashed through his head. The more miserable he was during the day, the hotter his dreams were at night, the desperation and aching sadness manifesting itself in other ways as he slept. He had climaxed in his sleep last night, waking up hot and sticky like a goddamn teenager.

He covered his face and groaned. "I can't even tell you how much I am not about to proposition Thomas for a quick romp in the sack before he leaves."

"Why not? Wait till his last day. If he's leaving, doesn't matter if he says yes or no."

"I don't just want to sleep with him, Finn. I..."

"You what?"

Luka blew out his breath. "Nothing. Thanks for your help. But I can't."

Finn narrowed his eyes at Luka. "This from the guy who told me to take the plunge with Rory."

"It's totally different!"

"Is it?"

"Of course it is."

Finn shrugged. "Think about it. You don't want him to leave and regret not even trying."

When Thomas settled back at his desk, Luka watched him out of the corner of his eye. Say he did take the plunge, make a move, proposition Thomas for one last, wild night... What then? Then he would be even more miserable once Thomas left, knowing what he was missing. No, it was a ridiculous idea. The dreams were torture enough.

* * * *

The gulf between them grew wider and wider. They kept their conversations short and about work, the easy familiarity that had developed between them now stilted. Thomas didn't come for drinks the next time they all went to the Exchange. Luka let it happen. Maybe it would make it easier when Thomas left.

Except by the time Valentine's Day arrived, Luka was miserable. He normally didn't mind the holiday, always managing to secure a date with someone cute — although of course last year he had spent it with Morgan on his couch. But this year it seemed cruel and unnecessary, a reminder of how very not with Thomas he was.

The team gathered in the conference room for an update on the campaign. Luka stared at the little bowls of pink and red heart-shaped chocolates Tawney had placed along the center of the table while Rory spoke. Then Ilona's voice cut in.

"Before we finish up here, I have some news," she was saying.

At the shift in her tone, Luka forced himself to give her his full attention.

"Aleandro has extended our contract for another four months," she announced happily. "Congratulations, everyone. You should be proud of your exceptional work."

The news was like hitting a wall. The air rushed out of him as his eyes snapped over to Thomas. Thomas was looking at his hands, a slow smile spreading across his face.

A wave of claps and small cheers swept through the room.

"Aw yeah!" Finn crowed as he high-fived Rory.

It was pretty wonderful news. There was no greater compliment than a client extending a contract. Luka did not give the slightest shit about that right now. His skin tingled with goosebumps. He looked at Thomas again. *Four more months.* Four more months of sitting next to him, being able to talk to him whenever he wanted, making him smile, watching the way his eyes crinkled and he tipped his head back when he was laughing hard. His smell sweeping over him, swirling around him like fucking fairy dust when he reached past him for a file. He wanted to cry with relief. *I still get him for four more months.*

"Does this mean Thomas is staying?" Rory asked, with a sidelong glance at Luka.

Thomas nodded. He looked up at Luka instead of Rory.

It doesn't really change things, Luka's brain was telling him. *He's still leaving soon.* But Luka couldn't fight the smile that spread across his face as they looked at each other.

Thomas smiled back.

* * * *

Finn slapped him on the back as they left the room. "Congrats, boys. You guys crushed it."

"We all crushed it," Luka corrected him. He was almost giddy. "We need to celebrate! Who's free for a drink after work?"

Finn laughed. "Sorry, Moreno. Valentine's Day, remember? We've got plans." The look he shot Rory threatened to melt the paint right off the walls. Rory blushed.

"Oh. Right. Well, I don't have any plans." Luka looked at Thomas. "Do you?"

Thomas shook his head. "No."

"Okay, this might be crazy, but...do you want to grab a drink anyway?"

Finn rolled his eyes behind Thomas' back so hard Luka thought he might hurt himself.

"Uh..." Thomas looked a little panicked.

"Just to Exchange or something," Luka babbled, thinking of the least romantic place he could.

Thomas nodded. "Sure."
This is fine. Not weird.

* * * *

Luka pushed open the door to the Bitter Exchange and froze. *Shit. This is weird.*

Thomas stumbled into him. "What are you... Oh."

They gaped at the formerly dingy pub, now transformed into a pink and red wonderland of hearts and crepe paper streamers. Balloons bobbed from every surface.

"I..." Luka was at a loss for words. *Jesus. I brought Thomas here on Valentine's Day.* "This is...unexpected."

Thomas burst out laughing. "Yeah." He gestured forward. "Shall we?"

Luka laughed too, the awkwardness melting away. "After you."

They made their way to the bar where Kazio was glowering.

"Happy Valentine's Day, Kazio," Luka said, taking a seat on a stool. "I have to say —"

"Yes, yes, I know," Kazio interrupted. "Tasha thought it would be funny."

Luka and Thomas shared a grin. "It is pretty funny."

Kazio sighed. "Bloody Mary?"

"I don't know," Luka said thoughtfully, studying the chalkboard above. "Got any Valentine's Day drink specials?"

Kazio glared at him while Thomas snickered. "A Bloody Mary is red, isn't it?"

After they got their drinks, they found a small table in the middle of the room. The place was busy, with other patrons equally confused by the decorations.

Luka pushed the balloon bouquet aside so he could see Thomas.

"Well, cheers," Luka offered, clinking glasses.

"Cheers."

They each took a drink.

"So…it's great that you get to stay longer," Luka ventured, trying to sound offhand.

"Mmm." Thomas placed his glass on the coaster and turned it so it was square with the table. "And now I won't miss your show."

Of course that's the thing he'd be happy about. So sweet. "I guess you don't normally stay in one place so long?"

Thomas shook his head, then looked up. His eyes were molten. Luka's stomach jumped.

"I need to thank you, Luka."

"Thank me? For what?"

Thomas tilted his head. "For many things. Your incredible work, first of all. But mostly, your friendship. I don't really have any friends, and it's been nice, having someone to talk to and hang out with." He folded his hands. "So thank you."

His stomach in his throat, Luka reached across the table and squeezed Thomas' arm. "You don't need to thank me. I like being your friend."

Thomas cleared his throat, then picked up his drink. He took a long gulp, then wiped one finger at the corner of his mouth.

Fuck. Luka licked his lips, wanting, with every fiber of his being, to suck that finger. *He's your friend,* he told himself as Thomas smiled at him. *He's your friend.*

He is your friend.

His head, heart and dick were at war and, frankly, it was fucking exhausting.

The only solution was to order another drink and engage Thomas in a game. "So. Here's my question. How many people here legitimately wanted to go on a date for Valentine's Day, and how many are distinctly *not* on a date, came here to avoid the whole thing and are now stuck in Cupid's lair?"

Thomas arched in his eyebrows in amusement. "Okay, like who?"

"For example"—he dropped his voice to a whisper—"definitely on a date." Luka pointed at the table beside them. The couple were holding hands across the table, feet twined together. "Definitely *not*," he continued, nodding at their other side. Two men in suits were frowning at their phones, slumped in their chairs.

"Well, those ones are too easy," Thomas said, eyes twinkling. "What about the two over on the end of the bar?"

"Hmm." Luka studied them. The two women were perched on stools, chatting easily, posture relaxed and comfortable, dressed in office attire. "No. Work friends, I think. Both single, keeping each other company on Valentine's Day."

Thomas frowned. "Disagree. It's a date."

"What makes you say that?"

"Just a feeling I have." As Thomas spoke, one of the women slide her foot over and hooked it around the other one's ankle. The other woman turned to smile shyly at her companion.

Luka gasped. "You called it!"

Thomas looked pleased with himself. "I knew it!"

"Okay, Mr. Smartypants. What do you think about the table under the giant teddy bear balloon?" Luka asked. The man kept smoothing his hair and tugging at his cuffs, while the woman was in jeans and leaning as far away from the man as she could.

"Hmm." Thomas slid his eyes to the side as he considered them. "She thought they were going as friends and she chose this place to keep it casual, and now she's freaking out because he thinks it's a date. So both."

Luka repressed a snicker. "You're too good at this game."

A few drinks and many laughs later, Thomas stilled and gave Luka a long look. "What about us?"

Luka almost swallowed an olive. "What about us?" he repeated dumbly after he coughed it back up.

Thomas gave him a small smile. "If someone was playing this game for us, what would they think?"

"Oh." His mind raced, yet he drew a complete blank. "I don't know. Probably just friends. What do you think?"

Thomas looked thoughtful. "It's hard to say, isn't it?"

Luka's cheeks were about to catch fire. "Sure is."

Chapter Seventeen

Could I?

With the renewed contract came a mountain of fresh projects to tackle. The office was a hive of activity again, phones buzzing, people hurrying past each other in the hallway with nothing more than a quick nod. Thomas started eating lunch with Luka again. "The gym is way too crowded over the lunch hour," he had said. Luka allowed himself to sink back into the friendship and roll around in it a little, knowing he still had a few more months to enjoy it.

But when the day of his open mic performance arrived, Luka was a mess. He'd barely slept the night before, and when he looked in the bathroom mirror, all he saw was the dark circles under his eyes and flat, pale skin.

Thomas took one look at him when he came in that morning. "Are you okay?"

Luka forced a smile. "Yeah. Just a little nervous about tonight. Didn't sleep much."

"You're going to be great. Are you sure you don't want me to come?"

"I'm sure." Chances seemed high he might vomit right on stage and he did not want Thomas to see that.

"Well, I'll be supporting you from my living room."

"I know. I appreciate it."

Thomas did his best to distract Luka for the rest of the day, peppering him with questions and asking him his opinion on an endless array of tiny set-design options. Luka knew Thomas didn't need his help, but he was grateful for the effort.

He had brought his guitar and a change of clothes with him, so after work he grabbed his bag and slipped into the washroom. He went with dark, slim-fitting jeans and a navy button-down, left open over a gray Henley. His hair was sticking up on one side and refused to sit when he combed it. He wet his hair and tried to flatten it again while his stomach twisted, mouth flooding with the nauseating taste of fear.

Thomas was still waiting in their office when Luka went back. Luka stretched his mouth into a fake smile for him.

Thomas didn't buy it. "You're going to crush it, Luka. You can do this."

He tried baring his teeth to see if that was more convincing. "Yeah, thanks."

Thomas stood, collecting his things. "Is it okay if I go with you?"

Luka blinked at him. Right. Jitters was across the street from his building. "Of course. I just don't think I'll be very talkative."

"That's okay. I can talk." So he did. "Did I ever tell you about the time I was in a band?" Thomas asked as they made their way out of the front door. Their shoulders bumped together on the crowded sidewalk, just two of dozens making their way home.

"What? *You* were in a band?"

Thomas chuckled. "I know I'm just a stuffed shirt in dark suits now, but I went through a bit of a rebellious phase as a teenager."

"How have you not already told me about this?" Luka demanded.

Thomas looked pleased with Luka's reaction. "I guess I was waiting for the right moment."

Luka shook his head. "Spill."

"Well. I was in tenth grade. I was confused about who I was, knew I wasn't like the other boys and I was still pretty short. I didn't really grow until the end of high school. So I was just this scrawny kid trying to figure my shit out. Some guys were looking to put a band together to get girls. My dad had some old drums and my rhythm was good enough."

"A drummer! Okay, so rock?"

"I wish."

"Tell me."

"Death metal."

Luka stopped in his tracks, throwing his head back to laugh. A woman bumped into him from behind and glared.

"Yup." Thomas grinned at him as they continued walking.

"Please tell me the name was, like…" Luka chewed on his lip for a moment. "'The Devil's Screaming Pain Machine' or something."

"Worse."

"Well?"

"Savage Throat."

"No, it was not!" Luka cackled again as they made their way down the stairs into the station.

"I swear."

"Will you sing me one of your songs?" He was still giggling.

"I honestly don't even know what any of the words were, but I remember some of the titles. We had one gem, what was it... Uh, *The Brutality In My Eyes and the Deluge Of His Nefarious Vengeance*. Oh, and there was *Fucked by Hate*."

Luka let out another peal of laughter as they crammed themselves onto the crowded train. They held onto the pole in the middle, facing each other. Luka wiped a tear in the corner of his eye. He hardly noticed the people jammed in around them. "How long did the band last?"

"About five days. Turns out I hated the music and I wasn't looking to get girls anyway, so..." They laughed together in the quiet train.

"Tell me more. You guys definitely talked about an album cover."

The ride passed by quickly as Thomas laid out the plans for Savage Throat's inevitable tour and album cover photo shoot.

Luka wiped more tears away, trying to catch his breath as the train rattled on. "What did your dad think about it?"

"He supported me, of course." Thomas smiled. "He even let us rehearse in our garage. He was a subversive bastard, never quite liked to fit in. I think he'd be horrified by my closet full of suits now."

"Are you kidding? He'd be so fucking proud of you." Luka didn't even have to think twice about it.

Thomas' eyes met his from only inches away. "Thank you."

The train jostled, and Luka swayed into Thomas' chest. For a second it felt like he was going in for a kiss.

He cleared his throat and looked away as he righted himself.

"I'm sure your parents are so proud of you, too. Did you tell them you were performing tonight?" Thomas asked.

"Not yet. We'll see how it goes." His mom would have herded Oscar into the car for the five-hour drive if he'd told her.

They continued to chat as they made their way up the stairs and back onto the sidewalk. Luka didn't even notice they had arrived at Jitters until Thomas stopped walking.

"Here we are. I'd offer to come in again..."

Luka shook his head. "Thank you, but...no." His stomach heaved. The pool of anxiety that had drained away when Thomas had been talking came flooding back.

Thomas put a hand on Luka's shoulder and squeezed. "You're going to do so great."

Luka nodded. "Thanks."

Thomas looked at him again, then he put his hands in his pockets and turned to stride across the street.

Luka took one last huge gulp of cool air before pushing open the door, the weight of his guitar heavy on his back. The place was jammed, the typical background hum of a coffee house now a dull roar. His nerves fizzed as he made his way over to the counter. The chalkboard read, *You can't buy happiness but you can buy coffee and that's almost the same thing.*

True enough.

"Where do I check in?" he leaned over to ask above the noise.

The barista pointed to a man hovering at a table with a clipboard on the other side of the room.

As Luka made his way over, a sharp crack of laughter burst out from a group he was passing by. He flinched.

He took another step, his mouth drying up. The table was packed full of beautiful men and women, looking way too glamorous for a coffee house open mic night. One of the men met his eyes, and he could swear a sneer curled around his lips. A woman's gaze swept up and down his body. A bored look crossed her face as she turned back to her giggling friends.

This was junior high all over again. What was he doing here? He hesitated in the middle of the shop. The sign-in table was still so far away. Clipboard guy hadn't noticed him yet. *I can't do this.*

He turned and bolted for the door. He pushed his way back outside, ducking against the cold wind as it stung his cheeks. Back to the subway station, home to wallow in failure. *So stupid.*

But then he heard a voice call to him from across the street. "Luka?"

He stopped and looked up. Thomas was standing in front of his building.

Guess the wallowing was starting now. He was so embarrassed that Thomas had seen him running with his tail between his legs. He stood frozen to the spot as Thomas hurried back across the street.

"What happened? Are you okay?" Thomas asked as he got closer. His brow was pinched in concern.

"Yeah. No. I, uh… Fuck. I bailed. I'm sorry." Another blast of cold wind hit them, more winter than spring. He hunched his shoulders against the icy fingers down his neck.

Thomas was silent for a moment. "Oh."

Luka stared at his feet. "I don't think I can do it."

"What happened?"

Luka knew he meant just now, inside the café. But it was a much longer answer. He sighed. "How much time do you have?"

"As long as you need."

So he told Thomas all about the *Say Hi* Horror, right there on the sidewalk. Thomas listened, his attention not leaving Luka's face for a second. A few brown curls escaped Thomas' bun and blew in the wind, but he didn't even break his concentration to brush them off his face.

"I know it's stupid, but..." Luka scuffed his toe at a mark on the pavement. "It scarred me for life. I can't perform in front of groups. I just can't. Singing to even just my friends is..." He shook his head "Really, really hard. Even karaoke, drunk at a party with people I know... I only did it because I didn't want Morgan to sing with you." He gave an abashed chuckle, still looking at his feet.

"Luka..." Thomas took a deep breath. "I'm so sorry. I didn't mean to pressure you at all."

"You didn't pressure me. Honestly, the way you believed in me was the one thing that got me in the door."

Thomas was silent for another moment. "Well, maybe you can go back in there. Because I just think the world needs to hear your songs. And I'd love to come and watch. I know you feel like that would be harder, but...maybe you need a friend there."

Luka's eyes watered in the wind. "I don't think I can..."

"I know you can."

Luka bit his lip, looking up at Thomas.

Thomas reached out and took Luka's hand, his grip almost hot in the cool air. "I'll be there with you. No matter what."

* * * *

"You're late," Clipboard Guy said matter-of-factly as he checked off Luka's name with a small, efficient stroke.

"Yeah, I'm sorry. I got a bit...stuck. But I'm ready now."

"Good, cause you're up next. You can leave your stuff in the manager's office, just down that hall." He pointed before he looked at his watch. "Better hurry. She's got one song left."

Luka turned to face Thomas again. The noise was a little fuzzy in his ears. His stomach flip-flopped. *'I can't'* was on his tongue again, ready to spill out.

Thomas put a warm, reassuring, hand on his forearm. "I'm going to find a seat. I'm right here. You can do this. And, you know, when in doubt, you can always play *The Brutality In My Eyes and the Deluge Of His Nefarious Vengeance.*"

A giggle escaped Luka, despite himself. "Thanks. I'll keep that in my back pocket." Thomas squeezed his forearm again before Luka turned to find the office. He tried to move quickly without too much thinking. *Open door, take off jacket, pull out guitar, find pick. Check.* He had done all of those things a million times before. He put the guitar strap over his shoulder and strummed a few chords. *A minor, C, G... Breathe.*

He stepped back into the hallway and made his way toward the crowd. A petite blonde woman was finishing up her song, a bouncy folk-rock piece, and the applause swelled as her last chord snapped to a finish. Luka tried to peek around the corner to find Thomas but he couldn't see his head sticking up over the crowd anywhere.

Clipboard Guy bounded up onto the stage. "Let's hear it again for Lottie!" She got a few whistles this time as she smiled and bobbed her head. She hopped off the stage and came over to Luka, flushed and smiling. "Good crowd tonight," she said as she passed. "Have fun!"

"Yeah..." His heart threatened to pound straight through his ribcage as he stepped up onto the tiny stage. It wasn't even a stage, more of a platform. He looked out over the crowd and saw nothing but junior high students, unsmiling hard faces. Everything in him screamed to bolt, an invisible force tugging him toward the door. But his eyes continued to sweep, frantic, until there was Thomas at a small table toward the back. His jacket and tie were gone, the sleeves rolled up and a few buttons undone on his shirt.

Thomas' gaze found his. Luka was flooded with warm, honey-colored sunshine. It smoothed out the rough edges in his stomach, dissolved away the line pulling him toward the door.

"Please give an extra special Jitters welcome to a first-timer, Luka Moreno!"

The applause washed over him, adding to the warmth. But he just watched Thomas, who was not looking away. He plucked the first note of *I've Just Seen a Face* then the next, and the next, settling into the slower, softer version he had done at Thanksgiving. Now his fingers were moving on their own. He sang to Thomas, who was still looking at him, still a beam of sunshine.

Luka tried to tear his eyes away, flick them around the room, but they kept finding their way back to his anchor, his safe space. And Thomas was always looking back...looking at him like he was the only person in the room. In the world, in fact. As he struck the last chord and the applause swelled around him, it came to him.

I love him.

The realization hit him squarely in his chest, his lungs emptying. Thomas was smiling, clapping for all he was worth, looking so goddamn proud of him. Luka swallowed, desperately sucking in air. *Oh, shit. I love him. I am in love with him.*

"Thank you," he said to the crowd, hoping they didn't hear the crack in his voice. The world was tilting sideways, toward Thomas Badgley. With apologies to Fleetwood Mac and Clipboard Guy, he changed his mind about his second song.

"This next song is one I wrote. It's called *Could I*?" He began to play.

"Could I be here
With you?
Could I have you
For a day..."

The chatter slowed in the audience, hands stilling. More and more faces turned to watch him.

"Could I touch you
Hold your hand
Could I smile at you
Is there a way?
Is there a way
For us to be..."

Thomas was leaning forward over the table, hands clasped to forearms, lips pressed together, like he was holding onto what oxygen he could. Like he was breathless.

"Could I love you?
Kiss you, hold you
What will it take
For you to say…"

Thomas' eyes crinkled as his smile grew. The audience seemed to take a collective breath, sensing something was happening. A few people even craned their necks around, looking to see who Luka was singing to.

"Is there a way
For us to be…
Be the one
Be your love
Be forever yours."

The music faded to nothing, and a silence fell over the room. The quiet held for another breath, until one person clapped, then they all did.

Luka's face hurt from how big his smile was. But he was only smiling at Thomas.

And Thomas was smiling back.

The host jumped back up on stage and took the mic. "Luka Moreno, everybody! Let's hope he'll be back again soon!"

Luka stepped off the stage, slinging his guitar around onto his back. He nodded absentmindedly at the kind comments being thrown at him, because he could only think about one thing at that moment.

Thomas had unfolded himself from his seat and was working his way through the narrow space toward Luka. Their eyes were locked, gold on blue, and the rest of the room had fallen away.

Luka threw his arms around Thomas as soon as he could reach, hugging him fiercely. Thomas' hands slid around his waist, then were warm on his back. His nose was pressed to Thomas' neck and he inhaled deeply, the now familiar spicy citrus scent like a drug in his veins. Thomas hugged him back. It was a long hug. Their hearts were beating at the same too-fast speed.

Luka pulled away to look at Thomas, but only a few inches. Their noses were almost touching.

"You did it." Thomas' face was split in a grin that mirrored Luka's own.

"I did it."

"You fucking did it."

Luka took a shaky breath. His hands were now squeezing thick biceps. A laugh bubbled out of him. "I can't believe it."

"I can." His anchor was unmoving.

Luka searched for words. "Thank you for being here. I wouldn't have been able to do it without you." *And, um, I love you.* They still held each other.

"I wouldn't have missed it, Luka." Thomas' gaze drifted down to Luka's lips then back up.

"You waited outside."

"Yeah, sorry, I know you said no, but… I just wanted to be there for you."

"No, don't be sorry. You were right. I needed you."

Thomas blinked and dropped his hands from Luka's waist, taking a step back. He looked embarrassed as he pushed a stray lock of hair behind his ear, eyes shifting down to his feet for a second. "We should go for a drink to celebrate."

"Sounds great." Luka swallowed, missing the warmth of Thomas' body against his. Suddenly he was aware that the next performer was starting and his guitar was still on his back. "Let me go grab my stuff."

Well, now what? he asked himself as he packed up his guitar. Voices in his head whirled in confusion. *You weren't supposed to go and fall in love with him, dummy,* one voice said. *Luka, you just performed an original song for a crowd full of strangers!* another one whooped. He wanted to laugh and cry at the same time, do a victory dance and curl up in bed. Throw himself into arms like tree trunks, and run away and hide.

Instead, he walked back out into the café, smiled at Thomas then followed him into the night.

Chapter Eighteen

Now Who's the Liar?

It was strange, arriving at his office and seeing Thomas sitting there, like any other day, fingers flying over his keyboard. How could he look so normal when he was the center of Luka's universe? Shouldn't there be planets whizzing around him? Comets hurling toward him, only to be flung back out into the void for another long, cold orbit, unable to break free of his pull?

"Morning," Thomas said when he saw Luka standing in the doorway. "I didn't think rock stars got out of bed before noon."

Luka let out a nervous chuckle. "Well, you know. They sent a limo, so..."

Thomas turned to face him. "I can't get over how amazing you were. I know you were so excited just to get through it, but Luka, you had those people eating out of your hand."

"Oh..." Luka flushed. The confusing whirl in his head had continued all night. He still couldn't believe he had done it, had stood in front of a crowd and shared a piece of his soul with them. But...what was that compared to the very fabric of his existence being rearranged?

"And I think they all knew," Thomas added.

Luka's mouth dried out. "Knew what?"

"That you're something special."

It was almost too much, having Thomas look at him like this. His eyes stung again. He slid into his chair and busied himself powering up his laptop and logging in.

Thomas smiled to himself as he went back to his typing. They managed to get their day going, since they had a few more internet ads to splice together that were supposed to be finished by tomorrow.

But as the end of the day approached and they were putting the final pieces together, Luka had to go and ask Morgan where the final cuts of the music were.

Morgan was at his desk, crumpled papers on the floor all around him, one palm pressed to his forehead. He jumped when Luka rapped on the doorframe. "It's not ready," he snapped.

"Ooookay." Luka stepped in. "When do you think it might—"

"Look," Morgan interrupted, changing gears, his voice thin and reedy. "I need your help."

Luka sighed. "All right, let's hear what you have."

"Well, I don't actually have any tracks laid out yet. Just…" Morgan waved a hand at a lone piece of sheet music on his desk.

"You—" Luka stared at the page of scribbles, dumbfounded. "You are *unbelievable*." He turned to march out.

"Luka, wait," Morgan pleaded. "Please. I need you here, just for a few minutes. I can't do it like you."

"No."

Morgan sighed. "I hate to do this, but...maybe I will have to go chat with Ilona."

Now? He was trying to pull this shit *now*? A rage bubbled up in Luka's chest. Maybe it was the newfound confidence... Maybe it was that everything in his world had shifted. He rested his hands on the desk and leaned forward until his nose was almost touching Morgan's. "*Do it.* I fucking *dare you.*" He spun on his heel. His heart was still racing when he got back to his office.

Thomas looked up at him, then his eyes widened. "Are you okay?"

"Ummm." Luka paced the room. "Yes. No. I don't know. I may have a problem. Fuck."

"Tell me." Thomas swiveled in his chair.

"Shit. *Shit.*"

"Luka." It was a low rumble.

Luka paused his frantic pacing.

"Sit down, take a breath, and tell me. It'll be okay."

So Luka sat and told him the whole sad story.

When he was finished, Thomas looked stunned. "You've been doing his work for him?"

"I mean...not all of it. Just some, here and there."

"I knew it," Thomas muttered. His face was a thundercloud as he stood. "Let's go talk to Ilona."

"But I didn't disclose the relationship either! What if I get fired?"

"You won't get fired. I promise." And he was off, striding down the hall. Luka scrambled after him.

Thomas paused to knock on Ilona's door before he opened it and barged in. "I'm sorry to interrupt, but I..." He stopped.

Luka peered in from behind him. Morgan was sitting across from Ilona.

"Luka. How fortunate you're here. Morgan has just been sharing some information with me. Please, come in."

Luka glared at Morgan. He wanted to smack that smug little smirk off of his smug little face. Ilona waved a hand at Morgan for him to continue.

"So as I was saying, I just couldn't live with myself anymore, keeping this secret from you. I *begged* Luka, but" — Morgan sighed — "he wouldn't let me tell HR about our relationship."

"I — You — What?" Luka sputtered. "You —"

"Luka," Thomas interrupted. "Let's all sit and talk about this." His fists were clenched.

"Go on," Ilona nodded to Morgan once the other two were settled.

Luka took a deep breath, trying to calm his racing heart.

"I've been wracked with guilt, and I just wanted to apologize, and disclose our relationship to you. Better late than never, right?" Morgan gave Ilona a self-deprecating smile, hands folded in his lap.

Ilona's eyes shifted over to Luka and narrowed. "Luka?"

"*I* wanted to disclose it, but *he* said no!" Luka protested.

"And yet, here I am, the one coming clean," Morgan said primly.

Luka fumed, at a loss for words.

But then Thomas cut in. "Luka did disclose it, to me. *Months* ago."

"I —" Luka stared at Thomas wide-eyed. *I did?* He flipped through his memories until it came to him — Thomas had overheard him and Morgan by the printer his first week here, and he had told Thomas about their relationship. Very briefly, but… "I did!"

Morgan's mouth flapped, his polished demeanor gone for a second.

Ilona's eyebrow arched. "Hmm."

"And," Luka added, "he's been blackmailing me! He's been threatening to tell you about us unless I do his work for him."

Morgan gasped and put a hand to his chest. "Luka! How could you say such a thing?"

Luka stared at him, agog. "Are you *kidding* me?"

Morgan batted his eyelashes at Ilona. "Ms. Hoszek, Luka is obviously upset that I've come forward, but to hurl these horrendous accusations at me? Luka, I'm…disappointed." He tugged at his pants, smoothing out a non-existent wrinkle. "Anyway, I just can't see how you would have any way to *prove* it."

Now it was Luka's turn to open and close his mouth, wordless.

"Would you two excuse us, please?" Ilona said. "I need to speak with Thomas."

Temples throbbing, Luka cast a look at Thomas who was watching him steadily. *It'll be okay*, his eyes said. Luka wanted to believe him.

He plunked down in one of the chairs outside Ilona's office and crossed his arms. Morgan stretched out in the chair next to him.

"What's your plan here, Morgan? To get us *both* fired?" Luka hissed, trying so very hard to keep from losing his shit entirely.

"Why would I be fired? I came to Ilona, and you're the one making up horrible lies about me."

Luka made a strangled noise. "Oh, save me that bullshit. It's just you and me here."

Morgan smirked. "I'm sure I have no idea what you're talking about."

Luka gripped the armrest of his chair, knuckles white, and sucked in a deep, calming breath. Well, a breath, anyway. "I can't believe you would do this. I mean, I knew you were a selfish prick, but this is a whole other *universe* of selfishness."

Morgan snapped his head over. "*I'm* a selfish prick? Me?"

Luka couldn't do anything but laugh. "Yes, you. What are you saying, that I'm the selfish one?"

Now it was Morgan's turn to laugh acerbically. "No, never you. Not perfect Luka!"

"Don't hold back, Morgan. Let's hear it."

Morgan clenched his jaw for a moment before it all came out in a torrent. "You dumped me. Out of nowhere, like it was no big deal. You couldn't have given less of a shit about me. And then I had to watch you chase after Thomas like a lovesick puppy, drooling all over him. It's sickening. He is *never* going to go for you, you know." The pitch of his voice climbed as the words spilled out.

"Oh, fuck you, Morgan."

"No, really, it's pathetic. Everyone is laughing at you."

Luka ground his teeth together. "I'm not trying to get with Thomas."

"Ha! Now who's the liar?"

Never before had Luka so badly wanted to punch someone. He shook his head. "Think whatever you want. This isn't about Thomas. It's about you being a fucking asshole."

"'Not about Thomas,' right. Cute guy comes along, pats you on the head and suddenly you're too good to even listen to my work anymore—"

"*Listen* to your work?" Luka spat. "*Do* your work, you mean. Maybe you didn't think this through. If I get fired, who will be there to bail you out when you've got *nothing*?"

"Well, you'll never know because your ass won't be here anymore."

Luka wanted to throw a chair. He sat there, stewing over Morgan's words instead. Then it dawned on him. "This is all because you're jealous of Thomas."

Morgan rolled his eyes. "You wish." It was not convincing.

"You *are*. You're jealous. If you can't have me, no one can."

Morgan crossed his arms and turned his head to glare at the wall on the other side.

"Morgan...think back to our relationship. You didn't care about me, not really. You cared about *having* me."

Morgan had nothing to say.

"You didn't even want to tell anyone we were together! Why? Why keep it a secret?" The question hung in the air. Luka sighed and shifted in his chair, giving up on getting an answer.

But after a long pause, Morgan spoke, low and hurried. "Because I knew you'd break up with me eventually, then everyone would know."

Luka blinked. "What?"

"It would be too embarrassing." He picked at a cuticle.

Luka reeled. "I don't..."

"And I did care about you." He said it so quietly Luka could barely hear.

Something softened in Luka for a moment, then he scoffed. "Yeah, cared so much you're about to get me fired."

Morgan pursed his lips and shook his head, still looking away.

They fell into silence as the minutes dragged by. The door opened and Thomas waved them back in.

They sat down again and faced Ilona. Her face showed nothing. Luka snuck a quick glance at Thomas. He didn't look as confident as he had before. Morgan was staring at his feet.

"Well," Ilona began. "As to your relationship, Luka did disclose it to a superior. As you did, Morgan…eventually. It seems the relationship was short-lived, never too serious and didn't cause any conflict at the time you were involved."

Luka's leg jittered. He forced himself to keep breathing.

"However," she continued, "the allegation that Morgan blackmailed Luka into doing his work is much more concerning. What I would like from you, Luka, is a timeline of events—when Morgan approached you for help, when he blackmailed you, what you worked on—and any proof you might have…emails, texts, witnesses. And then Morgan will have a chance to reply and offer his own proof."

He nodded dumbly. He was so fucking angry at Morgan. And himself.

"Can we meet back here tomorrow at ten o'clock? Is that enough time?" Ilona asked.

They both mumbled their agreement, then Luka sprang out of his chair. He couldn't stand being in the same room as Morgan for another moment. He strode down the hallway, Thomas close behind.

"I'm sorry, Luka. It's going to be fine," Thomas said once they were back in their office.

"Is it?"

"Ilona wants to believe you, but she can't just take your word over his. She's confident you'll be able to prove it."

Luka met Thomas' golden eyes. "You believe me." He didn't phrase it as a question.

"Of course I do."

Luka stared at him, emotion welling up in his chest.

Thomas turned to shuffle some papers. "If you say Morgan is blackmailing you, then Morgan is blackmailing you. But, to be honest, I've suspected for a while that he was getting help. His style and quality were all over the place. I'm just sorry I didn't say anything sooner."

"Don't be, it's my fault." Luka dug a pad of paper out of his desk and stared at the blank lines. He picked up a pen and wrote down the name of the jingle that Morgan had first asked for help on, way back when it had seemed like a good idea. He put the pen down again and ran his fingers through his hair.

Thomas watched him for a moment. "What did you guys talk about out there? Why is he doing this?"

"We just… He said…" Luka squirmed. *I'm drooling after you? People are laughing at me? You'd never go for me?* "He was just being an asshole. I don't know."

"Okay. Let me know if I can help with anything. Want some coffee?"

"Sure. Thanks."

His list grew as he scribbled, then he started wondering how he was going to prove the blackmail.

They had never texted about anything, so that was out. There might be some sheet music or notes he had written, but he doubted those would help prove it. He pulled a file drawer open and began pawing through, looking for any scrap that might help, but there wasn't much beyond a few scrawled notes. He had probably left most of that stuff with Morgan when they were done. Sighing, he closed the drawer again. He'd have to look at home tonight, on the off chance he might have something there. Maybe he'd have more luck with emails. He didn't expect to find anything blatant, but perhaps something vague enough to cast doubt. It would take him a while to comb through that mess.

Of course, there was Tawney. He hated to bring his best friend into it, but she knew he'd been helping Morgan all along. She hadn't *heard* Morgan saying anything incriminating, but she knew most of the tawdry details along the way. That had to count for something.

Not wanting to interrupt Tawney's day, he decided to attack his email before bothering her. In the meantime, they had work to get done. That didn't help the day pass any quicker. The seconds ticked by. He could tell Thomas was trying to distract him and keep him busy, but it didn't help, not with this massive weight hanging over his head.

"I'm going to head home," Thomas said a little after five. Luka was studying his list again. "You ready to go?"

Luka shook his head. "Nah, not quite yet. Gonna take a crack at the emails first."

"Okay." Thomas shrugged his coat on. "Text me if I can do anything."

"Thanks." He watched Thomas leave, then stared at his laptop. His inbox was a bit of a disaster. He kept up on reading his emails—mostly—but he was terrible at filing them in any sort of order, and never deleted any. He sighed and clicked the 'Search' button.

He narrowed it down to emails to or from Morgan, and set the date range for when Thomas had arrived. That left him with several hundred. He rubbed his face and began reading. It wasn't looking promising. They were mostly brief and brusque. 'See attached.' 'Let's try it in another key.' 'Chat at lunch.' There was one where Luka had added 'Hope you're happy.' It was a stretch to call that proof. He slammed the lid shut and decided that he needed a drink. His feet took him to Bitter Exchange out of habit now.

He slumped at the bar. It was quiet, and it wasn't long till Kazio came over and stood, waiting.

Luka sighed. "Whatever you feel like making."

A Bloody Mary appeared at his elbow in record time. Luka examined it. "Are Bloody Marys really the reason you don't like me?" He wasn't sure where the question came from, but it fell out without him even having a chance to think about it.

"No." Kazio was still there. He wiped at a few stray drops of condensation on the wood in front of him.

Luka looked up at him, eyes tired. "Well?"

Kazio sighed and propped himself against the counter. "One night, a few months ago, Morgan was in here, heartbroken. Said you dumped him, out of nowhere."

"What?" Each word was a stone dropped into his chest, rippling outward. "He *said* that?"

"So you didn't?"

Luka reeled. "I guess I did...but..."

Kazio waited.

"Heartbroken? *Really?*"

The bartender nodded.

Luka's mind staggered under the weight of this new information. "Wow, I... Wow. I mean, he seemed pissed, but not...sad. I had no idea he actually gave a shit about *me*." Morgan was indeed capable of human feelings. *Huh.*

"It seems he did." Kazio wiped at another drop and made his way down the bar to a waiting couple.

Luka downed his Bloody Mary, trying to make sense of this new information. He felt too unsettled to sit there long and he headed out after the one drink. Kazio's eyes were on him as he left.

He picked up a veggie pizza on the way home and was eating a slice standing at his kitchen counter when his phone buzzed. It was Thomas.

How's it going?

Emails weren't very helpful. I don't know how I'm going to be able to prove it.

There must be something. We'll figure this out, Luka.

Thanks. I'll have to talk to Tawney, I guess.

Having Thomas on his side felt good. He took a deep breath and grabbed another slice of pizza.

After he ate, he had another look at the timeline he had scribbled. He had done a lot of work for Morgan. God, he was a dumb motherfucker. Berating himself, he flopped onto the couch and picked up his guitar. He plucked a few chords, hoping it would help him relax.

He thought about the first time he had played for Morgan, early on. Maybe the third time Morgan was there, when they had left the bed long enough for him to spot Luka's guitar. Luka had flat-out refused at first. There was no way he'd be brave enough to perform for a professional like Morgan. But their relationship was still new and exciting, and Morgan had a lot of cards in his hand. He wheedled and cajoled and pleaded as he played all those cards, including the ones that had involved being naked. Luka had relented.

He had chosen *Blackbird*, an old favorite. It was one of the first songs he had taught himself. He remembered plodding through the finger picking that now came to him as easily as breathing. He had tapped the beat with his foot on the hardwood as he played.

When he finished, Morgan had stared for a second. "You're really good," he had said.

Luka had blushed as a little thrill had gone through him. "Thanks."

"No, I mean, *really* good. I had no idea."

He had been so happy at the time. But the memory blackened and curled around the edges when he thought about what Morgan had done with that knowledge. Anger built again, as he pictured Morgan's smug, lying face in Ilona's office.

Something shifted as he strummed, and he saw Morgan's face that night at his apartment when he had thought about kissing him again. He heard Kazio's voice saying Morgan had been heartbroken. He heard Morgan's mumbled confession in the hallway today—"*I did care about you.*"

It clicked... Morgan wasn't just jealous of Thomas... He was hurting. *Because of me.* Hiding Luka's mug and markers in his desk wasn't him being a dick—it was

235

him clinging to a piece of the guy who broke his heart. He had let the elevator doors close because it had hurt too much to share that tiny space with him. Morgan had gotten dumped, and not only had he had to see his ex every day at work, he'd had to watch him get closer and closer — and okay, flirt — with the stunningly beautiful new VP.

I am the selfish prick.

It was probably way too late, but it needed to be done. He grabbed his phone and tapped out a message.

I'm sorry I hurt you, Morgan. I didn't mean to. I didn't even realize I had. I was a jerk when I broke up with you. And I'm really sorry.

Send.

Three dots as Morgan read the message. Then nothing.

He phoned Tawney.

* * * *

Just before ten the next morning, Luka and Morgan arrived at Ilona's office at the same time. He held Morgan's eyes for a second as he opened the door for him.

He placed a folder on Ilona's desk and took a seat. Thomas followed him in. Morgan sat in the farthest chair, head hanging.

Ilona watched them, looking as polished and perfect as ever in her deep purple pencil dress, although Luka could see the tension in her jawline. "Thank you. Let's have a look." Ilona flipped open Luka's file.

"Wait." Morgan jerked his head up, his voice quiet. They looked at him. Morgan took a deep breath. "It's true. What Luka says. I...I blackmailed him."

Luka's jaw dropped. They all stared at Morgan in silence.

Then Ilona spoke. "Thank you, Morgan. Thomas, Luka, will you excuse us, please?"

Still stunned, Luka got up and followed Thomas out. Before the door shut, he turned to look back at Morgan. Morgan was watching him with wide, wet eyes.

"Holy shit," Luka said, falling into his chair when he got back to their office. "Holy *shit*."

"Yeah." Thomas scrubbed his face. "Wow."

"I can't believe he did that. I guess he did care about me..." He shrugged, cheeks warm. "In his own fucked up way."

Thomas nodded slowly. "Maybe you cared about him a little, too."

The words settled in Luka's chest. "I guess I did."

Luka found it hard to get back to work after that, his thoughts drifting to the conversation Ilona and Morgan would be having. About thirty minutes later, someone cleared their throat from the doorway.

It was Morgan, wearing his coat and carrying a cardboard box. "Hi."

"Hey."

There was a pause while they watched each other. Thomas pretended to keep working.

"Thank you for telling the truth, Morgan," Luka said, gripping his armrests.

Morgan nodded.

"I mean, you were a dick for doing it in the first place, but thank you."

Morgan snorted, the corner of his mouth twitching up. "Fuck you."

"Back at you." They almost smiled at each other.

"Well…" Morgan shifted the box. "Maybe I'll see you at Exchange or something."

"Sure, Morgan. Take care."

"You too." He turned to leave, then paused in the doorway. "He's still never going for you, though," he said, nodding his head at Thomas. "Just saying." And with a smirk, he was gone.

"Christ…Morgan." Luka buried his face in his hands. "What was I thinking?"

Thomas gave a low chuckle. "I hope the sex was good, at least."

"Fuck," Luka said, half laughing, half moaning. "It was. Still not worth it." He shook his head. "I don't even know how I feel right now. I thought Morgan getting fired would make me happy, but…"

"Hmm." Thomas studied him. "Did I ever tell you about the time I got fired from a calendar factory?"

"You…what?"

"Yeah, all I did was take a day off."

Luka blinked at him, then put his head in his hands and laughed until he cried.

Chapter Nineteen

Blossom

"Chasing after Thomas like a lovesick puppy, drooling all over him."

"He is never going to go for you."

"It's pathetic. Everyone is laughing at you."

The voice echoed through Luka's head the rest of the week. He was busy telling himself to ignore it when Ilona called, summoning him to her office.

Luka hung up the phone and frowned at Thomas. "Do you know what she wants?"

Thomas shook his head, not looking away from his screen. "Nope."

Luka headed down the hall, a little nervous as he settled across from Ilona, flashing back to the last time he had sat there.

"Luka." She appraised him. "We're looking at doing a little restructuring now that Morgan is gone. How would you like to be a Vice President?"

Luka stared at her. "What?"

"You and Thomas will be the leads on Sartini Wines. You'll have people working directly under you to head up each department, but you'll oversee the entire team."

The same role as Thomas. Luka's mind spun.

"There's a raise, of course. And you'll still work with Thomas as long as he's here."

"Um, yeah. Yes. Yes, I would like that."

"Excellent." Ilona stood to shake his hand. "Congratulations."

He went back to his office, insides fizzing with excitement.

Thomas turned to smile at him. "Congratulations."

"You knew?" Luka's legs were rubber as he fell into his chair.

"Ilona wouldn't let me say anything."

"I can't believe it."

"You deserve it." Thomas' eyes sparkled.

Luka flushed. "Thank you."

Word spread around the building. Finn and Rory arrived shortly after Luka had returned to his and Thomas' office.

"Exchange after work, Mr. VP! You're buying!" said Finn.

Then Tawney threw her arms around Luka and kissed his cheek multiple times. "I'm so proud of you, you brilliant boy!"

Later on, when Thomas was off checking some numbers with Rory, Aleandro stuck his head in. "My most sincere congratulations to you on your promotion, my friend."

"Thank you very much, Aleandro." A thought tickled at his brain. "Actually...can I ask you something?"

"Of course." Aleandro came in and shut the door, sinking gracefully into a chair.

"I was just curious, if you don't mind me asking. You hired Penelope before you fell in love with her, right?"

Aleandro's face melted into a soft smile. "Indeed I did."

"Did you ever...worry about dating someone you worked with?"

Aleandro laughed. "Constantly. I agonized about it for weeks."

"What made you decide to go for it?"

"Well..." Aleandro took a moment to collect his thoughts. "When I was a young man volunteering for the Red Cross, my supervisor was this grizzled old cowboy from Texas. He had the hat and everything. But he was the most organized and relentless person I'd ever met. One night we were talking about our work and I complained how ineffective I felt, how we were barely making a dent in the misery of the world. He pulled his toothpick out of his mouth and said, 'Yeah, but we made a difference for these people right here today, didn't we? That's all life is, Al. You do what you can to make things a little bit better for today. Just today.' And I realized... A day with Penelope compared to a day without her? It wasn't even a question. Why would I not take that chance? If I can make today better, why wait for happiness?"

The words settled heavy in Luka's stomach.

"My advice for anyone would be to seize love if you have a chance for it."

Luka swallowed. "Thank you, Aleandro."

Aleandro smiled as he stood. "You're welcome."

The door clicked open and Thomas came in. He nodded at Aleandro as he flipped through a stack of papers.

Aleandro returned the head bob. "Thomas." Then he turned to look back at Luka, his eyes flicking over to Thomas again. "Good luck," he said with a wink before he slipped out.

Luka watched as Thomas sat and made a few notes. "How did that go?"

Thomas picked up his coffee. "Good. I set up another meeting with them at two—"

"I was wondering if you'd like to go to Montecalvo with me on Saturday?"

Thomas put his coffee back down. "With Tawney?" he asked after a pause.

"No." Luka tapped his fingers on his leg. "Just us."

His eyes brightened as he took a deep breath. "I'd love to."

"Great!" Luka's heart hammered. "I can pick you up in the morning."

"Hmm... Have you ever been on a motorcycle?"

* * * *

Luka was waiting in front of his condo Saturday morning when Thomas roared up on his bike. Luka's stomach flipped at the sight of Thomas wrapped in black leather again, hair loose under his helmet, powerful engine vibrating between his legs.

But that was nothing compared to climbing onto the bike, straddling Thomas' hips, and snaking his arms around his rock-hard torso.

"Hold on," Thomas said over his shoulder before the motor rumbled back to life.

"Don't worry," Luka muttered as he tightened his grip.

* * * *

They pulled up in front of the restaurant about two hours later. The ride had been exhilarating, a heady mix of high speeds and an intense awareness of Thomas' body. Luka slid off the bike feeling rather windblown and stiff. He tried not to stare as Thomas took his helmet off and ran his hands through his hair like he was in a goddamned shampoo commercial.

The restaurant was a converted folk-style Victorian house, wrapped in a veranda, vines climbing the clapboard and curling around the sash windows. It was perched on the bank of a small river that rushed behind it.

Next to the restaurant was the entrance to a park that ran along the river. Cherry trees lined the path, their blossoms an explosion of cotton-candy pink. In silent agreement, they stopped at the entrance to the park, mesmerized by the petals fluttering into the river, then swirling away in the current.

"Think we can order lunch to go?" Thomas asked, eyeing the benches along the path.

"You read my mind."

Twenty minutes later, with a bundle of pork pastries tucked under Luka's arm, Thomas carrying the coffee, they made their way into the park.

The trees were heavy with blossoms, drooping low. They found an empty bench surrounded by weeping branches and tucked themselves away from the world.

The pastries were even better than Luka remembered, the crust impossibly flaky, melting away on his tongue.

Thomas closed his eyes in bliss after his first bite. "Mmm. You weren't kidding."

They polished off three each, then, fingers greasy and stomachs full, settled into companionable silence as they sipped their coffee. There was nothing but the two of them in their sweet cocoon, and the river drifting by, a swirl of blushing petals and gentle blue-gray foam.

Then a gust of cool spring wind blew through, unleashing a flurry of petals that fell onto them like soft pink snow. Laughing, Luka turned to look at Thomas. He looked like a fairy prince, a crown of flowers in his long brown hair. Thomas looked back and reached over to brush at the petals on Luka's head, smiling at the cascade of pink he loosened.

It was too much.

Words piled up on Luka's tongue. Then they fell out, refusing to remain unspoken any longer. "Thomas."

"Yes?"

"I...um... I like you." It hung between them for a moment, finally free. "That is... I care about you, a lot." Well, it wasn't 'I love you', but it would have to do for now.

Luka watched Thomas' face change, from uncertainty to joy, then back again.

He looked down at his hands where he clutched his coffee, then up at Luka. "I care about you, too. A lot."

Luka's heart leaped into his throat.

"But..." Thomas continued, then it crashed into his shoes. "I'm leaving soon."

"Yeah." Luka nodded and looked back to the river. "I know."

"It will be easier when I leave...if we don't..."

Luka found it hard to swallow through the lump in his throat. "Right." He already knew that, of course. That didn't stop it from feeling like a sword through his chest. "And...you're leaving for sure?"

Thomas nodded, his face tight. "That's what I do. That's...my life."

Silence fell again, this one tortured.

Thomas took his hand. "I'm sorry."

Luka held Thomas' hand for a moment, studying the strong fingers laced through his. A petal drifted down onto his nose. He flicked it away. "Me too." He squeezed Thomas' hand, then let go and stood, brushing the blossoms off his clothes. "Shall we walk?"

They strolled along the river for a while, Luka chattering away about anything and everything trivial that came to mind. He asked Thomas questions about his bike, and told him about how he and Tawney had found this place by accident the first time because the GPS had refused to let them U-turn. He commented on the adorableness of passing dogs and babies, and contemplated what other sorts of things the restaurant should stuff into their pastry. When he ran out of things to talk about, he took some pictures of the trees to send to Tawney. He even managed to convince Thomas to let him take his picture.

"I don't do selfies," Thomas mumbled.

"Well, it's not a selfie if I take it. Come on, just a little smile. You don't even have to look at me, just…stare pensively at the river."

Thomas quirked an eyebrow at Luka, then turned to look at the rushing water. His mouth was soft, not really smiling, but not really not. He even let Luka take one of the two of them together under the blossoms, petals in their hair again.

When the sun was hanging low in the sky, casting long shadows down the path ahead, it was time for them to go home. Luka took one last look at the trees, knowing that he would never be here with Thomas again. He brushed a few petals off his sleeve and slipped them into his pocket.

Luka rested his cheek on Thomas' shoulder on the way home, closed his eyes and breathed him in. Remembered.

Chapter Twenty

The Heart Wants What It Wants

When he got home, Luka pressed the cherry blossoms in the pages of his battered copy of *Pride and Prejudice*. "Am I a sentimental idiot?" he asked himself, smoothing a hand over the cover. "Yes, yes I am." He left the book on his bedside table.

It was an agonizing weekend, torn between the euphoria of Thomas liking him back, and the torture of knowing nothing was going to happen. He was nervous at his desk Monday morning waiting for Thomas to arrive. What should he say? What should he *not* say? Luka had hugged Thomas again when they had gotten off the motorcycle, wanting to stay wrapped in those strong arms for an eternity or two. But then they had parted ways with little more than a quiet "See you Monday."

Thomas came in holding a tray from Jitters. "Good morning. I got you an iced coffee and a muffin." He held it out with an uncertain smile.

Luka melted. "Thank you. That was so sweet." He took the tray as tears pricked behind his eyes. Oh, God, it was hurting. Was this what it was going to be like now? "What did the chalkboard say?" he asked to distract himself as he pulled his cup out.

"It was, um… 'Today's special, and so are you'."

"Ha." A nervous laugh was the only response he could muster. Butterflies danced in his stomach as he nibbled at the muffin. They made a plan for their day, and spent some time debating which voice actor they wanted.

"I still like Samuel," Thomas said. "His voice just has this quality to me…"

"You think he sounds hot, don't you?" Luka said, trying to keep things light.

Thomas turned bright red. "No, it's not that…"

"I'm just teasing," Luka said. "His voice is nice, but I prefer Tyrone. So deep, authoritative. I'd do whatever he told me."

"Uh." Thomas turned even redder.

"Like…go to a restaurant, I mean." Luka laughed, a little higher-pitched than normal, and flipped through the stack of resumes with sweaty palms. The tension between them was better — and worse — than ever. *Jesus. You need to pull it together, Moreno,* he scolded himself, offering Thomas a watery smile when he looked up. "But we can go with Samuel. He's great too."

The day continued in much the same way, prolonged silences and jokes landing flatter than pancakes. By ten o'clock, Luka wanted to crawl inside his own skin and hide. They were in the middle of awkward pause number five hundred and seventy-three when Finn and Rory came in, holding hands and grinning from ear to ear.

Luka raised an eyebrow at them. "Uh, what's with you two?" Their smiles were infectious, and he grinned back despite himself.

"Are you two free this evening?" Finn asked, sharing a glance with Rory. "We'd like to take you to dinner."

Luka narrowed his eyes. "I'm free...but what are you up to?"

"Nothing!" Rory insisted, their smile growing.

Now Luka and Thomas shared a look.

"Hmm," Thomas rumbled. "I am also free and suspicious."

"Great!" Finn said loudly. "We'll meet you back here at five."

"Where are we going?" Luka thought to ask.

"We were thinking... *L'Empereur*."

Luka whistled. He'd been one time, when he had briefly dated an heir to a shipping fortune. The guy had been an egomaniac, but the food was incredible. "So you're taking us to the fanciest place in town on a Monday for no reason whatsoever? Sounds normal."

"My cousin works there — remember Dimitri, the one I mentioned at Thanksgiving? — and I told him to call me when they had a cancellation. Can't a happy couple take their friends out to dinner on a whim?" Rory asked, eyes wide with innocence.

"Not this couple." Luka gave them a wry look. "I'll be on my toes tonight."

* * * *

As planned, Finn and Rory appeared again at Luka's office at five, practically wiggling with excitement.

Luka chuckled as he pulled on his coat. "What time is our reservation?"

"Seven," Rory said sheepishly.

"Seven? It doesn't take two hours to get there."

"Well…we have a stop to make along the way."

"Aha. Not suspicious at all."

"I'm sure we have no idea what you're talking about." Finn took Rory's hand again. "Let's go!"

Luka rolled his eyes at Thomas and off they went. They took the train downtown. There was a light rain falling, but the night was still warm, the air rich with the smell of spring. They ducked under awnings where they could, and they were almost at the restaurant when Finn and Rory stopped.

Luka looked up. They were at City Hall, a gothic brick building at least one hundred years old. "What are we doing here?"

Finn and Rory looked ready to burst.

"We're getting married!" Finn blurted.

Luka gasped. "What?!"

Rory nodded, squeezing Finn's arm with their other hand. "Finn proposed on Saturday."

"He did?" Luka threw his arms around the two of them. "Congratulations!" He was shocked, but then reflected that maybe he shouldn't be. They'd been together for six months, inseparable, and Luka had never seen Finn happier in the more than four years he'd known him. If anything, he was surprised Finn hadn't proposed earlier.

Thomas took his turn hugging them as well. "Congratulations. I'm thrilled for you."

"And you're getting married *now*?" Luka asked.

"We couldn't wait. We came down at lunch to get our license and decided to just do it today," Finn explained. He was bouncing on his toes. "We bought rings and everything."

"With just us here?" Thomas looked sideways at Luka.

"Yes. We'll do some sort of proper reception later, but we hoped you would stand up with us and be our witnesses." Rory smiled at them hopefully.

Luka's lips trembled. "I'd be honored."

"Me too." Thomas' voice was a low rasp that made Luka's skin prickle.

"Then let's get this motherfucking show on the road!" Finn cried. He pulled Rory up the steps. Thomas and Luka followed.

They rode the elevator to the registrar's office and checked in with a clerk who was expecting them. She showed them where to hang up their coats, and there was another form to fill out before they were waved into a small but official-looking chamber. A Justice of the Peace stood waiting for them in her black robe. She was about forty with long, dark blonde hair.

"Finn, Rory, welcome. My name is Kate." She shook their hands. "I'm thrilled to be officiating your ceremony today."

Luka and Thomas introduced themselves, and the four of them lined up in front of the Justice's podium. They were all still in their work clothes — Finn was in khakis and a pale blue dress shirt, Rory in black trousers and short-sleeved black dress shirt with subtle gray flecks on it. In some ways they looked like complete opposites, but Luka had no doubt they were perfect for each other.

"If you're ready, we'll begin?" Kate asked.

Finn blew out a breath. "Been ready since the day I met them."

Rory turned to give Finn one more look. "Me too."

Kate began. "This couple has come here today to be joined in marriage, which is the voluntary union of two persons to the exclusion of others. If any person can show just cause why they may not be lawfully wed, let them speak now or forever hold their peace."

Finn peered at Luka. "No smart comments from you, Moreno."

Luka made a show of holding up his hands and pressing his lips together, but the truth was, he was ready to kill anyone who interrupted at this point.

Kate turned to Finn. "Repeat after me, please. I, Finn Owens, do solemnly declare that I do not know of any lawful impediment why I may not be joined in matrimony to Rory Barrett."

Finn repeated the words, then she did the same for Rory before continuing.

"Marriage is not a single event but rather a progression, which is not to be undertaken recklessly or irresponsibly, but rather carefully and honestly. Marriage is the faithful union between two persons, the result of which is the formation of a family whose members shall help, support and enjoy each other in good times and in bad. It is the relationship these two persons wish to have declared and celebrated."

The words echoed in Luka's head — *formation of a family*. He wondered if they were sticking with Thomas, too. He wanted to be Thomas' family.

Kate continued. "Please face each other as you repeat your vows."

Finn spoke in a loud clear voice, repeating the words that Kate murmured. "I call upon those present to witness that I, Finn Owens, do take you, Rory Barrett, to be my lawful wedded spouse." Finn's eyes shone even brighter than his hair. "Rory...I feel so lucky to have found you. I still can't believe that someone as kind and patient and brilliant as you puts up with me and my bullshit. I love you more than I can possibly say, but I will try to show you every single day. I promise to love and cherish you, be there for you no matter what and fall asleep with you in my arms and in my heart for the rest of my life."

The tears he had been trying to hold back filled Luka's eyes. He sniffled. Thomas handed him a tissue behind Finn's and Rory's backs. He took it gratefully and dabbed at the tears, wondering how Thomas had happened to have a tissue ready for him.

Then it was Rory's turn. "I call upon those present to witness that I, Rory Barrett, do take you, Finn Owens, to be my lawful wedded spouse. Finn. You are my beacon. My bright, shining light of love and enthusiasm and passion for life. You've taught me to look at the world with my eyes wide open, not letting any opportunity for joy and laughter pass me by. Your love gives me strength, sustains me and makes me a better person. I will always love you, and I can't wait to share my life with you."

Finn's sniffles joined Luka's, but he had his own tissue ready.

"Do you have the rings?" They each pulled a simple band of white gold from their pocket. "These rings are a symbol of your marriage, your love and your life together. Please place the ring on the third finger of the other's left hand and repeat after me. With this ring, I shall love, honor and cherish you, and this ring shall be the symbol of my love." They exchanged rings, each repeating the words in strong, clear voices.

"I, Kate McCurdy, by the powers vested in me by the city of Oakport, do hereby pronounce you to be married. I wish you long life, happiness and prosperity, and may the vows you made to each other today sustain you forever. You may celebrate your marriage with a kiss."

And kiss they did.

Luka and Thomas applauded. As Luka watched his two friends, so happy, so in love and using an awful lot of tongue for City Hall, he wanted it for himself more than anything. His gaze slid over to Thomas, and he wasn't at all surprised to find Thomas looking at him. They held each other's gaze. *For the rest of my life*, he imagined saying to Thomas. Luka dabbed at another tear, but this one wasn't for Finn and Rory.

After they all signed the marriage register, the clerk offered to take a few pictures. She waved the happy couple over to stand in front of the city's seal on a marble wall. They looked so proud, faces glowing brighter than the sun, as they stood side by side.

"They're pretty adorable," Luka said to Thomas, as Rory tried to pick Finn up like a bride. They laughed as Finn slung his arms around Rory's neck, holding on for dear life.

"They are," Thomas agreed.

"Do you think you'll ever get married?" It popped out, unbidden. He grimaced.

The smile faded on Thomas' face. "I don't know," he said, now watching Finn plant a kiss on Rory's cheek. "Maybe."

"So…one day you'll stop moving around? Pick somewhere to settle?" *Pick someone to settle with?*

"Luka." Thomas swallowed hard. He looked back at Luka and his eyes were unbearably sad.

"Sorry, never mind, it's none of my business."

"I—"

"Hey, you two. Get over here!" Finn called. He put an arm around Rory and held the other one up in invitation. "Family photo."

Luka ducked under Finn's arm. Thomas stood next to him, so he slipped his arm around Thomas' waist. His torso was warm where it was pressed up against Luka's. He took a breath of Thomas' scent and smiled for the camera.

"Who's ready to celebrate?" Finn crowed when they were done, spilling out onto the sidewalk again. The rain had stopped, puddles gleaming in the streetlights.

L'Empereur was even fancier than Luka had remembered. There were only a handful of tables in the entire place, each in its own little world, tucked into an alcove with small bow windows and thick, cream-colored drapery with gold accents. The maître d' sat them one at a time on plush, button-tufted velvet chairs, then placed linen napkins on their laps. Once they were settled, they couldn't even hear or see any other tables. It was quiet, violin music playing in the background, the lighting low and soothing.

Rory's cousin, Dimitri, was their server, and appeared as soon as the maître d' left them.

"Rory!" He kissed them on both cheeks. "*Toutes nos félicitations!* And Finn." He kissed his new cousin-in-law's cheeks, too. "*Bienvenue dans la famille.*"

"Thank you so much, Dimitri. And thanks for getting us in tonight!"

Dimitri waved a hand. "*C'est rien.* I am thrilled to be a part of your wedding day!"

"These are our friends, Luka and Thomas."

"*Enchanté*." Dimitri shook their hands. Luka noticed Dimitri noticing how stunning Thomas was—lips parting, eyes widening—but he also seemed to react the same way to Luka.

"Rory, you said your friends were attractive, but you have drastically understated it."

Luka wasn't sure how to respond, but he didn't need to, because Dimitri breezed right through, collecting the menus the maître d' had just left.

"You won't be needing these, *mes amis*! I will take care of you. This evening, for hors d'oeuvres, we are featuring *Palourdes au Gratin*, baked clams with garlic butter and bread crumbs, and *Quiche Lorraine*. I will bring those out with some fresh bread and a bottle of red for the table to start. *Bon*?"

He was pretty hot, like Rory had said at Thanksgiving. And who didn't like a French accent? Luka willed himself to let his eyes linger on Dimitri's muscular frame, admiring his thick, ashy brown hair and dazzling smile.

Dimitri seemed to be taking his time looking back at Luka, too. He touched Luka's shoulder when he passed him. "Sparkling or flat water?"

"Sparkling, please."

"I will return *tout de suite*."

True to his word, Dimitri was only gone a few minutes before he came back with water, wine and a basket of warm crusty rolls with herb butter.

"How have you been, Dimitri?" Rory asked, taking a roll.

"*Ça va, ça va*. Max got nipped by a Yorkie at the park the other day, *mon pauvre bébé*. He had to get stitches. But he will be okay."

"Oh, yes, Rory mentioned you have four dogs?" Luka piped up.

"Five now, *mon dieu. C'est trop*! It is too many, but I seem to collect them. Do you like dogs?" He poured a sample of the wine for Rory to approve.

"I do. I always wanted a dog growing up, but my parents said no. I figured I'd get one as an adult, but I never did."

"They can be a lot of work!" Dimitri continued pouring wine around the table. "If you decide to get one, please let me know if you have any questions. I am somewhat of an expert!" He laughed.

"I will, thank you." Luka took a sip of his wine. Oh, it was good. *Very* expensive. It was so rich and smooth, the flavor bursting on his tongue. He took another sip.

It was clear Dimitri was an excellent server, very knowledgeable about the food and attentive to their every need. He answered their questions without hesitation, fawned over the newlyweds and always appeared the instant they looked for him.

As the night went on, every time Dimitri asked Luka a question or cleared his plate, he would gently touch his shoulder. It was nice—it made him feel important and appreciated. But once he started watching for it, he could see that Dimitri didn't do the same thing with the other three. They just got the odd tap, maybe once or twice each.

For dinner, they each had a taste of the two main courses—there was *Lemon Poussin*, roasted chicken stuffed with duck confit, served with truffle risotto and thyme and rosemary braised lamb shoulder with slow roasted vegetables. Every single thing was heavenly, and Luka was sure he would eat until he wouldn't be able to walk home.

"So, are you moving into Finn's place?" he asked Rory, after savoring the first few bites. The risotto was particularly exquisite.

Rory furrowed their brow. "I'm trying to remember the last time I slept in my apartment. I don't even think I've been there in weeks. But yes." They leaned over to kiss Finn. "I'll be giving my notice tomorrow."

"Will you go on a honeymoon?" Thomas wondered.

"Hmm, we haven't talked about that. What do you think, love?" Finn asked Rory.

"Yes, please. Can we find a cabin somewhere without cell service, and just hike and sit around a campfire and read and…just be together, only the two of us? For at least a week!"

"That sounds perfect." They kissed again. Finn reached up to push a piece of hair behind Rory's ear. Luka sighed.

The evening was winding down, their plates almost empty, when Dimitri brought up the topic of dessert. "I hope you have saved room?"

"Oh, gosh. I couldn't possibly." Luka groaned and rubbed his stomach.

"*Je suis désolé*, the chef requires that I bring it out as a gift from *L'Empereur*."

Luka realized that Dimitri was primarily talking to him. Finn and Rory were in their own little world, feeding each other bites of food and whispering sweet nothings. And Thomas… Well, Thomas was glaring at him as Dimitri's fingers fluttered over his shoulder again.

"Five dogs, hmm?" Thomas said, out of nowhere. "You must have dog hair all over everything."

Luka looked at him askance but Dimitri didn't seem to notice the jab. "Eh, *peut-être*. Three of them do not shed and I have a robot vacuum. *C'est pas mal.* It is not bad."

"Do they chew your furniture?"

Dimitri chuckled. "You are not a fan of dogs, Thomas?"

"Oh, I like them fine. I also like my apartment being in one piece."

"*Bien sûr.* But the feeling of coming home to such an outpouring of love? It is worth it, *non*?"

Thomas glowered in silence.

What's his problem? Luka wondered. Dimitri was charming and — *Wait, is he mad that Dimitri isn't flirting with him?* To be fair, Luka wasn't sure how anyone could see Thomas and flirt with him instead.

He looked at Dimitri again as he loaded his tray. He should feel an attraction to him. Cute, friendly, hardworking, clearly a decent human... He looked over at Thomas. He was looking back. His stomach flipped when their eyes met. *Fuck. There's no hope for me. I'm destined to love a man who doesn't want me back.*

It was approaching midnight when Dimitri cleared the last of their dishes.

"*Mes amis*, the first bottle of wine was a wedding gift from me, and, as I have said, the desserts were on the house. And the rest of your bill has been taken care of."

"What?" Finn blinked at him.

"By whom?" Rory wondered. He looked around the table. Thomas was avoiding his eyes.

"Thomas! You didn't!"

He looked a little embarrassed. "As a wedding gift."

"No, that's too much!" Finn insisted. "We wanted to take you out."

"It is already done," Dimitri interjected. "He snuck his card to me earlier."

Finn and Rory thanked him profusely, while Thomas grew increasingly pink.

When they left, Dimitri hugged Rory and Finn again, and shook hands with Thomas and Luka. Dimitri's other hand came to rest on Luka's elbow. "You will be back again soon, *n'est-ce que pas?*" He held Luka's gaze for longer than expected, giving him a soft smile.

"Definitely," Luka replied. "Thank you for an amazing night."

"*Le plaisir était pour moi.*" Dimitri waved without taking his eyes off Luka.

They strolled down the street after, Finn and Rory clinging to each other. Thomas and Luka followed behind, perhaps a little unsteady on their feet as well.

"I can't tell if they're drunk or I am," Luka murmured.

Thomas took his arm. "Both, I think. I can hold you up."

Luka leaned into him, brain and tongue thick. "Okay."

When they got to the station, they parted ways with Finn and Rory, with many more hugs and congratulations and thank yous all around. The newlyweds waved through the window as their train pulled away. Luka's train was next. Thomas and Luka walked over to a different platform, Luka still holding tight to his arm.

"That was a fun night," Thomas said when they arrived and turned to face each other. "I'm so happy for them."

"Me too," Luka agreed. And he was, truly. But, there was no denying it… It hurt a whole fucking lot, seeing their happiness and knowing that wasn't going to be the same for him and Thomas.

"Too bad the waiter was such a douche," Thomas added.

"What?" A surprised laugh burst out of Luka. It echoed in the station. "You thought he was a douche?"

"Uh, yeah. 'Coming home to such an outpouring of love'," he said in his own terrible, exaggerated French accent.

Luka snorted and shook his head.

"What?"

"Nothing, I just thought..."

"Thought what?"

"That maybe you liked him."

Thomas cranked one eyebrow up to an Olympic level of incredulity. "I did not like him. He sure liked you, though."

"Yeah, he was flirting a bit... Is that why you were glaring at him? Are you *jealous*?" The idea was both maddening and appealing at the same time.

Thomas studied his feet. "Sorry. I know I'm ridiculous, and I have no right." He rubbed his chin. "He seemed nice."

"Yeah. Nice enough..." He stared at Thomas, willing him to look up.

Then he did. "Luka..." The next train arrived in a blast of warm, industrial air.

"Mmm?"

Thomas was staring at his lips. His heart skipped a beat.

Thomas leaned toward him, and for a heart-stopping second, he thought Thomas was going for his lips. But of course he wasn't. His arms went around

Luka in a careful hug. "Your train is here. Text me when you get home, okay?" The words vibrated in his chest.

Luka let go of Thomas with great effort. "I will."

"Goodnight."

"Thomas?"

"Yes?"

"Thank you for dinner."

"You're welcome."

* * * *

Luka's head was a little fuzzy the next morning, tongue dry, stomach uneasy. Thomas seemed no worse for wear, already on the phone and pacing around the office when Luka arrived. He had forgotten how intimidating Thomas could be when he was the Big Bad Wolf.

He was taking another painkiller and chugging some water when he got a text from Rory asking him to stop by their office when he had a minute. Luka stuck his head in after lunch. He never failed to be mesmerized by Rory's setup. Four huge screens spread around them, thousands of numbers dancing across each in some obscure pattern that made sense to Rory.

"You two didn't take today off?" Luka said by way of greeting.

Rory spun around and smiled at him. "Saving it for our honeymoon. Come on in."

Luka sat across from them. "Thanks again for including us yesterday. Me. Thanks for including me, I mean."

Rory smiled. "Of course. Thank you for being there." They paused and drummed on their leg. "So. Dimitri asked me for your number."

"Me?"

"Yes, you."

"Not Thomas?"

Rory shook their head. "What made you think he wanted Thomas' number?"

"I don't know, I just…doesn't everyone?"

Rory gave him a curious look. "No, it's definitely you. And Finn says you'll say no. He says you're in love with Thomas."

Luka leaned back in the chair and closed his eyes. His heart throbbed. "Sadly, that is true." *Who am I even fooling anymore?*

"Yeah, I thought so."

"I'm sorry. Dimitri seems great. I just… Fuck."

"I get it. The heart wants what it wants." They studied Luka for a minute. "Look, Luka, it's not my business, but…have you told Thomas how you feel?"

"I did, actually. On Saturday. And he turned me down."

"Oh."

"Yeah."

"Did he say why?"

Luka shrugged. "Like I knew all along. He's leaving. Why get involved and get your heart broken in a month or two?"

Rory gazed at him. "Is your heart not already breaking?"

Chapter Twenty-One

This Is for You

Things weren't quite as awkward after the wedding. They got used to just being friends again and, at least from Luka's perspective, it was preferable pretending he hadn't in fact thrown himself at his colleague. That wasn't to say that there still weren't moments that were a sharp pain in his chest. Every time his mom called, for example.

One day at lunch Luka decided he needed some fresh air, so he offered to run out to the deli down the street to pick up some sandwiches. His phone rang on the way back. When he glanced at the display and saw it was his mom, he thought about letting it go to voicemail for a hot second, but his conscience wouldn't allow it.

"Hi, Mom," he answered, tucking the bag of food under one arm.

"Oh, hello, my son! Long time no talk!" She always opened with either that, or 'Well, hello, stranger!'

"Mmhmm, how are you?"

"Why aren't you at work?" she asked. "I hear cars."

"Just went to pick up some lunch. On my way back."

"Did you get something for Thomas?"

"Yes, Mom, for both of us."

"How are things going with him?"

He wanted to laugh hysterically. "Good."

"Good, good. That's great, Luka. Well, as you know, Easter is coming up…"

Luka gulped. Asking Thomas to go to Andchester for Easter when he had just flat-out rejected him… *Oh, God*. He shuddered at the idea.

But his mom had other plans.

"So, my parents have decided to come visit me for Easter," Luka blurted as they unwrapped their sandwiches. His leg jack-hammered. "They've been meaning to get up here for a while, and my sister is taking her girls to Disneyland, so…" He trailed off and licked his lips.

Thomas looked up with interest. "That will be nice."

"Yeah. It will. The thing is…" *God, just say it, Luka.* "The thing is, I haven't told them we 'broke up' yet. I just wasn't feeling ready to handle the ensuing interrogation. My mom would probably deliver Cynthia's son to my doorstep herself if she thought I was single again." He realized he was babbling and gave an embarrassed chuckle. "So…you don't have to, but—"

"Luka."

"Yeah?"

"I'll do it."

Luka blew out a breath. "Really?"

"Sure. I'd be happy to meet your mom and dad anyway." He shrugged. "I don't mind pretending to be your boyfriend."

"Yeah, well, you haven't met my mom."

* * * *

"Luka!" Marta barreled through the door, throwing her arms around her son. She kissed him on both cheeks before she looked around. "Where's Thomas?"

"It's nice to see you too, Mom. He's not here. Hi, Dad. How was the drive?"

"Oh, fine. Your mother insisted on stopping at every fruit stand we passed." Oscar came in, towing two suitcases behind him, a bag of cherries slung on his arm.

"The cherries aren't ready in Andchester yet. Why isn't Thomas here? Did you two fight?" Marta frowned.

"He doesn't live here, Mom. He's coming for Easter dinner."

"Not until Sunday? But I'm dying to meet him!"

"I think he's busy."

"Don't be silly. We're going to the market tomorrow, yes? Invite him to come with us!"

Luka chewed his lip, weighing his options. Suffer the embarrassment of Marta fawning all over Thomas for a few extra hours, or endure a solid day-and-a-half of nagging leading up to Easter dinner?

"Fine. I'll ask him."

* * * *

Luka had his door cracked open the next morning, peering down the hallway. When Thomas' wide frame rounded the corner he began whispering in a frantic stream. "Oh my God I'm so sorry, thank you, so, so, so much. I owe you so huge. You didn't have to do this—"

Thomas stepped up to him and put a large, warm finger over Luka's mouth. He smiled gently. "It's fine."

Luka nodded, taking a deep breath when Thomas removed his hand. Then he took in Thomas' appearance. His hair was half pulled back into a knot this time, the other half hanging loose and brushing his shoulders. It was...so sexy. A huge, bright spring bouquet was tucked under his arm, contrasting with his soft gray T-shirt and faded jeans.

"You look nice. Oh my God, you brought my mom flowers. I hope she leaves you in one piece."

"What do you—"

"This must be Thomas!" a high voice exclaimed from behind Luka.

"Mom, Dad. This is Thomas." Luka held the door wider.

"Thomas!" Marta trilled. She pushed past Luka and reeled Thomas in for a hug. "Look at you! Finally, a handsome man for our Luka." She kissed both cheeks, up on tiptoe.

"Mrs. Moreno." Thomas smiled. "It's so nice to meet you. These are for you." He handed her the flowers.

"Please, call me Marta." She cradled the bouquet like a beauty queen. "Aren't you too sweet? Thank you, Thomas. This is Oscar." She patted her husband's chest.

"Sir." Thomas shook his hand.

"None of that 'sir' stuff," Oscar blustered, but he looked pleased.

Luka knew the burst of pride he was feeling was ridiculous. Of course the best man he'd introduced his parents to was a fake boyfriend. Then he realized Thomas was still holding flowers.

"And these are for you," he said, handing a second bouquet to Luka.

"Oh." Luka took them, Thomas' hand lingering on his. He buried his nose in the flowers to distract from the thumping in his chest. "Thank you, Thomas. They're beautiful. I love flowers."

"I know. You're welcome."

Marta beamed at the two of them. "I'll put them in water." She held out her hand to take Luka's bouquet and bustled into the kitchen.

"How's the temperature out there?" Oscar offered to fill the silence. "Weather forecast said it would be chilly this morning."

Luka cringed. *Really? The weather?*

But Thomas smiled affably. "It's warming up nicely."

Marta reappeared, pulling her windbreaker on. "We're so glad you could join us, Thomas. Luka has told us nothing about you—"

"That's not true, Mom."

"—and it's time we got to know each other!" She took Thomas' arm. "Let's go, shall we?"

"Sorry," Luka mouthed at Thomas when he caught his eye.

Thomas smiled and shook his head slightly, before turning his attention back to Luka's mom. "I'm afraid I'm not that interesting, Marta. But what would you like to know?"

They took the train to the old part of town where the Farmers' and Crafters' Market set up every Saturday. Marta and Thomas chatted the entire time, Luka's insides clenching whenever his mom asked something too personal. But Thomas was a champ, taking every question in stride, responding good-naturedly to everything she wanted to know.

"Have you had many serious relationships, Thomas?"

"Mom! Christ!"

"Not really. I'm on the move so much, and it's hard to meet people," Thomas answered.

Luka watched his mom beaming up at Thomas when a lump formed in his throat. Because the relationship that he was watching form in front of him was real, even though it was based on a lie. He did his best to swallow it down. What else could he do, besides enjoy the time with his parents and his friend? It was a sunny spring day, after all, the kind that made it seem like summer was right around the corner. The perfect day for a market.

They stopped first at a stall where an artist took reclaimed wood and turned it into picture frames and treasure boxes. Luka was admiring one frame in particular when he noticed his mom studying him and Thomas. He thought about taking Thomas' hand for a moment but couldn't quite get up the courage to do it. Then Thomas glanced at him. They held each other's gaze for a second. Thomas' gaze shifted over to Marta, then he took Luka's hand and smiled at him. "I'm hungry. Who wants a soft pretzel?"

Luka's heart turned into a puddle. "Me."

They found the pretzel vendor down the next row. Luka ordered his with cinnamon and sugar on top, and Thomas asked for the same. It was heavenly, thick and warm, the sugar dissolving on his tongue. Thomas paid for all four.

"What a gentleman," Marta said, patting his arm. "Thank you, Thomas."

They wandered on, munching their pretzels, taking in the rows and rows of pottery, flowers, jewelry, art and candles, not to mention the food—fruits, vegetables, bread, popcorn and sausages, for starters.

"So good," Luka said as he finished off the last bite of his pretzel, brushing the remaining crumbs off his fingers. He noticed a sparkle on Thomas' cheek. Without thinking, he reached up to dust the sugar away. Thomas froze. Luka watched as his fingers, almost of their own volition, lingered on his cheek, then swept along Thomas' jaw.

Thomas gave him a look that sent Luka's heart skittering into his rib cage. Then he leaned forward and brushed his lips against Luka's cheek. "Thanks," he murmured.

Fireworks exploded behind Luka's eyes, while his throat squeezed out a strangled gasp. "You're welcome." His cheek burned where Thomas' lips had touched him. He forced himself not to reach up and press his fingers to the patch of skin.

Thomas straightened up and took a deep breath. "All right, Marta," he asked, without looking away from Luka. "What do we need to find for dinner?"

Luka knew it was all an act, but his pulse was racing, throat squeezing. Thomas' lips had just made contact with his body. He wanted to throw his arms in the air and scream, but settled for wiggling his toes inside his shoes when they paused in front of the first vegetable stand. Once they had loaded up on potatoes and carrots and all sorts of other veggies, they were ready to go. Luka held tight to Thomas' hand, even though he knew his palms were sweaty. They passed by the reclaimed wood artist again on their way out.

"Wait…" Thomas said, letting go of Luka's hand and shifting his heavy bag to his other hand. He had insisted on carrying most of their spoils. "I'll take this one, please," he said to the artist, picking up the small frame of bleached white driftwood Luka had been eyeing earlier. The man wrapped it in brown paper for him. Thomas tucked it carefully on top of one of his bags.

"That's nice," Luka said.

"Mmm," Thomas mumbled. "I have just the picture in mind." He took Luka's hand again, and they turned to stroll off.

"Luka! Thomas!" a voice called out.

Luka turned to see Tawney waving and headed right toward them. Then she saw they were holding hands. Her eyes widened and she gasped, mouth hanging open.

Luka dropped Thomas' hand and dove toward Tawney, hauling her in for a hug. "It's not what you think, it's for my parents, please be cool," he whispered, frantic.

He pulled back. Her face was a mask of confusion.

But then Marta appeared at their side. "Tawney, my dear! How are you, sweetheart?"

"Marta! Hi! I didn't know you were in town."

Marta clucked. "I hope Luka hasn't been neglecting you since he and Thomas started dating."

Luka stared at her hard, trying to explain the situation telepathically. Tawney looked back and forth between them, then studied Marta and Oscar. Something like understanding washed over her face. Then a glint of evil. "Oh, a little bit." She tilted her head and grinned, enjoying herself way too much. "But I can't blame them. They've clearly been in love since the day Thomas arrived."

Luka narrowed his eyes at her as his face grew hot. "Well, thanks for saying hi, Tawney. We don't want to keep you."

Marta beamed, ignoring him. "How adorable. Can you believe Luka didn't say a word until Christmas?"

Now it was Tawney's turn to give Luka a reproving look. "My goodness. Not until Christmas? Remind me again how long you two have been together?"

Oh, she was going to pay for this. "Just after Halloween," Luka said through gritted teeth.

"That's right. How could I have forgotten?" Tawney smacked her forehead. "It's actually because of me they're together, if you think about it! Did he tell you the story?"

Tawney took Marta's arm and strolled with them all the way back to the train station, elaborating on how the whole thing was thanks to her and her stomach bug. "I expect a mention at the wedding," she said, winking at Luka.

"If you get invited," Luka replied sweetly.

Tawney snickered as they waved at her on their way down into the station.

Luka exchanged a relieved glance with Thomas. That had been a little too close.

They had only been back at Luka's condo for a few minutes, unloading their bags in the kitchen when Marta asked, "Won't you stay for dinner, Thomas?"

"No, Thomas can't stay, Mom," Luka interjected. He'd already gone above and beyond. The poor man had earned a break.

"Thank you, Marta, but I have a few things I need to do before dinner," Thomas demurred.

She pouted for an instant.

The corner of Thomas' mouth twitched. "But I look forward to seeing you again tomorrow." He took her hand and squeezed it.

"Well, fine," she said, mollified, "but promise you'll at least come early."

"Mom —"

"I'll be here nice and early," Thomas assured her.

* * * *

Later that night Luka stretched out on his bed.

Thank you thank you thank you, he texted Thomas. *My mom has never loved another human so instantly before.*

It was no problem. I'm sorry, though, I should have asked before I kissed your cheek. We didn't talk about what was involved with the 'fake boyfriend' role.

This time Luka allowed himself to press his fingers to the spot where Thomas' lips had been.

Totally fine. It was very convincing. I didn't mind.

Okay, good.

I owe you so huge for this.

I might cash that in one day.

An emoji followed his message. "Winky face?" Luka gaped at his phone. "Is he kidding?" He held his breath and typed.

Did you have a particular favor in mind?

He hit 'send' before he could change his mind. Three dots.

I have a few.

Luka held back a scream. *Is this happening?*

Are you gonna ask me?

Hmm, I'll guess you'll have to wait and see. Night.

Luka fanned his face, thinking about all the favors he would like to do for Thomas. Unfortunately, with his parents next door, he couldn't do much more than think.

He had a lot of trouble falling asleep that night.

* * * *

There was a sharp rap on the door at two o'clock the next day. True to his word, Thomas arrived for Easter dinner nice and early. Luka held the door wide, admiring Thomas' light gray slacks and crisp white dress shirt. His hair was back in its customary knot again.

"Hi," Thomas said as he came in. This time he carried a pale blue box, with a brown paper gift bag hanging from one hand.

"Hey." Luka gazed at him, wavering for a moment as the air grew hazy around him. He so badly wanted this tiny, innocuous moment to be real. Just greeting his boyfriend at the door. For a second, the hurt was too much to take. For a second, his heart was in a million pieces.

Then Marta came bustling in from the kitchen. "Thomas!" She had Luka's red apron over her pink pants and flowered blouse.

"Marta. You look lovely." He let her squish him for a long hug, holding the box to one side. Then Thomas handed it to her. "I brought dessert."

Marta took the box from him with an excited "Ooh" and peeked inside. "Eclairs! My favorite!"

Thomas grinned. "Luka may have mentioned something."

"Oh, you!" She let out what could only be described as a girlish giggle.

"And this is for you." Thomas held the bag out to Luka.

"For me?" Luka took it, their fingers brushing for longer than necessary again. He reached inside to remove a rectangle wrapped in brown paper, and peeled it off to discover the driftwood picture frame from the market. He turned it over and found one of the pictures he had taken of him and Thomas under the cherry blossoms. They were both smiling, Luka at the camera, but Thomas' eyes were shifting over to look at Luka. The smiles were soft, and, Luka knew, a little sad.

He felt that ache, that hazy feeling, wash over him again. "*This is for you.*" He blinked quickly and looked up at Thomas. "Thank you. I love it." He stepped closer, slipped an arm around Thomas' back and leaned in to kiss him on the cheek. Thomas' eyes fluttered closed as he took a deep breath. There was a tightness in Luka's own chest.

"You're welcome." Thomas cleared his throat and turned to Marta. "What can I help with?"

"No, no. Luka and I have it under control. You keep Oscar company. He's got the game on."

"That I can do." Thomas' smile shifted from Marta over to Luka. His eyes softened. Luka didn't think he was imagining the sadness reflected in them now. "Let me know if you need me."

Luka wasn't sure if he was about to laugh or cry. "Will do." Marta gave him a strange look as they headed back into the kitchen. Luka put the picture frame out of the way on the counter where he could see it as he worked.

* * * *

"This looks incredible," Thomas said in awe, taking in the spread.

Marta waved a hand. "It's nothing."

A ham sat glistening on the island, next to a bowl of steaming scalloped potatoes. There was a tray of asparagus and a dish of roasted onions, snow peas and carrots, plus a salad and rolls.

They sat down, all four in a row along the counter, and served themselves. It took Marta about three seconds to turn the conversation over to their relationship.

"Luka gave us so few details at Christmas, he would barely talk about it." Marta shook her head. "Like you're in the CIA."

Thomas chucked. "This guy, not talking? That doesn't sound like him."

Luka gasped in mock outrage.

Thomas slid a hand onto Luka's knee and squeezed, and Luka forgot what he was offended about.

Marta laughed. "You can say that again! I wish I had known, though. We would have loved to have had you over for Christmas."

A tiny warning bell began jangling in the back of Luka's brain, but it was hard to follow the sound with the heat of Thomas' palm still lingering on his leg.

"Luka said you spent the holiday with your family in Solano?" Marta continued.

Ah, fuck. That was it.

Thomas quirked an eyebrow at Luka, giving him a minute.

"Um…" Luka offered.

"What?" Marta looked back and forth between them.

Damn it. "I might have…made that part up."

"What part?" Marta frowned.

"Thomas wasn't with his family over Christmas," Luka said, cringing. He couldn't look at his mom, so he looked at Thomas instead. "I just felt so bad that I hadn't invited him and I didn't want you to give me shit. I'm sorry." Luka curled his mouth in a sheepish smile.

Thomas jumped in, bless him. "It was just me and my dad, Marta, and he passed away a few years ago from cancer. And it's okay, our relationship was still really new at the time. I didn't expect Luka to invite me."

Marta glared at her son. "Luka Francis Moreno. Lying to your mother at Christmas and leaving your boyfriend alone? We raised you better than that!" Then she turned to Thomas, her expression softening. "I'm so sorry about your father, Thomas."

"Thank you."

"Well. You'll have to come for Christmas this year. You're part of our family now." She glared at Luka again.

Family. The lump was back in Luka's throat. God, he was such a fucking dick. *Family.* Luka's brilliant plan to pretend he and Thomas were dating had just made the situation worse. He had, once again, been entirely selfish, worried about his own skin when he had to tell his mom that they broke up. But he was fucking around with real people and their real feelings. Thomas didn't have a family, and here was Luka, asking him to pretend he had one, when it was all a lie.

He'd have to wallow in his own selfishness later. For now, there was a conversation to hold together. *Christmas. Great.* "Sure, Mom." He stabbed a piece of asparagus. "How are lessons going these days?" That was a safe topic for distracting his mother.

"Oh, good." She sighed. "The Peres twins still refuse to practice. I didn't think it was possible to get worse every week, but they're managing it. Rebecca is heading to Phoenix for the next six months, so she'll miss the recital. And I have a new little guy starting the guitar. He reminds me of you, Luka. Comes so easy to him and cute as a button. Doesn't know how good he is." Her smile was a little distant as she cut a piece of ham.

Thomas looked over at Luka with a raised eyebrow. Luka hadn't told them he had performed yet. He had wanted to tell them in person. With Thomas there, if he was being honest. He gave Thomas a little nod.

"Did Luka tell you?" Thomas asked. "He performed at an open mic night last month."

Marta gasped deeply enough that it threatened to suck all the air from the room. "You did?" she warbled. "Oh, my baby." She dropped her cutlery with a clatter and pressed her hands to her mouth.

"That's wonderful, son," Oscar added. He kept eating.

Marta was shaking her head, eyes wet. "I'm so proud of you."

Luka looked at her, finding his eyes were also a little wet. "It was thanks to Thomas." He glanced over at him. "I never would have done it if it weren't for him."

Thomas' eyes were shining, too. "He was incredible, Marta. You would have been so proud."

"I'm always proud." Marta reached over to touch Luka's arm. "But you'll tell us next time you perform?"

"Mom, you don't need to drive ten hours for an open mic night."

Marta shrugged and reached for another slice of ham. "Oh, Luka. I'd drive a hundred."

Thomas had his head down now, spearing small pieces of carrots one at a time onto his fork. Luka wanted to apologize for the whole thing, for asking Thomas to pretend, but all he could do now was put his hand on Thomas' knee and squeeze.

* * * *

A while later, plates scraped clean and eclairs devoured, a comfortable, sleepy silence settled over the table.

Then Marta sat up straight and cast a mischievous look over to Luka and Thomas. "Well…now that dinner is over…"

Shit. "Oh God, Mother. You did not."

Marta retrieved two pairs of bunny ears from somewhere under the counter. "It's time for the egg hunt!"

"Mom."

"Oh, don't be such a spoilsport! Come on! I didn't get to do one for the girls this year." She stuck out her lower lip and batted her eyelashes at Luka and Thomas.

"Hmm, so that's where you get that from," Thomas said wryly, nodding at Marta.

"What—I—" Luka sputtered, quite sure he had no idea what Thomas was referring to.

Thomas grinned at him, then stood and took the bunny ears from Marta.

"You can't be serious." Luka gawked at him.

Thomas' eyes were twinkling. "I bet I find more eggs than you, Luka Francis." He plunked the pink ears on his head.

Again, with the heart squeezing. Luka reached for the pair of blue ears. "You're on."

* * * *

Luka closed the door after Thomas left. He turned to see his mom and dad smiling at him.

"What?" he asked.

Marta's eyes were wide and shining. "He's a special one, Luka."

Luka ignored the throb in his chest. "I know, Mom."

"Don't let him go."

Chapter Twenty-Two

Can't Help Falling

"Morning." Luka's gaze swept up and down Thomas' frame as he arrived in their office. He never got tired of that man in a navy suit.

Thomas paused his typing. "Morning. Did your parents get on the road okay?"

"Yup, when I left for work." Luka shook his head. "I feel like I need a couple days off to recover from Hurricane Marta." He sat at his desk.

"She's great." Thomas chuckled. "If not a little intense."

Luka's heart ached. "It's gonna crush her when you move."

Thomas turned to look at him. "I can be your fake long-distance boyfriend if you need…to keep Cynthia's son away from you."

Jesus. How did he get to a point in his life where he was contemplating a fake long-distance boyfriend? Where it seemed better than nothing? Despair and guilt bubbled up his throat. "Long-distance doesn't work."

Thomas looked down at his hands where they rested on his laptop. "I know. But…it can if it's not real."

"Yeah." Luka smiled sadly. "I guess. I'll have to let her down eventually though."

"Maybe not for a while. You can start dropping lines into your conversations about what a jerk I'm being."

"Ha. She'd never believe it."

Thomas smiled. "She's sweet."

Luka felt sick. The apology fell out. "I'm really sorry, Thomas."

"Sorry for what?" he asked, brow wrinkling.

Luka picked up a stack of sticky notes to fiddle with. "Sorry for…letting you pretend."

Thomas still looked confused. "It's fine. I offered to help."

"Yeah, but…" The words sat heavy on his tongue. "It was a lot. It was too much. My mom already adores you. She said you were part of our—" He stopped. The next word refused to follow the rest out.

"Oh." Thomas nodded. He understood. "It's okay."

"It's not. It wasn't fair of me." He pulled a note off, folded it in half. "You don't have to pretend anymore. As soon as you move, I'll just tell her we broke up because you left. It'll be easy to act sad." To his alarm, tears started to well up. *I am a fucking mess.*

"Luka…" It looked like Thomas was shifting his weight to stand when his phone rang. "Thomas," he answered. "Mmm." He hung up. "Ilona wants to see us."

Luka blinked hard and took a deep breath, trying to smile. "Okay."

"Hey." This time Thomas did stand. "I'm not going anywhere just yet."

"Yeah." Luka nodded. "I know."

Thomas took his hand and pulled him to his feet. He squeezed it before he let go. They headed down the hall, shoulders bumping, hands brushing more than once, drawn together like they were supposed to be holding on still. It sent a spark up Luka's spine each time.

"Great news." Ilona smiled at them as they sat down. "You know how we've been trying to land the Grand Plains account for ages? Shamsi finally agreed to meet."

"That's fantastic!" Luka said. Shamsi Moghadam was the director of Grand Plains, a huge university-hospital, renowned for its world-class healthcare and pharmaceutical research.

"The two of you can leave for Elander tomorrow around three, then you'll meet with her at nine the next morning," Ilona said. "I know it's rushed, but that's what she offered. We have some preliminary work done for you to review, and you've got some time before you go."

"The two of you." Oh God. Luka was once again torn. The excitement of a road trip with Thomas, just the two of them together for a whole day…and agony of just the two of them together for a whole day.

"Sabrina will book you a hotel near the university. Take the firm credit card for gas and meals and other incidentals. Do you mind taking your car, Luka?"

Luka looked over at Thomas, who was staring back.

"No, I don't mind at all."

* * * *

"Luka Moreno and Thomas Badgley, checking in."

"Welcome to the Elander Foothills Resort, gentleman." The man behind the counter nodded as his fingers flew over the keyboard. "Ah, yes, Mr. Moreno and Mr. Badgley, here you are… And it looks like congratulations are in order! We have the honeymoon suite all ready for you."

"The what?" Luka squawked as Thomas' eyes grew to the size of dinner plates.

"The honeymoon suite. Are you not…?" He trailed off as he got a look at their expressions and emphatic head-shaking. "Oh. Oh, dear. Hmm, let me just see…" His fingers danced over the keys again. "Ohhh. We had you booked in a double, but there was a leak on the third floor last night and that block of rooms is now unavailable. We only have the honeymoon suite remaining for you this evening."

They blinked at him.

"At no additional cost to you, of course. There's a pullout couch…" he finished helplessly.

"Um…" Luka turned to look at Thomas. "Well."

"That will be fine," Thomas mumbled. "Two keys, please."

* * * *

Thomas pushed the door open. Luka held his breath as he peeked in. They were high above Elander, the curved wall of floor-to-ceiling windows providing a stunning view of *les Sommets de Maurac*, a jagged, snow-capped mountain range to the east. Then his gaze found the bed. The only bed. An expansive king-sized one, draped in rich, textured cream and white linens. It was strewn with red rose petals, a bucket of champagne chilling on a silver tray in the center.

Luka's snort turned into a cackle. "Of course." He dragged his suitcase into the room and flopped onto the couch, shoulders shaking with mirth.

Thomas gave an embarrassed chuckle. "You can have the bed. The pullout is fine for me."

"Oh, no, please, you take the bed," Luka said in between giggles.

"No," Thomas said firmly. "I insist."

"All right." Luka wiped a tear from his eye. "I won't fight you too hard. I've always wanted to sleep in a bed of roses." Still snickering, he lifted his suitcase onto the bureau and zipped it open to hang up his suit for tomorrow.

"You brought your robe?" Thomas asked as Luka pulled it out.

"Well, of course I brought my robe. I don't think you understand how much time I spend in this thing." Luka placed it on the bed and gave it a fond pat.

"Hmm." Thomas was trying not to smile.

"What?" He put his hands on his hips. "You wear your wolf cufflinks all the time."

"Yes, I do."

They stared at each other.

Fuck. "Shall we get dinner?"

Sabrina had made them a dinner reservation at the hotel restaurant as well. It was busy, but quiet and dim, and they were seated in a booth tucked away by the bar.

They were studying their menus when two men in tuxedos appeared next to their table.

"For the happy couple," one announced, handing them each a rose, while the other started playing *Can't Help Falling in Love* on a violin. "On behalf of the Elander Foothills Resort, we wish you all the best as you begin your new life together." Before Luka or Thomas could even make a sound, he began to sing along.

Luka threw a panicked glance at Thomas. His face was frozen in a mask of alarm and incredulity. Luka realized he'd better look elsewhere or he'd lose it. He forced down the laugh that wanted to bust out of him and studied the violin. *Hmm, that's a Maestro Stradi, I think, very nice, great tone...* He kept his lips pressed together, studiously ignoring Thomas.

When the musicians finished their performance, Luka and Thomas applauded, smiled and nodded, along with the people seated around them until the men left. They looked at each other with wide eyes. Then it burst out of them, and they pressed hands to their mouths, hunched over the table, shoulders shaking.

"Oh my God," Luka gasped. "This is the best honeymoon ever."

Thomas laughed, pushing a stray hair back off his forehead. "Definitely the best one I've had." He straightened the rose lying next to his plate.

Dinner was delectable. Thomas ordered the prime rib, and Luka went with the roasted duck.

"This is unbelievable, Thomas. You need to try it." Luka held out a bite on his fork.

Thomas lifted an eyebrow at him in a look that said *'Really?'*

Luka grinned and shrugged. *Why stop now?*

Thomas leaned over, tongue flashing pink as he put his lips over Luka's fork. He held them there a second, then pulled back, all without breaking eye contact. "Mmmm," he purred, a low rumble in his chest. "Delicious."

Luka's mouth dried out as his heart slammed into his ribcage. *Fuck.* His dick twitched at the sudden flow of blood. "Right?" His voice cracked.

"You have to try mine, too." Thomas held out his fork in turn. Luka opened his mouth and let Thomas slide his fork in. The juicy slice of beef nearly fell apart on his tongue.

"Incredible," Luka said, licking his lips. "So tender."

"Mmm." Thomas' foot bumped against his under the table, where it stayed for the rest of the meal. Luka felt hotter and hotter under Thomas' gaze. By the end of the meal he'd removed his blazer and undone two more buttons on his shirt.

In the elevator on their way back to their room, Luka leaned against the wall and brought his rose to his nose, inhaling deeply. He realized he was humming *Can't Help Falling in Love*.

Thomas chuckled and shook his head. "Enjoying the honeymoon?"

"Well…" He batted his eyelashes at Thomas "…it could be better…" He hoped it came across like a joke. Although, he wasn't sure if he was actually joking.

Thomas' smile softened. His gaze lingered on the open neck of Luka's shirt before he looked up at the number above the door. "Yeah…" He cleared his throat. "We should go over the presentation before bed."

Luka sighed and nodded. *You're here for work,* he reminded himself.

They rode the rest of the way in silence. Neither spoke until Luka stepped into their room. "As I suspected. Turndown service. Chocolate-covered strawberries. Why fight it?" He threw his hands in the air. "May I pour you some champagne?"

Thomas undid his cuffs and rolled up his sleeves. "Yes, please."

Luka retrieved the bottle from the ice bucket and got an idea. "Come here. Let's see how far we can launch the cork. Grab the glasses." He beckoned Thomas to follow him out on the balcony. It was a warm night and they were high above a garden, higher than even the tallest trees. He pulled the foil off the top and unwound the metal bracket from around the cork as Thomas joined him.

"It's so beautiful," Luka said, pausing to look around as Thomas leaned up against the railing next to him. The trees and shrubs, dark green and lush in the thickening night, gave way to the rolling foothills before the mountains shot up to touch the inky black sky.

The breeze ruffled Thomas' hair as he looked over at Luka. "It is." His voice was slow and heavy. The stars dotted the night. Luka swore they were reflected in Thomas' eyes.

Luka turned his attention back to the stubborn cork, which didn't seem to be moving. He braced the bottle against his stomach and pressed his thumb under the ridge trying to push it out. Nothing.

"Be careful…" Thomas said, reaching over to ensure the bottle was tilted away from Luka's face.

"Can you help?" Luka asked. "I'll hold it steady, you try to get the cork out."

Thomas moved closer and wrapped his hands around the neck of the bottle. Luka pictured Thomas wrapping those strong, sure hands around something else. A surge of heat flooded his face. He tried not to look at Thomas. Except he did. They could kiss right now if he just leaned forward an inch or two…

He jumped when the cork erupted with satisfying pop, launching itself out into the night, disappearing amidst the foliage. He laughed, relieved he hadn't just made a horrendously awkward move. "That was a stubborn one. This bubbly better be worth it." They were still standing together, both holding the bottle.

Then Thomas stepped back to pick up the glasses he had brought out. "Let's find out."

The bubbles felt like heaven rolling across Luka's tongue, fizzing up into his brain. The champagne was light and crisp, with just a hint of sweetness. Luka wanted to stay there the entire night, watching Thomas in the moonlight, but... "I suppose we'd better get to work," he said reluctantly.

Tilting his head back, Thomas swallowed the rest of his glass. He licked his lips. "I suppose." He didn't sound that happy about it either. They went back inside, Luka taking one last lingering look at Thomas' profile against the dark night.

Thomas powered up his laptop and spread out some papers on the coffee table while Luka slipped into the bathroom to change into his robe. Thomas stared at him when he came out.

"What?" Luka asked, a little self-conscious—and a little buzzed—from downing his first glass so quickly.

"Nothing," Thomas smiled. "You're just...you're adorable in that robe."

Luka ducked his head as he poured them each another glass. "Agreed. Here, eat some strawberries," he said to get Thomas to stop looking at him like that.

Thomas' eyes glinted at him as he took one off the plate and brought it to his mouth. Something snapped in Luka's brain and he started giggling. He couldn't say why, just that the whole situation was completely and objectively hilarious. The strawberries, the champagne, the roses, the motherfucking stars twinkling. The most gorgeous fucking man in the whole world looking at him like that. The universe was such a bitch. He laughed harder.

Thomas smiled at him. "What's so funny?" But he was already giggling too.

Luka flopped onto the couch, gasping for air, stomach aching. "This," he managed to wheeze, waving his arm around the room. "Our honeymoon!"

Thomas laughed harder too, although he was mostly watching Luka fall apart. It took Luka a long time to calm down, wiping the tears from his eyes and taking deep ragged breaths. "Oh, God. I'm so sorry." He took another breath. "I'm okay. I've got this." He picked up a strawberry. "All right. These bad boys aren't going to eat themselves. Let's get to work."

By the time the bottle was empty, their presentation was finalized, and it was time for bed. Thomas came out of the bathroom shirtless, pajama bottoms slung low around his hips. Luka let his gaze linger for longer than was appropriate, but when he flicked his eyes up to Thomas, Thomas was smiling at him.

Luka cast about for words. "Hi," was all that came to him.

"Hi." Thomas pulled the tie out of his hair and tousled his waves, biceps flexing.

"You're really fucking impossibly gorgeous, you know that, right?" *Oops. That's the champagne talking.*

Thomas looked down at his toes. "Thanks."

"No, I mean…" Luka shook his head. "It's not fair."

"Hmm." Thomas padded over to the couch, cheeks pink. "You are too," he mumbled as he pulled the cushions off and dropped them to the side.

Now it was Luka's turn to flush—again—but he tossed his head. "Well, yes, we agreed I'm adorable, but you—"

"You're more than adorable." Thomas' gaze was heavy on him as he tucked a strand of long hair behind his ear.

Luka felt like his heart might explode right out of his chest if he didn't kiss Thomas this very second. *No. No, no, no, Luka.* "Have you always had long hair?" he scratched out instead, hoping it would prove to be a sufficient distraction.

"My dad did, so I did too. And at my first real job, just in the mailroom at a law firm, some ass told me I should cut it. So...I didn't."

"I'm glad."

Thomas flushed and bent to grab the handle for the foldout bed. He gave it a tug. It didn't move. He frowned and gripped it with both hands, giving it another yank. This time it rattled out with a shriek. He unfolded the rickety frame for the bottom half of the bed but the mattress was so limp and thin it didn't spring open.

"Well, that looks...comfortable," Luka said with a raised eyebrow as Thomas flipped the mattress open. The coils were trying to burst through the thin cover.

Thomas grunted. "I'll be fine."

"The offer still stands to share the bed. I don't bite...unless given permission first." He waggled his eyebrows at Thomas. *Oh, Jesus. I can't stop.*

Thomas suppressed a smile as he shook his head, pulling extra bedding out of the closet.

Luka took his turn in the bathroom, chugging an extra glass of water to counteract the half bottle of bubbly he'd consumed.

When he came back into the room, Thomas had made the bed and was settling in, frame squeaking.

Luka wiggled out of his robe and flopped onto the king-sized bed in his pajama bottoms. "Oh, Thomas. If you knew how perfect this mattress is, you might not give it up so easily."

"Hmm. We'd better get some sleep." Thomas rolled over a few times trying to get comfortable, to no avail.

Luka listened to Thomas tossing and turning for a good thirty minutes, the bed creaking and groaning with every movement.

After Thomas growled and bunched up his pillow for the twentieth time, Luka sat up. "Thomas. Would you just get over here?"

Thomas propped himself up on an elbow. The springs protested. "It's fine."

"It is very clearly *not* fine. This bed is huge. There's plenty of room for both of us. Will you please stop thrashing around and get over here? Neither of us will sleep a wink if you stay there."

It was silent for a moment. "I could sleep on the floor."

"The floor? Now I'm insulted."

Thomas sighed. "Okay."

Luka was already lying on one side of the bed, but he scooted over even closer to the edge.

Thomas circled around to the other side, his skin shining in the moonlight, muscles thrown into stark relief. He pulled the covers back, sliding in. "Ahhh," he sighed as he burrowed.

Luka rolled over and grinned at him. "What did I tell you?"

"It's good." Thomas was lying on his back, eyes closed.

Luka watched him for a moment, a smile playing on the edges of his lips. "Goodnight, Thomas."

"Goodnight, Luka."

He studied Thomas a while through half-closed eyes, lulled by the way his chest rose and fell with deep, even breaths. Eventually he drifted off, still smiling.

* * * *

At seven, Luka's alarm woke him from perhaps the best sleep he'd ever had, and it took him a second to figure out where he was, and who the large, warm, very firm body was under his arm. He took a slow, contented breath, then his eyes flew open at the scent. He was staring at a bare chest, head tucked under Thomas' chin. They each had an arm flung over the other's waist, and Luka's knee was notched between Thomas' legs.

He tried not to squeak as his next breath whooshed out of him. *Oh, fuck. What do I do?* He started to shift his weight back, but as soon as Thomas' wrist slipped on his waist, the big man mumbled something and pulled Luka closer, burying his nose in Luka's hair. His face was pressed against Thomas' collarbone.

This time Luka couldn't help it—he did squeak. Then Thomas froze.

"Ummm... Good morning," Luka said, a little muffled.

But instead of darting away from him, like he expected, Thomas relaxed again. "Morning."

"So..." Luka groped for words. "This is nice." A little too nice. Luka had been half hard when he awoke and the situation was not improving.

"Mmm," Thomas replied. Luka could feel the rumble in his chest. Then Thomas inhaled.

"Are you smelling my hair?" Luka asked.

"No."

They were quiet again. Thomas dragged his fingers in lazy circles on Luka's skin. The tingle threatened to wrench his brain in half. His body was responding one way, and his mind was a tangled mess. If he let himself go down this path, there would be no coming back. This path was dangerous. This path would leave him shattered.

"I think… I need to pee." Luka rolled over and slid off the edge of the bed, hating the feeling of Thomas' warm fingers slipping from his skin. His bare feet padded on the carpet as he darted for the safety of the bathroom. He closed the door behind himself and leaned back against it, head spinning.

When he came out, Thomas was sitting on the edge of the bed, waiting. "I'm sorry."

"It's okay."

"That wasn't fair of me."

Luka took a breath. "I know I was joking around last night, but if we can't… Then I can't…"

"I know. You're right. It won't happen again."

But that's not what I want either… His chest ached. "Okay. Thank you."

"Well…" Thomas stood, smoothing his pajama bottoms. "We'd better not keep Shamsi waiting."

Chapter Twenty-Three

So It Goes

Luka paused when he came out of the bathroom, seeing the look Thomas was giving him. "What?"

"A green suit?"

Luka huffed and examined himself in the mirror over the desk. "I'll have you know that green is the color of *healing*, Thomas, and I have a strong feeling that Shamsi is the type to appreciate a pop of color."

"Hmm. Is it a 'pop' when it's head-to-toe?"

"Oh, fuck off, Mr. I-Have-Suits-in-Fifty-Shades-of-Gray."

Thomas snorted and opened his mouth to respond.

"Anyway"—Luka pushed ahead through his blunder to cut off Thomas' reply—"I look fantastic." He patted his hair.

Thomas smiled shyly. "You do."

They had breakfast in the restaurant, now much louder and brighter than dinner had been, a few tables of large families adding to the buzz.

"It's our honeymoon, you know," Luka said to their server when she arrived with coffee. "We're on our way to the coast."

"Congratulations," she said as she poured.

"Thank you," Luka replied, tilting his head and sighing at Thomas. "This one planned the whole thing. Wine tastings, whale watching, romantic dinners on the beach... I'm so lucky."

Thomas rolled his eyes but played along, nodding at the server.

"How sweet." She offered a small smile as she stood there, holding the pot.

"Indeed it is. He begged me, you know. Got down on *both* knees and said if I didn't marry him, he'd die from a broken heart."

"That's nice." She paused. "Did you want to order, or...?"

"He hired a sky-writer, too. 'Marry me, Luka, or I'll *literally die,*' it said, in giant letters across the horizon."

"Okay," Thomas interrupted to put the server out of her misery. "Sorry about him. We'll both have the buffet, thank you." She gave him a relieved look and scurried off with their menus.

"There was a marching band!" Luka called after her.

Thomas shook his head, trying not to laugh. "I'm glad you amuse yourself."

Luka grinned. "Thought I'd see if I can get us some free mimosas."

"I don't know if Ilona would love the idea of us showing up for a meeting with the biggest possible client of all time buzzed on mimosas that we scammed from the breakfast buffet."

"She would never know," Luka said with an evil finger waggle.

After a mimosa-free breakfast, they checked out, loaded their suitcases into the car and made the short drive over to the Grand Plains University-Hospital. It was a massive, sprawling campus, built around the foothills of the mountains. Poplars lined the drive up to the hospital itself, a soaring building made of gray stone.

Walking into Shamsi's office was like stepping back in time — shelves covered in leather-bound books, jars, skulls and other treasures in a display of artful chaos. Tall windows looked out over a lush courtyard garden.

She stood when they came in, her white coat a stark contrast to the pleated burgundy dress underneath. Her short black hair framed a no-nonsense face. But her expression softened when she smiled, eyes crinkling. "Welcome to Grand Plains. Won't you have a seat?"

Luka felt like he could curl up and take a nap in the richness of her voice. They shook hands and settled onto the upholstered wooden chairs.

"Thank you so much for agreeing to meet with us, Doctor Moghadam," Thomas said.

"Oh, everyone calls me Shamsi. And you can thank Ms. Hoszek for the meeting. She is persistent."

Luka and Thomas shared a glance. "Indeed she is," Luka said.

"You didn't drive down from Oakport this morning, did you?"

"No, last night. We stayed at the Elander Foothills," Thomas replied.

"How nice. I've heard it's lovely."

"Yes, it was…very special," Luka agreed, his heart squeezing the slightest bit.

"Excellent." Shamsi leaned back in her chair. "Now, why don't you tell me what Breakpoint would have to say about Grand Plains?"

* * * *

"That went well," Luka said when they stepped back out into the sunshine.

"Hmm. She loved you."

"Well, I'm loveable." Luka sighed, brushing imaginary lint off his sleeve.

Thomas barked a short laugh and shook his head.

The ride home was quiet. Luka rolled down the windows and let the warm air blow through his hair. Thomas turned on some music, then leaned back in his seat and closed his eyes. Except for when he was glancing at Luka, out of the corner of his eye.

They stopped at Ilona's office when they got back. She grinned up at them from the stack of papers on her desk. "I already heard back from Shamsi. She's in. We're drawing up the contract."

Luka and Thomas smiled at each other.

"Great work, gentlemen." She nodded. "Thomas, could you stay a minute longer? There's something else I need to talk to you about."

As Luka turned to leave, Ilona called after him. "Oh, and Luka? Shamsi liked your suit."

Luka shot Thomas a look of triumph. "Of course she did."

"Please, don't encourage him," Thomas muttered, trying to keep his face stern.

"Well, someone's got to," he heard Ilona reply as he left.

Luka found Finn and Rory waiting outside his office and they trailed in after him.

"How was the trip?" Finn asked as he fell into his usual chair. Rory pulled up another and sat next to him.

"It was great! Shamsi is going to sign with us. Ilona is working on the contracts."

"Cool, cool, I meant with you and Thomas, though."

Luka shook his head. "There's nothing to say, Finn. It's not happening."

"Okay..." The redhead shared a glance with Rory, then looked back at Luka. "Tell me again why not?"

"I tried, all right? I told him I liked him, and he said no. He said it would be easier if we didn't get involved. And he's right. He's leaving in a couple months."

"So what are you going to do?" Rory asked.

"What do you mean, 'what am I going to do'? I'm doing nothing."

Finn rubbed at his beard. "Well, that's bullshit. He doesn't have to leave. No one is holding a gun to his head. Tell him *you're in love with him* and ask him to stay."

Luka made a strangled noise. "He likes his life. He likes not being pinned down. He said it's simpler this way. I can't ask him to change everything just for...for me."

"Look. You encouraged me to go for it with Rory, and I did, and it's been the best thing that's ever happened to me." He paused and looked at Rory, who was watching him with the softest eyes Luka had ever seen. Rory reached over and took Finn's hand. Their wedding bands glinted.

"And" — Finn continued, holding up his other hand before Luka could interrupt — "I know you think it's different with you two, but it's not."

Luka ran a hand through his hair. "I appreciate you trying to help, but… What's the point of falling in love if you know it's going to end in heartbreak?"

"What's the point?" Finn looked baffled. "Luka, you don't get to choose who you fall in love with."

Luka opened his mouth to tell a big fat, futile lie, something along the lines of 'It'll be fine', or 'I'll get over it', then Thomas walked in. He looked like he'd been punched in the gut.

Finn and Rory took one look at Thomas' face and scooted out with mumbled excuses, closing the door behind them.

"What's wrong?" Luka asked as silence fell around them.

Thomas had frozen in his tracks, staring hard at Luka. "I'm leaving."

A knot of dread curled up in Luka's stomach. "Yeah, I know, in two months—"

"No. Now. This week."

"What?" The knot grew, cutting off his air.

"You guys are all set with the Sartini and Grand Plains contracts. Ilona says they're looking at doing some more hiring, you're a VP now and I'm…moving on. Head office said they need me elsewhere." His voice was flat.

"Wow." Luka couldn't breathe. Was this what it would feel like to be a planet ripped from its orbit, hurled into the infinite darkness of space?

"Yeah."

"I mean, I guess we knew it was coming…" *No. Not now.* This time it was so much worse.

Thomas nodded. "My last day is Friday."

Luka swallowed hard. "Friday." Two days away. Every cell in his body screamed at him that his world was ending. He wanted to cry. Weep. Throw himself at Thomas and beg him to stay. Curl into a ball on the floor and never get up again. Instead he forced himself to smile and take a shaky breath. "Well, I'll need your help getting Grand Plains off the ground before you go. Coffee?"

Thomas scrubbed his face. "Sure. Thanks." He didn't meet Luka's eyes as he sat down again.

That night Luka stared up at the ceiling for hours. His heart was being torn in two, a sharp ache in his chest. Even though he had known all along it was going to happen. Even though it was ridiculous to feel like he was losing something he never had. Even though it was better this way. The sooner Thomas left, the sooner he could get over him.

The next two days were the shortest of Luka's life. The time slipped through his fingers, every hour gone in a minute, every minute taking a second. The seconds evaporated before they even existed. He did his best to grin and joke and get the job done, but the grins ached, the jokes hurt and his brain could do nothing but chant at him, *He's leaving. He's leaving. He's leaving.* The pain in his chest just got sharper and sharper, until it hurt so bad the tears were always there, threatening to spill.

Tawney organized a goodbye for Thomas at the end of the day on Friday. They gathered in the conference room around a 'We'll Miss You, Big Bad Wolf!' cake. It had the Three Little Pigs waving goodbye and everything. Luka took in everyone smiling and chatting and eating, patting Thomas on the shoulder or shaking his hand, and he wanted to scream at them, *Don't you get it? He's* leaving. *He's* gone. He envied the way they had just another weekend stretching ahead of them, instead a dark, yawning chasm of nothing.

As five o'clock approached, people began to head back to their offices to take off for the weekend. Rory gave Thomas a hug, then squeezed Luka's arm on his way out. Once Ilona had said goodbye and they could avoid it no longer, they made their way back to their office. Luka's office.

Luka watched Thomas close his laptop for the last time. "So…you're out of here tomorrow morning?"

"Yup. I'm all packed. Movers come at nine, then train to the airport."

"Well…stay in touch."

"Of course."

The tears stung in Luka's eyes as he hugged Thomas goodbye. "Take care," he said as he pulled away, blinking rapidly. "I'll miss you."

"Luka." Thomas swallowed hard.

"Yeah?"

Thomas shook his head, his jaw tight. "I'll miss you too. I'll text you once I'm settled."

"Great. My mom will want to know how you're doing." Luka's voice cracked.

He made it to the elevator before the tears spilled over.

Chapter Twenty-Four

Shall I Stay?

The air in his condo was stifling. Luka went through the motions—dropped his keys on the counter, dumped his bag on a chair, slouched into his bedroom and robotically peeled off his work clothes. He paused to stare in the mirror for a moment, but the empty eyes staring back unnerved him. He frowned at his robe lying on the bed and reached out to run his fingers down the sleeve. It felt cold. Unfamiliar. Wrong. He tossed it into his closet and pulled on some old sweats instead.

He jammed a container of leftovers into the microwave for dinner, but couldn't do more than slump on his couch and pick at the rice. A new episode of *The Great British Bake Off* did not help distract him. The contestants were making muffins. Thomas had brought him a muffin. Stood there, gorgeous and perfect, holding out the tray. Luka swore. The tears were back.

How can it hurt this badly? Luka curled up and wrapped his arms around his knees. *Thomas was never mine. I never had him. I haven't lost anything.* Except he had. He could see it. All of it. Holding hands with Thomas coming back from the market on Saturdays. Laughing while they made dinner, aprons on and music playing. Thomas' eyes crinkling while Marta gushed all over him at Christmas. Rolling over in bed to watch Thomas sleep, his dark curls spilling across the pillow...golden brown eyes opening, watching him...

He was going to be sick. The sweet oblivion of sleep was the only thing that sounded tolerable, so he turned the TV off and pitched himself straight into bed without even brushing his teeth. Unfortunately, his brain didn't get the memo. He continued to torture himself, tossing and turning with 'what ifs' for hours. *What if I had told him I liked him months ago? What if I never see him again?*

What if I had asked him to stay?

At some point he must have fallen asleep, because then he was on a path lined with cherry trees, a carpet of pink petals beneath his feet. He looked around but there was no one in sight, so he wandered, not knowing where to go.

"Thomas?" he called, starting down a path at a slow jog. There was nothing but trees and blossoms and a muffled, unsettling quiet. He ran faster, the pink a blur around him, until his lungs burned. When he stopped, panting, he was right where he had started. He turned in a circle, looking for a sign. "Thomas!" he yelled into the thick silence. "Thomas!" He jolted awake with a gasp.

Oh God... He checked the clock, rubbing his puffy eyes. 9:02. Thomas' movers would be arriving right now. He stared at his phone resting on the bedside table, fingers itching to send a text. Just something simple. A goodbye, good luck. Don't fucking leave. *Fuck. No. Not a good idea, Luka.*

He blasted himself with hot water in the shower, scrubbing the dream away till his skin was red. Then he got dressed, grabbed his keys and bolted, desperate for fresh air and to be far, far away from his phone. He had no idea where he was going to go—he just had to get out.

When he pushed open the front door of his building, a gust of wind and rain swept over him. He looked up at the heavy, gray clouds, squinting as the fat drops hit his face. *How fitting. Rain on me, Misery. Do your worst.* He turned to make his way down the sidewalk, then he saw him.

Thomas.

Standing in the rain. Chest heaving. Looking back at him.

Luka's heart swelled as the rest of the world fell away. "Thomas," was the word that came to him, voice cracking. "What are you...?"

"I ran from the station," Thomas said, short of breath. His hair was loose and plastered to his head. His sweater was soaked. He took a few steps closer and dropped the duffel bag he was carrying.

Luka shook his head, trying to clear the static. "You're drenched."

Shifting his weight to his other foot, Thomas nodded. He opened his mouth, paused then pushed the words out. "I'm sorry."

"Sorry?" Luka tried to keep his heart in his rib cage... *Breathe...* The rain soaked his hair and trickled down the back of his shirt. He shivered.

"Because...I've been such a fucking idiot."

All Luka could do was nod. "Kind of. But...how, exactly?"

Thomas took two more steps, until they were an arm's length apart. The raindrops clung to his eyelashes and ran in rivulets down his jaw. "This morning...alone in my empty apartment, I realized, what the *fuck* am I doing? Why am I leaving?"

Luka nodded some more. "That's what I was wondering too," he agreed in a small voice. His heart was now forcing itself up his throat, throbbing with raw, painful hope.

Closing the distance, Thomas took his hand. "What if I stay?"

Luka's eyes flooded with tears. He was hardly able to believe what was happening. "Yeah. Yes. Stay. For the love of God, please stay."

"Luka..." Thomas pushed out a long breath, then squeezed his hand. He raised his golden eyes. His lower lip trembled, then he said it. "I love you."

Luka's lungs emptied with a wheeze as his legs threatened to buckle. Tears spilled onto his cheeks, mixing with the rain. "You what?"

"I love you. And...fuck, I'm so sorry."

Another tear fell. "I told you I was loveable." Luka sniffled

Thomas laughed and took Luka's other hand, his smile shy. "Do you still —"

Luka threw himself into Thomas' arms, pressed their lips together and kissed him for all he was worth. Kissed him for every longing glance, every lingering touch, every skipped heartbeat. For the hundreds of days he hadn't kissed him. For the accidental couple's costume, for the honeymoon suite, for the cherry blossoms. For every wish, every ache, every dream.

The kiss went on, wet as the rain poured down on them. And on, until they were dizzy.

"So," Luka panted when they pulled apart, lips tingling, arms still wrapped around the other. The smell of the rain was intoxicating and he wanted to drown in it. "You love me?"

Thomas hummed, pushing a wet strand of hair off of Luka's forehead. "You do realize I could have gotten my own office at any point, right? I've loved you since the moment I saw you."

"Really? Like, the *moment*?"

"Well…" Thomas looked up, thinking. "Maybe not the *moment*."

Laughing, Luka smacked him, then tightened his grip around Thomas' torso again. "I love you, too." *I love you, too.* It had never felt so good to say those four words. Any four words, ever. They hung in the air, wrapped around them, anchored a planet to its sun.

Thomas smiled, holding his gaze. Luka blinked more tears away, then kissed him again. His heart was pounding…or was that Thomas'?

Then Thomas' eyes widened. "Fuck. All my stuff is on its way to Mansfield."

Luka laughed again, because any problem felt small when they were together. "Let's get out of this storm, shall we?"

Thomas called the movers on their way in and explained that he would in fact not be moving to Mansfield today. They were confused, but, fortunately, hadn't even made it out of the city yet. He held the phone away from his mouth and whispered to Luka. "Where should they take it? I can't go back to where I was — it's already been rented."

"Uh…" Luka thought quickly. "Here? I have room for some stuff, and my storage area in the basement is almost empty."

"Thanks." Thomas gave them Luka's address then hung up.

They stared at each other in Luka's hallway, pools of water gathering on the tile floor beneath them.

"Shall we get you out of these wet clothes?" Luka asked with a grin.

Thomas smirked.

Luka slid his hands under Thomas' sweater and T-shirt, then peeled them off, discarding them in a sopping heap. Goosebumps sprang up on Thomas' bare skin, and Luka let his eyes roam greedily over the muscles, mouth watering. Then he lifted his hands and placed them on Thomas' shoulders, sliding them down his arms. "Fuck, you're beautiful." He leaned forward and placed a soft kiss on his collarbone.

Thomas wrapped his hands around Luka's waist and pulled him close. He kissed him again, his tongue gently probing.

Luka let out a muffled groan then forced himself to take a step back. "I can't believe I'm saying this, but…the movers will be here soon. You'd better get dressed."

"Hmm." Thomas gave him a disapproving look.

"I'm not happy about it either. Believe me." Luka found some baggy clothes in his closet that he figured Thomas would be able to stuff himself into, then eyed him hungrily when he came out of the bathroom. "The way that T-shirt is clinging to you…"

"Hold that thought," Thomas muttered, eyes hot on Luka's skin as his phone buzzed.

* * * *

Thomas' sparse furnishings and other small pieces fit into Luka's storage space. They stacked his boxes and suitcases in the spare room.

When the door closed behind the movers, they lunged for each other at the same time. Thomas pressed Luka against a wall, his lips traveling from his mouth, over his jaw and onto his neck, teeth scraping.

"Oh God," Luka moaned, his voice shaking. "Is this really happening?"

"Yes," Thomas muttered, sliding his hands around Luka's hips to grab his ass, pulling them together. Thomas' hardness pressed against his, leaving no doubt. "I'm right here."

They gripped each other frantically, their kisses desperate, until Luka had the presence of mind to tow Thomas toward his bedroom. He pulled Thomas' too-tight T-shirt off then slid his hands into the waistband of the borrowed sweatpants. He gasped when he realized there was no underwear underneath.

"I've been dreaming about this for a long time…" Luka breathed, heart racing as he pushed them down and took in the sight of Thomas in all his glory. He gulped. His poor, sad imagination had done Thomas a disservice.

"Your turn," Thomas whispered. He removed Luka's clothes with steady hands like he had done it a million times before.

Thomas lay him back on the bed as he climbed over him strands of long, chocolate-brown hair tickling his face. He took Luka's lips again, slow and sure, until Luka was gasping, overwhelmed with the raw desire behind the kiss. Then Thomas slid his mouth down to

Luka's neck and lower, traveling the length of the quivering body beneath him. He explored every hard line, kissed every tender spot, licked places that made Luka shiver. Made him writhe and moan, his skin tingling, fire kindling inside him.

Finally, he could take it no more. "Please, Thomas," he whispered. "I need you."

Luka had had many dreams about this moment. There had been five in particular that were so passionate, so realistic, he had woken up dizzy and spent. The real thing left them all behind.

A while later, when they were soft and sleepy, curled up in bed, Luka laced their fingers together. "Do you think you can stay at the office?" he murmured into the hard plane of Thomas' chest.

"I think so. Ilona hinted a few times they could make things work if I wanted to."

"She did? So why didn't you?" Luka popped his head up and met Thomas' eyes. His stomach jumped at the intensity of his gaze.

"Luka...I've been alone for a long time, on the move. I was scared. Scared that if I stayed, you might not want me here anymore, and then I'd end up alone again, but now with a broken heart."

"Fuck. I'm gonna cry again." Luka wiped at one eye then leveled a firm look at Thomas. "Listen to me, Thomas Badgley. I love you. I love you so much it hurts. I am never letting you leave."

Thomas pressed a kiss to Luka's knuckles, blinking. "Good. I never will."

Luka wiggled even closer, breathing in as deep as he could, filling his lungs with the scent that had sent his stomach spinning from day one. "So when was the moment you knew you loved me?" he asked. "You know, once I had wiped off the toothpaste and changed my shirt."

The laugh vibrated through Thomas' chest. "Did you know there was an empty chair right by the door when you came bursting in?"

Luka's jaw dropped. "What? There was?"

"Yup. An empty seat right next to you, and you climbed across the whole entire room with everyone staring at you in complete silence, and you just looked so vulnerable and embarrassed—"

"That's because I was," Luka interjected, covering his eyes at the memory, now even more excruciating.

"—and cute. So fucking cute, your shirt all crooked, hair sticking up. The toothpaste..." They laughed together. "I wanted to protect you, wrap my arms around you. And I just...that was it for me. I knew."

"Right." Luka rolled over and reached for his phone.

"What are you doing?"

Luka frowned as he started typing. "Emailing HR."

"I don't think that's the best way to go about getting my position back—"

"Aaaaand...send." He mashed a button and tossed his phone aside. "Oh, no, just getting ahead of things. I requested a meeting first thing Monday morning to disclose our relationship. Just in case."

Thomas' reply was a deep, languid kiss. Luka rolled Thomas onto his back, hands smoothing down his chest and along rippled abs. "Well, now that that job's taken care of, there's another one I've been wanting to cross off my list..." Luka murmured as he traced his lips along the dip of Thomas' hip.

"Mmm..." Thomas groaned, threading his fingers into Luka's hair. "I've always admired the way you tackle your...*jobs*."

Luka rolled his eyes and chuckled, but his mouth was too busy to reply.

An hour or so later, when they could no longer ignore their growling stomachs, they dragged themselves out of bed. Luka put his robe on — rescued from the floor of the closet with a whispered apology — while Thomas went to dig through his suitcases. He put on a pot of coffee, popped some bagels in the toaster and began to scramble some eggs when Thomas appeared in the kitchen…wearing the same robe.

"What…" Luka shook his head, the smile spreading so widely across his face it hurt his cheeks. "You bought one for yourself."

"I bought one for myself." Thomas shrugged sheepishly. He walked up to Luka and took hold of the robe's belt, planting a kiss on his forehead. "I liked the idea of being curled up in my robe at the same time as you, even if we were in different places."

"You're actually a massive sap, aren't you?" Luka found his lips. The kiss went on until he realized the eggs were browning.

They sat on the couch, eating and laughing in their matching robes, knees touching. The storm had not let up outside, and the patter of the rain added to the coziness of their little cocoon.

"Will you play me something?" Thomas asked, eyeing Luka's guitar when they were finished eating.

"I'd love to." He knew just the song.

"I saw you across the way
Looking so good today
And I wanted to say
Now please don't be shy
Come over and say hi

I saw you smiling down the hall
So cute with your brown eyes and all
I wanted to say
So please don't be shy
Come on over and say hi
'Cause it's clear to see
That it won't be me
I guess I'm way too shy
Please come over and say hi."

Thomas stood and took the guitar from Luka's hands, carefully placing it back in the stand. He leaned over and kissed him, before he pulled back an inch. "Hi," he said, looking deep into Luka's eyes.

"Hi," Luka replied, so happy he could die.

"That's my new favorite song," Thomas said, pulling Luka to his feet and wrapping his arms around him.

Luka grinned at him like an idiot. "Like I said, sap."

Then Thomas whispered into his ear, sending goosebumps skittering down Luka's spine. "Let's go back to bed, and I'll show you just how much of a sap I can be."

So he did. Twice. Then later, tangled up in sweaty sheets, before they drifted off to sleep, Thomas murmured, "I'll have to find a new place to live."

Luka's gaze landed on his copy of *Pride and Prejudice*, still with the cherry blossoms pressed between its pages. "You can stay with me while you look."

Thomas never left.

Epilogue

To the Sea

One Year Later

"I can't believe we're doing this," Luka muttered as they approached the Bitter Exchange.

Thomas gave him an amused look. "You didn't *have* to agree to come."

Luka sighed. "No, but I'm a good person."

Thomas chuckled. "You just want to see if he crashes and burns."

"I am *shocked* and *appalled* at such accusations..." Luka began, pressing a hand to his chest.

Thomas rolled his eyes affectionately as he held open the door. "Mmm. After you."

The pub was packed, a small stage set up in one corner. Luka waved at the Breakpoint crowd as they headed over.

"Hey guys," Tawney chirped, kissing them each on the cheek. "Ooh, is that...is that an actual *color* you're wearing, Thomas?" She ogled his cobalt-blue button-down. "You look *gorgeous*."

"Ha!" Luka crowed, squeezing Thomas' waist. "I told you. We went shopping," he explained to Tawney. "There were threats if he bought anything black or gray."

Thomas grunted, trying not to smile. "Thanks, Tawney."

"Well, look who showed up!" Finn appeared, slapping Luka on the back. "You almost missed the show. Did you guys get, uh, 'held up'?" he asked with obnoxious air quotes.

Luka scowled at him while also blushing, because that was, in fact, the reason they were late. They had taken a shower together and... Well, things had gotten very dirty before they had gotten clean.

But Thomas stepped in smoothly. "Says the guy who walked into a wall the other day because he was sexting with his spouse."

Finn flapped his gums for a minute then flounced off toward the bar, muttering something about Rory starting it.

Luka snickered and leaned in to whisper in Thomas' ear. "I love you."

Thomas met his eyes, gaze soft. "I love you, too."

A thrill went through Luka. He never got tired of hearing it. He took Thomas' hand, about to tell him that, when Kazio started growling at them through a microphone.

"All right, everyone, sit down," he said from up on the stage. He paused to glare as the crowd shuffled to their seats. Luka and Thomas slipped into chairs next to Tawney.

"I normally don't do this kind of thing," he continued, "but, well, I give you... Symphony!"

Luka sighed.

"I know." Thomas patted his knee before Luka could, once again, tell him how much he hated that name.

Then there he was, strutting to the microphone as the patrons cheered. Morgan fucking Di Meo. He was wearing impossibly tight ripped jeans and a retro Queen tank top, a red electric guitar slung over his shoulder. He had let his hair grow out a little, and it was styled up in an artfully constructed tousle. He looked pretty hot, which irritated Luka to no end.

Then he kissed Kazio on the cheek. The barkeep gave him a look that was both affectionate and annoyed at the same time.

Luka's eyebrows shot off his forehead. "Oh, *really*?"

Then Morgan took to the mic and drowned out any further thoughts anyone might have.

"What's up, everybody!" Morgan hollered. "We...are...Symphony!" He struck a chord on his guitar and the band crashed in behind him. He had a drummer, bassist and a second guitar. It took Luka about four bars to decide they were...quite good. *Damn it.*

Luka bobbed along despite himself. Thomas opened his mouth to say something, but Luka held up a finger. "Do not, my love. I need a moment to adjust to this reality."

Thomas smiled into his pint.

"Oh my God, they're really good!" Tawney leaned over at the end of the first song. She spotted Luka's sulk and laughed. "Sorry, babe. I mean..." She glanced back at the stage. "He's a performer!"

Luka sighed and took a drink. The second song was even better. Thomas took his hand, rubbing a thumb in soothing circles. After the third song, he leaned over to murmur in Luka's ear. "You're still better than him."

Luka turned to give Thomas a half-smile. "Thanks, but...it's okay. I'm happy for him."

"Oh, well, then... Maybe he needs an opening act?"

Luka swatted at him and settled in to watch the rest. The truth was, Luka was drawing crowds of his own now. He had performed at two more open mic nights before the manager of Jitters had asked him about doing his own show. So he had done three of those, and experienced the very weird feeling of having *fans*. People who called him by name and showed up just to watch him. His most requested song was *Say Hi*.

And he was okay with Morgan being successful, too. Were there too many guitar solos? Yes. Was he still a raging egomaniac? Absolutely. Was Symphony quite talented, despite the pretentious and unusable name? Fuck. Yes, yes they were. Morgan took on a few notes he shouldn't have, but overall, Luka didn't hate it.

The band finished their first set to raucous applause. "Another drink?" Thomas asked, getting up from the table.

"Thanks, babe," Luka said as some surprise visitors settled themselves across from him. "Aleandro! Penelope!" he greeted them. "What are you doing here?" They had extended the Sartini contract again, but Breakpoint was between campaigns right now and Luka hadn't talked to them in a few months.

Aleandro returned the warm smile. "We were planning to stop by the office sometime to say hi, and Ilona suggested we come tonight. I quite enjoyed the band!"

Penelope tilted her head. "He was a little sharp in his upper register, though, wasn't he?"

Luka snickered. "Penelope, I don't think I've told you before how much I like you."

Her smile gleamed, then her gaze flicked over Luka's shoulder.

"Luka…?" Thomas rumbled.

"Yes, my love?" He turned around.

And there Thomas was, kneeling on the ground. On both knees.

"What are you…?"

The Breakpoint crowd stilled, and all eyes were on them.

"Luka," Thomas began, "it was a year ago today that I realized I had to stay in Oakport, to be with you. And it's been the happiest year of my life."

Tears flooded Luka's eyes as he pressed a hand to his mouth. "What…"

"So here I am, on both knees, *begging* you to marry me. And if you say no, I will die from a broken heart."

Luka laughed through the tears. "Oh my God. You—"

Thomas gave him a crooked smile, his own eyes rather wet as well.

Finn, Rory, Tawney and Ilona unfurled a giant banner. It read, *Marry me, Luka, or I'll literally die*, in puffy white letters on a blue background.

Thomas nodded at it. "It's not sky-writing, but…"

Luka laughed harder, wiping at the tears still spilling down his cheeks. He jumped up and hauled Thomas to his feet. "Yes, I'll marry you, you beautiful dork."

They kissed as the pub erupted in cheers. Luka's heart was pounding, and the tears would not stop.

He pulled back, sniffling. Thomas removed a tissue from his pocket and handed it over.

"Is there a marching band, too?" Luka wondered as he blotted his eyes.

"Well…" Thomas looked over his shoulder. Morgan and his band were back on stage. At Thomas' glance, they kicked into *Marry You* by Bruno Mars.

Luka felt like his tiny body could not contain the love he had for Thomas Badgley. As he looked into those golden eyes, with all his best friends — and Morgan — around him, he was perfectly, singularly, happy.

* * * *

They got married the next spring under the cherry blossoms. Luka wore his green suit, Thomas, his wolf cufflinks.

They stayed in the honeymoon suite at Elander Hills on their wedding night, then set out for the coast the next day — two weeks of wine tastings, whale watching, romantic dinners on the beach and making good use of their wedding present from Finn.

On their last night, they strolled down the shoreline hand in hand.

When they stopped to take in the sunset, Luka put his arm around Thomas and tucked his head onto his shoulder. "I'm so lucky," he said, overcome by the perfect moment. Tears welled up again.

Thomas looked at him. "Hey, shhh." He wiped a thumb over the drop that had escaped. "I'm the lucky one. I was alone, Luka. And now…I have you. We're a family."

And they were.

Want to see more from this author? Here's a taster for you to enjoy!

Falling Hard: A Hard Fit
Jennifer Moffatt

Coming November 2024

Excerpt

Love at first sight? Not real.

Probably not, anyway. Maybe it happened to some people, but not everyone. It was certainly not something Finn expected to happen to him.

Well, maybe it could.

It wouldn't.

But it might.

If it was going to happen, now was the perfect time — new job, fresh start, a whole city full of people. It would just take one, after all.

Worth trying, anyway.

His first date in Oakport was with Albert. They matched on a dating app. It was definitely *something* at first sight, although Finn suspected that something was lust... hard to tell the difference, in the moment.

"Albert?" he asked the man at the bar, even though he knew Albert from his profile pics. He was Finn's type — tall and lean, smiley, tousled hair.

"Finn?" Albert grinned.

"Great to meet you," Finn said, shaking his hand.

"You too." Albert studied him up and down in a way that made Finn's dick twitch. "Want to go back to your place and fuck?"

Finn laughed as he sat, considering the offer. "You're on the wrong app, Albert."

Albert's green eyes twinkled. "Doesn't change my question."

Finn pushed his ginger curls back, taking in the way Albert's cuffs were rolled up, displaying sculpted forearms. "Why arrange to meet here if you just want to fuck?"

Albert shrugged and tossed back the rest of his cocktail. "Making sure you matched your pictures." He eyed where Finn's T-shirt pulled tight over his biceps.

Finn rested an arm on the bar and leaned in. "So you like what you see?"

Albert nodded and inched closer on his stool, gaze now dropping to Finn's lap. "And now I want to see the rest."

Albert came back to Finn's place. And came at his place. Finn hadn't even gotten his breath back yet when Albert rolled over and looked at his phone. "That was great. I've gotta get going, though. I'll call you."

He never called.

So, lust—definitely lust.

It wasn't quite as easy to tell with Safa. They had sex on the first date, too, but then there were more dates. At least five, by Finn's count, plus he ran into her at the charity 5K. Anyway, they spent enough time together that there was something more than lust, but she broke up with him because, quote, *my cat thinks you're too loud.*

You're choosing your cat over me? was the question that came to Finn's mind, but that was where it stayed, because there were some questions he shouldn't have to ask. Plus, that cat was an asshole.

Travis was hot but had no sense of humor. He didn't laugh at a single thing Finn said, not even his standard first date dirty jokes.

Wynn was rude to servers. *Next.*

With Luka, gorgeous Luka, there had been promise, at least. When Finn had seen him for the first time, he had felt warm all over. Luka was new at their office — young and sparkling, brown hair flopping into his forehead, killer blue eyes, sharp dresser. The two of them were the only openly queer men at Breakpoint, and gravitated toward each other instantly. In fact, Luka asked him to go for a drink after work at the end of his first week. Finn said yes without hesitation.

Finn took him to the Bitter Exchange, a new pub that had opened only a few blocks from the office. It was dim and already grimy somehow, but the wings were excellent and the beer was cheap. After the requisite chit-chat and delivery of their pitcher, they started diving into more personal topics.

"So, where did you go to school?" Luka asked before taking his first sip.

"U State, you?"

"Bryerson."

"I dated a couple from Bryerson once." Finn remembered it fondly.

Luka quirked his brow. "Like...at the same time?"

Finn shrugged. "Not exactly. I went out with her first a few times, and then him, but when he brought me home, she showed up."

Luka grimaced. "Awkward."

The grin stretched across Finn's face. "It was at first, but then we had a threesome."

Luka almost choked on his drink. "How did that go?"

"It became a bit of a competition between the two of them to see who could get me off first, so…really, really good."

Luka's laugh warmed Finn's heart. He laughed a lot, at all of Finn's dumb jokes.

They swapped stories with not a single lull or awkward pause in the conversation the whole night until the place was closing and the owner was glaring at them from behind the bar. There was a moment, though, watching Luka lick a stray drop of beer off his lip, when Finn realized there was no zing, no lust *or* love. But there was a lot of laughter and warmth and the beginnings of friendship, and that felt exactly right.

Towards the end of the evening, Luka asked Finn for his hair care regimen. Finn did have the softest, shiniest hair around, and he spent a decent chunk of money on products to keep it that way. He couldn't leave those curls to their own devices.

"That would be telling," Finn said, narrowing his eyes at Luka. "Can't have you stealing my Sexiest Guy at the Office crown. Shiny hair might push you over the top."

Luka stuck out his lower lip. "Pretty please? I'll be your best friend."

Finn only paused for another second before giving up his secret. Luka ordered the whole product line right then on his phone.

Finn didn't mind if his new friend had hair just as shiny as his.

About the Author

Jennifer firmly believes that there are so many more stories to tell than the ones that have traditionally been lined up on bookstore shelves, and she wants to write as many of them as she can. She lives with her spouse and two children in beautiful British Columbia, Canada. This is her first novel.

Jennifer loves to hear from readers. You can find her contact information, website details and author profile page at https://www.firstforromance.com/

PUBLISHING

Sign up for our newsletter and find out about all our
romance book releases, eBook sales and promotions,
sneak peeks and FREE romance books!